Sandy stood in the open end of a long, narrow marble hall. Her shadow ran before her as long as the hall itself, a dark streak all the way to the other end. Sprague waited at the end. In his hand was the head of her shadow. He drew it close against him. He was chanting. Misshapen forms moved in the darkness behind him. Her shadow stretched like thick rubber and she felt his elastic pull upon her body. She felt urged to glide through the long hall until she was with him. But now there was something behind her. *Hideous*. Something too dreadful to turn and face. Claw-tipped hands touched her bare shoulders. Her body was accessible, vulnerable, she realized she was nude. The hand lay heatedly on her cool, naked shoulder. But she wanted to go to Sprague. He was pulling her shadow and hissing in sudden rage. She wanted to take Melanie and go to him. . . .

Fawcett Gold Medal Books
by Jere Cunningham:

HUNTER'S BLOOD

THE LEGACY

THE LEGACY

by
Jere Cunningham

A FAWCETT GOLD MEDAL BOOK

Fawcett Books, Greenwich, Connecticut

THE LEGACY

ISBN 0-449-13926-3

Printed in the United States of America

10 9 8 7 6 5 4 3 2 1

Prologue

Dusk gathered first in the deep pockets of the earth. Darkness pooled in crevices, shadows rising and overflowing. A black river ran through ditches and highways, its branches connecting, the oncoming night a web of long shadows connecting the depressions of the land.

The horizon glimmered. Men turned longing eyes toward that last light, not knowing why, saying the colors were beautiful. The great shadow moved over them from east to west across the face of the planet. In its wake electric lights blinked on, feeble and myriad.

Behind locked doors men sought the oblivion of television and sleep. The night did not belong to them.

In the dark was the unseen. In the stars was the unknown. As men dreamed nightmares, the creatures of the night gathered power.

The town of Bickford, Mississippi, lay near the river called Father of Waters. Its population was 639, twelve fewer than the previous year.

In the thickening night, twelve miles distant, the Mississippi River was a vast sluggish band of moving starlight. High on its eroded bluff a restored manor stood lifeless. No night birds sang in its eaves. Its high casements rejected the vitality of light. Its glass held darkness within. Like sentinels, ancient water oaks guarded its high walls and central tower. Thunder rolled distantly. Black tree limbs became wraiths against clouds inking out the last resisting stars. Lightning flashed across the river. A storm was coming out of the southwest, and its reaching light came against the house in lurid assaults.

Rain lashed down through trees. The gutters of the house filled and rumbled and gushed. A lightning bolt branched violently to earth, shearing a black, rainslick oak. And in almost the same instant the great house rang within to a single gunshot. The inner sound faded quickly in the ravaging storm.

From the doors of the manor a bent and rapid figure appeared. It did not pause, running through the black rain, bearing a second shape heavily across its back, disappearing through the trees as a thing howled savagely in the doorway, trapped in the black dryness of the house by the driving rain.

The man came from the trees. His watery face strained upward, panicky at the diminishing rain. His heart was old, it hammered with the weight of the corpse across his back. The white head lolled on his chest and the feet bumped the small of his back. From the gunshot head, blood and hair and brains oozed sodden down his heaving chest. Before him was his own manor, Whitewood. His eyes gladdened briefly at the sight of white clean majesty in flashes of receding lightning.

Gasping, he hurried on through the mown field. Passing stables, tennis court, garage, he came sagging to the small cemetery near the river bluff. Below him the water was no longer black. A light rain fell but clouds were breaking up. Moonlight dropped at oblique moments upon the horror of what he found himself struggling to do.

The corpse slid into the fresh-dug grave. It slopped head-first into a foot of water. His shovel mucked, the grave filled, he ran for the house. The rain had almost abated.

In his book-lined library, at the yellow lamplight of his old familiar desk, he slumped into his favorite leather chair without peeling off the wet clothes. The wet Smith and Wesson lay dripping on a stack of *New Yorkers*. Panting, he gazed across the desk into the open closet. In the open gray floor safe the clockwork device rested silently in its bell jar. Its archaic gilt discs did not stir, and he felt a benevolent calm replacing the hour of hysteria and near-madness.

He poured Wild Turkey from a Baccarat decanter into a shot glass engraved *Chester* and threw the mellow burning liquid back neat, reassured in the wake of its old familiar fire. He rubbed his face. He did not know whether what he had done would end the nightmare. He had committed murder in order to cause far more terrible things to cease. He had done the only thing he had found conceivable as a plan, within his limited and human forces.

Perhaps, he thought. Perhaps it will end now. Perhaps I will even survive.

His eye caught peripheral motion in the closet floor safe. The gilt disc in the clockwork device flicked.

His breath caught in his throat. The disc trembled. Lower gears and balances moved feebly, in tiny jerks that became more and more fluid. His body went rigid in the leather chair. His eyes dilated in horror. It was out there. *It* was coming.

His hand slid to the damp .38. Its touch was dead and cold but not threatening. His mouth hung open in dread. The disc whirred quite sweetly now, faintly humming. His fingers clawed the revolver. It could not stop the approaching thing, yet it could terminate his own consciousness.

He felt for the phone and dialed.

The heavy safe door suddenly crashed shut. The dial spun, clicked, and the closet door slammed shut.

His hand feebly put the receiver back onto its yoke. He thought he saw something huge, something dark pass the windows.

"David," he groaned, and dialed the phone again.

The study door, closed, began to groan, to strain as if pressed upon by some tremendous outer force.

"Hello?" asked the telephone receiver impatiently. The door was open and his hand clutched desperately for the mercy of the gun.

One

David opened the window. Dank midnight heat of the city poured in. Air-conditioning was out again, dammit.

From the town-house window he gazed out over the groomed courtyard below, scanning upward across the glittering Memphis skyline in the distance. Neon-tinged clouds bunched low over the Mississippi River bridge. The city hummed. He wondered what men were doing out there in the glaring city streets and the dark mouths of alleys. Night in the city. Stalkers. Lurkers. Watchers. Having grown up in the country on a plantation outside of Bickford, Mississippi, he never got used to the idea of what happened in Memphis at night. Or in any city.

Below him, the courtyard pool was a green shimmering rectangle. Underwater lights rayed through the lapping glassy surface. He thought how good a swim would feel—cold water rippling over the muscles, smell of chlorine, cold feet wet on the sandpaper concrete—not like a creek swim but still very very good.

He turned from the window, smiling, rubbing his lean bare chest. Sandra was a long curving shape on the bed. He stared. Sometimes he forgot how really lovely she was. He moved to sit beside her, then stroked the dark sprawl of her hair on the pillow. Her long lashes blinked open.

"Want a swim?" he whispered.

Her answer was a mock shiver. She took his hand, kissed it, and placed it on her left breast, his favorite.

Awake now, lifting her head, Sandra tickled David's ear

with the tip of her tongue, whispering impishly. She began to move her hands to feel for him.

In the heat of the room they made love like it used to be in the old downtown apartment when David had been struggling through med school. The asphalt nights had been a torture. But cold baths together and the old rickety bed had made them forget. They shared faith that David had a brilliant future in medicine.

Now, as then, they forgot the heat and the sounds of the city night. David's body slipped against hers. They twisted as one. Sandra moaned, drowning in pleasure and security.

They lay apart on the bed. She listened to the deep regularity of his chest. His hand found hers on the damp warm sheet. They both thought of that old apartment. The tough times with no money. A six-pack of Busch a real luxury. Married as freshmen at U. T. The child coming right away.

Sandra smiled to herself in the dark, so glad she'd decided against the abortion. Melanie was almost ten now, sleeping in the next room. Oh yes . . . having a kid so early had been rough. But she had found something true that she had always scoffed at (*you can't know how fantastic it is until you have one of your own*). Those old apartments, so dingy but so full of love and light.

Then, unbidden and harsh as it would, the thought of what that old man had tried to do with Melanie came at her. Her long legs tensed. She fought back the ugly images, but they came wedging in. Hearing Melanie scream. Running through the hall on warped splintery boards. Melanie running from that old man's apartment with torn jeans and blouse, her eyes wild. The wrinkled banality of that old leering disappointed face.

Sandra rolled on her side, face to face with David. She squeezed her mind tight to blot it clear. Her hand found David's again.

"Happy birthday," she whispered.

His eyes smiled back at her. It was dim but they almost sparkled.

His hand caressed her face. "I owe you, Sandy," he whispered.

She smiled like a little girl. "Don't worry, boy, you'll be making payments for the next fifty years."

He knew how true it was. Without her he never would have made it. It was at least half her drive that got him through tough years of college, med school, Melanie coming along, Sandra teaching piano in junior high and never begrudging the trickle of money that kept them going. It was a vast relief to realize that things were getting better. A little money of his own beginning to come. Interning at Methodist Hospital. Not long now. . . . In a couple of years he could hang out his shingle. Home free.

He pulled her arm, sitting up and whispering. "Nobody's outside, let's swim. Just like we are."

"No skinny-dipping tonight, son. Momma's not that tight." One night in a silly mood they had done it, almost getting caught by the fat rent-a-cop. She pulled him back to her, giggling at the image of wet naked bodies hotfooting it across the courtyard just in time.

David growled with mock antagonism. His hand groped toward the night table for the half-empty bottle of champagne she always bought to celebrate his birthday, sparkling burgundy for hers. The champagne was more expensive and French this time—Mumm's. It was no longer cold but still fizzed on his tongue with the bottle tilted to his lips.

"Barbarian," Sandra teased.

He handed it to her and she drank. Warm, sweet, and fizzly down her throat. Her eyes shut with pleasure—next year maybe some Dom Perignon, up, up and away.

She lay back smiling. With any kind of luck, bright as David was, he would be taken on by some rich East Memphis pediatrician. Sometimes he talked about doing a stint of welfare clinic pediatrics. She hadn't argued that point yet. Time enough when it came. The dues were almost paid now, the bad times over. The delicious warmth of lovemaking moved through her arms and belly and thighs.

The phone suddenly rang.

Their moods shattered, David and Sandy hissed curses together. The phone rang again with its irritating loudness-demand to be answered. David groaned and sat up. Sandra held onto him. The phone rang on.

Reluctantly, David pulled loose.

"It'll wake up Melanie." He grabbed the receiver.

Sandra sat up pouting. Probably the hospital wanting him to take off in the middle of the night. Some other intern flaking his E.R. duty.

David said hello and heard a long-distance crackle but no voice.

"Who is this?"

Sandra frowned. A mouth-breather call, ruining her natural high.

David hung up angrily and lay back down.

"No voice?" asked Sandra.

"I could hear breathing. Some freak getting his jollies." His heart was pounding, yet not in anger. He was troubled. Waiting, listening to that distant breathing, some knowing twinge had sparked in the recesses of his mind. Somehow he knew that someone needed him—that something had interfered with that need. It was like a familiar but unplaceable taste on the tongue.

Sandra rubbed his chest. "Thought it was your daddy, didn't you? I hoped it was. He could have at least called on your birthday."

David wished it had been. His father used to call once in a while, always on his birthdays, but not once in the past year. He thought of the plantation. Whitewood. The river Bickford seemed light years away. They used to drive down for weekend visits a couple of times a year. But since David's mother had died three years ago the visits had become strained. His father more distant than ever. In the past year even cold. More of a stranger than ever. Long silences. Unheard remarks. The old tensions revived manifold.

"People change," David sighed.

Sandra rubbed his chest. "He must be lonely, on that big place all alone except for Sam."

David smiled. Sam, who'd taken him fishing and hunting as a boy more than his father had. Sam, tall and black and proud long before it was fashionable, proud in a quiet self-assured way that needed no posters or proclamations, that drew admiration and trust rather than rage and reacting contempt. At least his father still had one friend like that. David's mind ranged back over the years. Chester, his father, was probably alone in his study right now, reading the classic kind of stuff he'd always liked, Herodotus or Pepys, Thucydides or Balzac, a constant bird dog curled snoring by the big dark red leather chair. Chester had wanted him to love the family land, take it over instead of going to Memphis to study medicine. So simple now to reduce it to that. A difference of opinion. A clash between generations of differing hopes and expectations. His father had said hard words, made strong statements. David had not yielded. So, like the Prodigal Son, he had left one night on his own. A new separate life. College supported by night jobs. Meeting Sandra. A wedding, to which mother but not Chester had come. Melanie. Then the beginning of sporadic visits, and Chester beginning to soften and smile. And then, three years ago, mother dying in agony of intestinal cancer. Cobalt.

Drugs. Specialists helpless. Chester blaming all doctors, not speaking to David. And in the past year not so much as a phone call.

David felt a sharp rise of guilt—had it been a year? really a whole year?

The phone rang, startling him from thought.

He answered. No voice. The long distance crackling. The faint breathing.

"Daddy?" he asked softly, listening. Then the dead clunk of disconnection.

"What, it's your daddy?" Sandra whispered with a sudden bright smile.

David shook his head and put the receiver down.

"No voice again?" Sandra asked.

"Nothing."

"Guess it's my lover. Told him you'd be here, not to call."

David grinned in spite of the uneasiness. He lay back down, craving a cigarette. Four years now without one and still it would taste damn good. He lay still for a few minutes and was abruptly sitting up, startling Sandra.

He dialed a long-familiar number in Mississippi area code 601. The sleepy drawl of the interchange operator: "What number you calling, please?"

"Area code six-oh-one, five-five-two-six-one-oh-one."

"That's Bickford, Mississippi, please?"

"*Yes*, operator." Come on . . . come on, for Christ's sake.

"That number is not in service at this time, sorry."

"It's got to be in service, operator." The idea of anything of his father's not being in service was too absurd. The perfunctory voice retorted.

"Trouble on the line, sir. Will you try later?"

David hung up and rose and went to the window, feeling Sandra's fingers slip from his back. He stared out at the neon-hazed clouds far off over the Mississippi bridge. *Guilt*, was that what he felt? As so often before? Leaving his father alone with grief? No . . . he had made his way alone. He had earned the right to live his own life.

"David? Come back to bed, honey."

He did. Lying against her sensual arm and thigh, her hand on his stomach, he knew that something was terribly wrong.

Two

Sandy woke. Pinks of dawn streaked the window panes. Beside her, David was struggling. Grunting. Heaving. His fists were clenched, his contorted face glittering with dawn-pink beads of sweat. She gripped his arm. Every muscle felt taut, strained, wiry with tension. She shook his face. His eyes rolled open, at first interior-turned, glazed, then blinking, returning to the exterior reality to which she belonged.

"Sandy?" he rasped.

She kissed his throat, eyes, lips. His body still quivered.

David exhaled a long sigh of relief, breathing deeply to the hammer of his heart in his brain. Rubbing his face, he sat up slowly.

"Oh . . . sweet Jesus," he gasped.

"What was it, honey?" Sandra rubbed his back. They had an agreement, share all bad dreams, get the bad out of yourself into the one who cared. "Let me make it all better," she offered maternally.

David's shoulders quivered. He couldn't remember the dream. Only the raw edge still lived. He felt the bliss of escape, yet there was a repressed and bitter undertaste of guilt. As if he had escaped torment by deserting a friend.

"I can't remember it," he said truthfully.

Sandra grinned. "Momma'll get Davie if he won't tell."

"Really, Sandy, I can't remember."

Without warning, she grabbed his ribs with both hands. He stifled a cry. Grinning, giggling, writhing back and forth, he slipped off the bed, gasping for breath. The phone crashed from its nightstand. He quit grinning. The receiver stared up at him, a black maze of tiny holes, buzzing, making the ticklish laughter die in his throat. Sandra's fingers slipped away. He released a long-held breath.

"Well, I get the shower first," he said.

Sandra jumped off the bed and ran into the bathroom, but David didn't chase her as he usually would. She peered round the bathroom door at him impishly, saw him just sitting there looking at the phone. With a puzzled frown she shut the door.

David rubbed his face. The shower curtain rattled. Water began to hiss.

He picked up the phone and tried to call his father again. Melanie was waking in the next room. Characteristic sounds. Streak's nails clattering on the hardwood floor. The thump of a rubber ball. Streak was Melanie's dog, a male Doberman who waked her with his frisky tongue or his rubber ball every morning.

The phone rang. David sat forward expectantly, forcing a workable smile upon his features (*Daddy? Hi, David, how are you?*). But he kept counting the rings without an answer. He wanted a cigarette, a straight Philip Morris or maybe a fancy-ass-good Balkan Sobranie. Irritated, he hung up. He glanced at the bathroom door. His look of consternation changed to playful glee.

Rising, he crept to the bathroom door and pressed it silently ajar. Steam poured over the curtain rod. David grinned. Sandra's contours were dim and sleekly female through the translucent curtain. How she could stand hot showers in the summer he didn't know.

In the stall, Sandra soaped her body vigorously. The rich lather was sensual, soothing but enticing. Suddenly hands grabbed through the curtain. She squealed. The soap squirted through her fingers.

Then David was stepping into the shower with her. She poked in good-natured revenge that quickly ended in wet naked kissing.

In her bedroom, Melanie sat on the old iron-framed bed pulling on a boot. Streak rolled his red rubber ball toward her feet with his nose.

"I've got to get dressed for school, dummy, it's the last day."

But Streak nuzzled her hand. She rubbed his silky cropped ear, making his long black head cock over in ecstasy.

"You big bad boy," she grinned. Streak loved his loving. She kicked the ball and he raced for it, nails skittering.

On her eighth Christmas morning there had been a big red tinfoil-covered box under the tree with little holes punched in the top and sides. Something thrashed and whimpered inside. Daddy and mommy pretended surprise that one of the presents was kicking up such a fuss. Melanie tore into the box with savage delight—a puppy! That morning, two and a half years ago, had begun a steadfast companionship. Streak tried to follow her everywhere. When he didn't, she was disappointed, though she scolded him for trying to follow her to school. She taught him things. Streak was an extremely bright pupil. He learned everything she could think of. How to sit and stay and come before he was six months old. To wait to go out the front door when she said "front." To wait to go out the back door when she said "outside." And if she ever said "go," Streak raced in wild acrobatic circles on his long graceful legs, knowing he was going somewhere in the car. He knew "down" and "fetch" and "shake." But she refused to teach him "roll over," thinking that too undignified for such a tall proud friend to have to do.

Streak opened long jaws, depositing the ball in her second boot.

"Like my boots, huh?"

They were cowboy boots mail-ordered from Austin, Texas. Mommy had denounced them, an outrage. But daddy said it was her allowance—she could spend it any way she wanted, especially for clothes—boots were clothes, sort of. When they were just about worn out she'd had them half-soled, out of her dollar-a-week allowance. Most of that she usually spent on Streak. Leash. New slip-chain or colored nylon collar sometimes. Saving up for his shots. Mycodex flea shampoo. Liv-a-Snap treats he craved. But the rubber ball was his all-time favorite thing. At first it had been red but the paint had been chewed off the first week. Now it was a brownish chunk of rubber.

He brought it again. She kicked and it bounced off the wall under her King Kong poster. Streak lunged after it, nails skittering, bringing it back between long white curving fangs, his aristocratic head arched proudly on its long graceful neck. She pried it from his jaws, making him snap at it, teasing. Her white hand passed over the blue-black luster of his tall back.

"Let's go to the kitchen."

She paused in the hall. Daddy and mommy were making splashes in the shower. No chance to use that sink. She wondered what they were doing in there, her baths were never any fun.

Streak trotted behind her to the kitchen with his ball locked between his canines. At the round Formica table she filled a bowl with Frosty-Os. Sunlight burned through the windows above the sink. Streak nuzzled her with his ball.

"You like old rubber balls and I like cowboy boots," she grinned. "Who cares if we're both kind of weird?"

She brushed her teeth at the sink and sat down to eat.

Sandra and David came swiftly through the hall into the kitchen, both late. David wore stiff clinical whites. The gold Cross ball-point Sandra and Melanie and Streak had given him last Christmas—a lean holiday—gleamed in his chest pocket. His hair, damp from the shower, was combed back and short the way Sandra like it. Hers was blown-dry—wet, it hung in long hopeless strings—dry, it was transformed, thick, long, and so lustrous David could hardly keep his hands off. She wore the boring brown dress Melanie called the Hostess Cupcake dress. Brown with white piping, not too expensive, it was perfect for teaching, chalk washed right out. God, Sandra thought now, as she did whenever she wore it, when can I have some really nice clothes? The family was first now with its needs, but in three years or four she could buy in New York if she wanted. All the dues were just about paid.

Melanie was at the fake-wood Formica table spooning down heaps of Frosty-Os. Streak gnawed his ball in a corner.

"Hi-ho," Sandra kissed Melanie's forehead and took two bowls from a squeaky cabinet.

Melanie grinned, "Gonna be late again, you two."

David stopped, struck by the morning light profiling Melanie's smooth aquiline features. Time stretched that moment. Soon his daughter would no longer be a child. The window-diffused sunshine made the down of her cheeks glow. Her hair was lit, a hallowing radiance about her luminous blue eyes. David found himself starstruck by his daughter more and more often these days. Even now as her cheeks bulged with cereal, her jaw munching industriously, she was breathtakingly beautiful. Rare. Blooming. His chest moved inside, a gentle tug of the heart. Life happened so fast. It seemed he was just starting school last year, Melanie an infant, another strain on them.

As he stood that way, he suddenly remembered the old man in the old apartments near med school. Fear. Obscenity. Revulsion. Old man putting greedy hands on her until she bit him and tore away. The urge to kill that man. Rage and hatred, torment that Melanie might have suffered psychic harm. But now he saw no trace of darkness in her young face. She glanced up at him from her Frosty-Os, a little rim of white milk on her upper lip. He realized he was staring.

Melanie's nose wrinkled with a smile. He winked back at her.

"Whatcha looking at, daddy? I got a booger?"

David laughed. He moved behind her chair to hug her. Streak rose, nuzzling his hand. David's fingers found Streak's velvety head, feeling strong bone structure and long fangs under silken thin hair. Christmas had come not long after the old-man incident more than two years ago. The Dobe puppy had been David's idea. A Doberman will turn on its master, people had warned Sandra, people who had never known or had one. But Streak had worked out just perfectly. The dog worshipped Melanie. One harsh word from her and Streak would lie down with a miserable whine. Nosing her hand until she relented. The idea that Streak would ever suddenly attack Melanie was too absurd. And David grinned, imagining what would have happened to that scabby old lecher if Streak had caught him or anybody like him making Melanie cry.

"Come *on*, David," warned Sandra. She hurriedly dumped Cheerios in David's bowl and Sugar-Frosted Flakes into hers, dark raku bowls a gifted potter friend had given them. She pulled the sugar bowl from Melanie's side of the table and sat down with a spoon. "Let's go, boy, shovel it down."

David sat and was pouring milk. The phone rang. He jerked. Milk washed over the Formica surface.

Sandra shoved her chair back with a start before milk could drip in her lap.

The phone rang again. She grabbed a wad of paper towels and threw them on the spill. "What's the matter with you this morning, David? You jumped like you were shot."

The phone rang again. David sat staring at it. Shadows ebbed at him from the dawn nightmare, attacking the edges of his thoughts. He thought of the phone ringing last night.

Melanie jumped off her chair to answer it.

"Yes, sir. No, this is his daughter."

David watched Melanie innocently stretch the long twisted cord from the wall toward him and he felt his stomach turn. It was only the hospital, he told himself, yet somehow he knew it wasn't. Hesitating, he took the receiver cautiously, as if it were the head of a snake.

"Is this David Rawlings?" The voice was distant but familiar, stretched and crackly over long distance.

David's heart skipped and his free hand rubbed his temple.

"Yes," he said. His wife and daughter watched him. Strangely. A sensation of impending doom increased.

"David, this is Grady Barksdale. How are you?"

Barksdale. His father's attorney in Bickford. David took a long breath, swallowed, said nothing. The voice coughed. Then continued.

"I'm afraid I have some pretty bad news. Real bad. I don't know how to put a sugar-coating on it for you."

David closed his eyes.

"David?" insisted the lawyer's voice.

"Yes . . . I'm here."

"Sam, you know—the man who worked for your father—?" There was a pause. Then a rush of hurried words. "Sam found Chester early this morning, in his study. Your father —he's dead, David. I want you to know how sorry I am. I hate to be the one to have to tell you."

David's eyelids tightened. His mind was burning, then chill, numbing and distant. He felt himself dodging the impact.

"What—happened?" His voice managed to perform. Perfunctory words. No suspension of disbelief. This was not happening. Other fathers died, not his.

The line crackled. Barksdale's voice was flaccid.

"Suicide. County coroner just left your father's plantation. I'm having the body brought to the funeral home in Bickford. That okay? David? I'm sorry, real sorry."

"What happened?" David heard himself saying.

There was a long pause. "David . . . it was a suicide. I know you'd want me to be honest with you. I fixed it with the M.E. so on the records and in the papers it'll be called accidental. He was as fine a man as I ever knew. Just tell me what you want me to do and I'll take care of things until you can get down." The voice paused, waiting for response.

"Davie?" frowned Sandra, worried.

David stood up. He dropped the receiver and reeled back from the chair, reaching for the table to support himself. The receiver was pulled from the table by the stretched cord. It hit the floor. The lawyer's voice made questioning sounds from the floor like a repeating toy demanding his name.

David looked down at Melanie. Her face gazed back up at him, frowning, her open mouth full of cereal. A bird sang in the tree outside the kitchen windows. Sandra got up and picked up the receiver.

David walked to the back door, feet shuffling as if he'd forgotten how to walk. Sandra's voice came from behind him, questioning, answering the phone. David looked out with a sudden curious amazement into the dawn-filled courtyard where men and women hurried from their apartments to carry on the business of their lives. In that instant he despised them all. They were alive and his father was dead. He reached again to feel pain but the numbness was thick. Shock held him at a distance. He wanted to cry out, to weep, but it was not possible yet. And he realized Barksdale had said suicide. That was utterly unbelievable.

Keeping an eye on David, Sandra spoke with the lawyer. She saw his shoulders shake once as if he shivered. The lawyer repeated his message to her. She pursued details. What must be done. She saw the next week of their life torn apart.

Almost reluctantly, Barksdale added: "I hope we can take care of the will right after the funeral. I know that might sound strange, but it's kind of a strange will. Unorthodox, to say the least. Your father-in-law brought it into my office just last week. Will you-all contact the funeral home in Bickford and make arrangements for coming down?"

Sandra performed. Her mind clicked into gear, the automatic controls taking over. Formalities. Burial, tears. Weekend in the country. It was ironic how badly they needed one. She remembered seedily the burial of her own father. Little girl with her mother's hot hand wrapped heavily around hers. The sweaty force of the maternal hand. Its trembling as they wept. The weeping. The platitudes. The moldy aroma of deep violated earth as the ornate steel ugliness of the casket went down on ropes forever. God, she didn't need this now.

Staring into the courtyard David tried to feel grief. Flecks of the nightmare caught darkly in the matrix of his thoughts. His father's face in horror. His father. He had dreamed of his father trapped in some dark place, and something hideous clawing to get in.

"Daddy? What's wrong?" Melanie's arms hugged his legs.

Sandra watched David turn, bend, and hug Melanie. His eyes were dreamy, disturbed and distant. But there was more. She strove to read it. A darkness in his eyes, like dread.

Three

Hardly aware of the yellow Scout, the traffic, the turns, he drove mechanically to the hospital. Dialogues toyed through his mind. My father, the suicide. I need a week off, sir. No, I'm not crying.

His mind reeled, pivoting, taking absurd tangents. Suicide. What had the texts said? Tenth leading cause of death. Divorced suicides highly ranked. Method? Barksdale hadn't said. Firearms highest percentage. Poisons. Gas. Hanging. Strangulation. Drowning. Jumping from high places. Cutting or piercing instruments. Classic features? Fatal cuts preceded by tenative incisions. Drowners piling clothes neatly. Chest bared before gunshot. What had Nietzsche said? *The thought of suicide is a great consolation: with the help of it one has got through many a bad night*. Where had he been? Not with his father, who he knew now had obviously needed him. Where were the tears? Big boys don't cry. Reference? Schottstaedt observes that when a mother admonishes her son who has hurt himself that big boys don't cry, she is teaching him stoicism.

But he knew it wasn't stoicism. It was shock, waiting to explode. When it happened, when it finally hit, he would calmly observe himself going to pieces in grief. He had loved his father. He still did.

He realized he was at the hospital. Its brick towers rose against a bright unclouded blue sky. This was what he had chosen. This over the land, over his father. It was as if he belonged nowhere now.

He parked the battered yellow Scout in the staff parking lot near the emergency entrance. It was half past nine. He would go through the motions, not feeling the full assault, hoping it wouldn't hit in the chief of surgery's office, explaining why he needed a week off.

He left the Scout in a packed row of Jags, Cads, Lincolns, and Mercedes and walked through the E.R. doors. He halted. A struggle was going on near the desk. A massive black man fought a clot of nurses and orderlies. He was gagging, growing weaker but still slamming his arms into them. Two shrieking little girls jerked futilely on a withered nurse's arms.

David forgot his own state of disbelief, his own suspended tragedy. The black man collapsed. He fell. His feet kicked. David was quickly among the orderlies and nurses. Kneeling, he forced the clenched jaw open. The tongue was cyanotic, blue. Something blocked the airway. Fingers couldn't reach. An intern came running with a scalpel. David took it, pierced the throat, saw blood bubble, heard air wheeze and hiss. The stiffened half-conscious man flopped back in apparently exquisite relief.

"Fish bone—fish bone!" one of the little girls cried.

David stood, blinking, shaking his head. Minutes later, at the elevator, he stepped back for a bevy of young nurses and felt their eyes. Their smiles were vital, fresh against the grim background of death that rose like a black wall in his mind, every common vitality a mocking contrast.

On the second floor he paused at the lounge door. Coke-sipping interns discussed blood platelets, cadaver grafts, and alveoli survival over baloney sandwiches. They saw him and waved invitingly. Saying nothing, he continued down the sterile corridor, mind fixed in disbelief. He stopped at a door marked Chief of Surgery. He knocked.

"Come in," a sternly familiar voice came.

As David gripped the doorknob, traces of the early-morning nightmare ebbed back suddenly. A thick wedge of heat rising in his throat like poison. He started not to open the door at all. He didn't have to explain, to say the words out loud that were rehearsing over and over in his brain—"My father is—Daddy is—Dead?"

"I said *come in,*" the voice repeated. David opened the door and walked in.

Through first and second periods in the music room at White Station Junior High, Sandra listened to advanced students banging away on the upright Vose school piano. Her present student had short thick fingers that could barely reach an octave. Her eyes were on the back of his moving fuzzy red hair, but she hardly heard the lurching gallop of his chords. She kept seeing the fear in David's eyes. Fear, more than hurt. And dread. She had seen that too. His grief hadn't poured out of him like it should have. He had insisted on going to work this morning, his dazed eyes like two-way mirrors—throwing back her own smiles and expressions of concern but holding in a pain she could only guess at. His mother's death had been ghastly enough. The encroaching cancer eating her from inside. Gradual decay. The lessening of life day by day. He leaned on her hard, needing her, and she knew that this was somehow much worse, straining every fiber of perception in an effort of approach and understanding.

He wouldn't tell me his dream, she remembered. Not like David.

She intuited some connection, but what? He would break down and tell, need her. She loved him so much she was jealous even of his private pain. She hurt for him now, feeling uneasy heat beneath her breasts as discordant as the agonized hammering of the old upright school piano, its keys racked by stubby fingers.

She heard girls squealing. She glanced through the music room windows. Fifth-grade girls playing soccer on the elementary field. Even at this distance she could distinguish Melanie from the others. She raced back and forth in a forward position on the blue team. Stealing the ball suddenly, she moved it toward the goal through a clutter of frantic opponents. She kicked and they screamed unhappily.

"You gorgeous tomboy," she said aloud.

"Huh?" asked the kid at the piano, turning a ruddy square face glinting with braces.

Outside, on the field, Melanie dodged and intercepted the white and black soccer ball. The ball popped the net. The girls screamed in delight and disappointment. The ball went into play again. Melanie trotted back to center field. Shouting at the head of her troops, long hair silken in the sunlight, her cheeks were as red as if rouged, her long smooth legs pumping, maneuvering, twisting.

She was running upfield after the ball when some of the girls began to squeal. Melanie looked, stopping. Streak was running across the field straight toward her. Girls fled in all directions. Streak reached Melanie, nipping at her, leaping and circling in delight. Red-faced and square-bodied like a female weight lifter in short-shorts, the gym teacher shouted angrily, without coming near the Doberman. It was the last day of school so Melanie paid no attention. She knelt, rubbing Streak's head.

"You bad boy, how many times have I told you you can't follow me to school? How did you get out this time?"

Streak just kept licking. The teacher kept shouting.

Sandra sat beside Melanie on the faded corduroy couch in the living room. The television was on, volume low. *Voyage of Sinbad.* A bald Hollywood sorcerer in a starry robe. Kathryn Grant cringing in his palm. Tiny princess in terror.

Sandra touched Melanie's hand. "The next few days will be kind of rough, honey. For daddy, and for you and me, too. I want you to understand that if daddy acts funny, it's because he's hurt. Understanding is what makes us family. Okay?"

Melanie winced. "I know how I'd feel if daddy—died."

"We want to do everything to help him feel better. He needs us a lot right now." Sandra rubbed her daughter's head, felt rigid contours of bone under silken hair. "I was just about your age when my own daddy died," she reflected, feeling an odd detachment. A hollow place that David had only partially filled. A desolation she hardly understood.

Streak brought Melanie the half-eroded rubber ball.

"Go on now," whispered Melanie.

Sandra looked up and saw David standing in the doorway, his eyes upon them glacially in turn. Then his face was softening. His eyes reddening.

Melanie ran to him. He knelt quickly, with open arms.

Four

Obituary from *Mississippi Delta Courier,* Greenville, Miss., biweekly:

ACCIDENTAL GUNSHOT DEATH OF PROMINENT BICKFORD PLANTER

Chester Harlan Rawlings, 53, of Bickford, owner of Whitewood plantation, was found dead in his home about 9 A.M. yesterday, Bickford sheriff D. Pounds reported. Pounds said Rawlings was found lying across the desk in his study by plantation employee and long-time companion, Samson Johnson. The medical examiner's office of Hatchie County has ruled the death an accidental self-inflicted gunshot wound.

Rawlings was well known in the Bickford community, and highly regarded. He was a combat veteran of World War Two, serving in Europe, and was formerly known in trapshooting circles. Leah Rawlings, his wife, had passed on three years ago. He leaves a son, Doctor David Rawlings, of Memphis. Memorial Funeral Home of Bickford is in charge. Services are scheduled for 2 P.M. Saturday at the home.

Addendum news item:

BICKFORD REACTS TO TRAGEDY—D. T. Hill

The mood of Bickford was one of shock as the news spread of Chester Rawlings' death. Samson Johnson, who found the deceased, was unavailable for interview, but this reporter found sorrow among townsfolk. Mr. Grady Barksdale, the deceased's attorney, said, "Chester Rawlings was well liked around Bickford. We'll all miss him. It's definitely a shame."

Rawlings' death is the second major tragedy of the year for Bickford.

In the sensational case only three months ago, young Bickford banker Hamilton Butler was found dead in his home in Bickford proper. The ruling was suicide. Holly Butler, his wife, was committed to Whitworth Sanatorium in Jackson. Their eleven-year-old daughter, Lisa, former student at Hine Elementary, is still listed as missing. In spite of all efforts, neither county authorities nor the FBI have turned up any clue to her whereabouts. Still current is a $10,000 reward offered by a prominent Bickford citizen, who remains anonymous.

All of us who knew Chester feel a loss. We extend condolences to his son, David, a resident of Memphis, and his only living relative of immediate family.

In the yellow Scout—its hatch space stuffed with odd and worn overnight luggage, topped with Melanie's comics, with Streak's stainless steel pan and a half-bag of Ken'l Burgers—they left Memphis on the expressway around its southern belly. The morning was fresh. David glanced back at low white clouds over the uneven gray river bluff skyline. Behind him was Beale Street, Elvis Presley's home, the Lorraine Motel where a Nobel Prize winner had died, a vastness of industry and hospitals and universities, of friendly suburbs and dangerous inner-city slums.

On the back seat with Streak, Melanie pointed as they passed the champagne-glass construction of the Memphis International Airport terminal. Then the city was receding. I–55 led south into Mississippi, toward Jackson. Sandra through chic sunglasses smiled as she always did at the corny sign—crossed cotton bolls and WELCOME TO MISSISSIPPI. It was a quarter past nine.

David felt the warm window breeze, smelled the thickening vegetation of the countryside, watched the land on either side of the expressway rise and fall in gentle slopes. He kept his thoughts from straying into dangerous grim formations of death and suicide, of the man he had most respected in this life.

In the back seat Melanie read *Spiderman*. Streak had his head out her window, red tongue lolling in the sixty-mile-an-hour wind, his eyes slits in the black sheen of fur. Sandra's profile was calmly sensuous. Loose white blouse fluttering in the breeze. No sign of introspection. He envied her. Then he knew better. She had liked Chester. Never known her own father. At least, he had.

A hundred miles out, Melanie pointed exertedly at a

Stuckey's sign. They exited. David despised the sugary plastic of the place, its red and yellow bogusness, but Melanie deserved any concession he could make to her. This afternoon, and especially tomorrow, the child would confront appalling, even frightening displays of adult emotion. A subtle change of watchfulness had come over the child. She seemed to be keeping an eye on him aside. He hoped she wouldn't suffer too much, no longer thinking of himself. . . . It was much easier not to.

They pulled out of Stuckey's and were riding again. Melanie sucked loudly on twin milkshake straws. She let Streak lick the cup. In front, David heard her giggling. He and Sandra both looked back—the cup was stuck on Streak's head like a long nose cone. The big Doberman, usually so-noble but now so-baffled, twisted his head back and forth in embarrassment, pawing the cup. David and Sandra traded suppressed grins. Then both strained faces broke with irrepressible laughter. Taking pity, muttering sympathetically, Melanie tugged the absurd cup off Streak's nose. He snorted, licking his jowls in humiliation.

David tried out the C-B, catching chatter on 17, a rich country twang: "Hey, little lady, what's your handle?"

"Afternoon Dee-light," a woman answered seductively.

David and Sandra laughed. Melanie leaned up over the seat.

"This here's Beaver-Pleaser, Afternoon Dee-light. What's your location?"

David switched it off. Amused, Sandra nodded approval.

"It was just getting good!" protested Melanie.

David grinned. Reaching back, he knuckled her soft cheek gently, lovingly. For now, they were happy, absorbed in each other rather than what lay ahead.

David exited the expressway. The blacktop turned west toward the Mississippi River. A bullet-pocked sign said *BICKFORD—29*. The landscape was more sentient as the distance from the expressway grew. Between sporadic farms were dense growths of gum and brier from which moss-hung oaks rose against the glaring blue sky. The wooded shadows were deep and secret. In open fields sunlight lay broken between sprouting rows of cotton and soybeans.

David felt the old timeless quality of hidden age in the soil and the woods, a gnawing nostalgia. Streak barked at cows and horses. Aloud, Melanie counted the farms . . . thirteen . . . eighteen . . . twenty-six. Like a tape in her mind, Sandra listened to Debussy, to Ravel and Satie.

The highway smoothed and straightened. Ragged ditch weeds were suddenly cut and trim. Houses popped from tame trees. White fences and mailboxes lined the road.

Slowing the Scout, entering Bickford, David felt a familiar and not unpleasant claustrophobia. Coming home to this town was like going back in time when he had been a boy with a boy's hopes and a boy's feelings. It was startlingly easy to see the town again through those boy's eyes he had long since forgotten. Déjà vu invaded him like a trance.

Lining the slowness of the main drag, inevitable old men sat in chairs tilted back on storefront porches. Their worn-out boots propped on railings, red jaws chewing. The only filling station in town was still a converted clapboard house, changed incongruously—almost making him laugh—by a new plastic Exxon sign revolving on a stark white pole. Its attendant wore long hair, the lone sign of any encroachment of city fashion.

"Funny town," stared Melanie, "like in a movie or something."

"You've been here before," said Sandra.

"No different than a thousand others just like it," David smiled. "Families living out generation after generation."

Sandra had taken off her sunglasses. She saw two old men staring as the Scout moved past a store, and she put the glasses back on.

"Weird," Melanie said.

"We were here just last year," said David.

Melanie shrugged. "I know, but I was a little kid then."

Sandra glanced at David to trade smiles but she saw his profile staring ahead. Looking forward she saw the elaborately corny sign on its wrought-iron post. MEMORIAL FUNERAL HOME OF BICKFORD. Looking again at David's profile she saw a flush of restraint. His eyes were too hard. His mouth too soft. She turned across the seat to hand Melanie a hair brush as the Scout slowed and stopped at the sign. The funeral home seemed to have been, once, a small but very nice Victorian house. Few cars were on the street.

Do I have to come? asked Melanie's eyes. Sandra nodded with a firmness in her lips.

But David surprised her. "You two stay out here. I won't be a minute, okay? I have to check on some things." His voice was not husky; rather, too light. Sandra leaned across the seat, kissed him, and let her eyes probe his.

David stared back at her. At moments like this he wondered truly how in hell he ever would have made it without her. He opened the door and slid from the seat. His feet struck hot Bickford asphalt, sticky and clinging under his soles.

Sandra watched him follow neat flagstones that dotted sun-dappled Bermuda grass. Double oak doors on a fresh white porch were flanked by tall narrow stained-glass windows. David went inside. I wish he didn't have to, she thought. Why do people have to die?

She tried to remember her own father but could only catch the heat of her mother's gripping hand. She smelled fresh earth, tasted the salty-wet kiss of her mother's tears, saw the ornate coffin lowered on ropes forever. Why do the ones who love us ever have to go away?

Streak barked at a squirrel on the lawn. Melanie hushed him.

Sandra turned to look. The nearness of death—with David in there—somehow heightened Melanie's beauty. Nuzzling Streak, her laugh was innocent and sweet. Sandra had a vision of youth that would irrevocably fade and crumble beneath the erosion of years and adult experience. Suddenly she wondered if maybe she wasn't even a little pleased that David's father was gone now, too . . . no longer envious because she'd never really had one. *Quit it right now!* she heard her secret voice warning. She hated it when she was morbid.

"Does everybody have to die, mommy?" asked Melanie, taking Sandra utterly by surprise.

She stroked her daughter's silken dark hair. "Maybe . . . we don't really die, honey." Of course she didn't believe that. It was a groped comment, a platitude. She hated any lie and was not religious. There was life, the end of life was death. But that stunning simplicity was too harsh to admit to the child she loved. "Maybe it's kind of like a change we go through," she suggested.

Melanie's brilliant blue eyes deepened in thought.

"You mean—like we go to heaven . . . or hell?"

"Nobody knows for sure," replied Sandra honestly.

Melanie sighed.

"Where did the idea of heaven and hell come from then?"

Sandra shook her head. "I guess from people who were scared and had to figure out a way not to be." Instantly she wished she had phrased it another way, some idyllic, pleasing lie. But her daughter merely nodded.

"I guess everything bad is scary. If I die I'll come back and tell you, or try to send like a message about how it was."

Sandra turned across the seat and kissed Melanie, surprising the child. "Honey, you're not going to die." She heard her own fervent lie, wanting to believe it, kissing the smooth soft cheek. Her daughter was everything precious in life, everything beautiful and defensible.

Stepping inside the air-conditioned hush of the funeral home, David steeled himself, smothered in padded silences. Overstuffed chairs in dull colors. Through a doorway he saw it. Closed casket resting on a velvet-covered bier. He moved through the room to the open door. The casket was closed. Its brass handles gleamed cheaply, brightly plated. Jesus looked down from pictures on the walls. Bent double, a tall aged black man sat on a low couch droning prayers in muted cadence. David stood staring without breathing. He knew the old man well. He heard the sharp edge of fear in sporadic muffled words—

". . . and deliver him from evil . . . Let your rod and your staff comfort him. . . . Yea, though he walk through the valley of the shadow of death, be with him. . . . He loved you, Lord, don't turn your face away. . . ." The words ceased. The long tear-sad face of Samson Johnson turned with sudden awareness of a stranger. Its leathery web cracked open in a sudden glad grin, handsome yet vulnerable.

"Sam," David said as the old man arose.

They met with open arms and embraced. Swaying, David felt Sam's massive frame tightening about him.

"Sam, Sam, Sam," he cried. He wanted the tears to come hard and unexpectedly. But though his face was hot, no tears came. Sam's head pressed his neck and shoulder. He smelled whiskey, felt Sam's tears smearing wet heat on his cheek. Huge hands patted his back. For that moment he was a boy again with the proud and rascally wise black man who had half-raised him, who had lived with his father nearly four decades.

Sam pushed David away. They gazed at arm's length. David saw a dark face bright with grief and smiling.

"Doctor," grinned Sam. His bull neck rose from a cheap starched white collar like a stump. A front gold cap gleamed.

David nodded. An irony flashed—Physician, heal thyself. The big hands tightened on his shoulders.

"I'm proud of you, boy—he was, too. Don't you never think your daddy wasn't proud of his son."

Sam's yellowish eyes probed into his, and David looked back and saw pain—yet there was something more, mixing secret and dark, something he had never seen in all his life in Sam's eyes—was it fear? Sadness, he thought, sorrow so strong it was brother to fear. Sam had never been susceptible to fear. And—fear of what?

Sam turned to the casket and lowered his head with a miserable sigh.

"So bad they couldn't leave it open, David."

"Why, Sam? Why would Chester do it to himself?" He realized he didn't even yet know *how*.

David put an arm around the tall proud old man. He could almost feel his pain flowing together with Sam's. There were many questions. But not now. Sam snuffled.

"I loved that man, boy."

David shuddered. Heat, huge and rising, simmered in his chest. His eyes burned drily. Unbidden, seductive, a montage of images rushed across his mental screen, sweet, happy, cruel—walking with Sam and Chester in fields of sage coppery with autumn light of dusk, the bird dog running ahead—the comfort of Chester's arms when mother had died, just three years ago—Chester's strong but sweet face, hair going white, deep eyes blue, sad, pure, the love in them naked as they sat in rapprochement together on the bluff and watched the great broad river gleam under blood-red sunset—Chester's mouth opening to laugh, the boom of it virile, stronger than he thought his would ever grow to be—the forgotten sureness of a strong hand gripping his wrist as he sank underwater time and awful time again until in the deep green creek he at last learned to swim—

"What made him do it, Sam?" He heard himself asking, "Was it mother?"

Sam sighed, shook his head. David saw the dark emotion flit across Sam's eyes again, like sudden fear. "He took it hard when she went, you know as well as me, David. But I thought he was over it. Then this year he started going off by himself, gone sometimes all night, never saying where. Tried to follow him once and he raised his hand to me. Onliest time he ever done that. I never followed no more. And if I'd ask, he'd give me a look like something was making him scared. But never said a word, like I didn't ask nothing at all. . . ." Sam heaved a deep long sigh. "Finally I left thc place three months ago. He made me go. Later I thought and I thought and decided to come back and he was. . . . He used his pistol, son." Sam pointed to his temple, put a hand wearily on the casket. "I wasn't there when he needed me."

"None of us were. . . . God." His mind fixed on guilt, David stared at the scrollwork motif on the casket lid, felt the impossibility of trying to imagine the bullet-shattered skull of the man he had loved. The man who had loved him. Somehow, he had known all along it had been a gun.

Bell chimes tinkled. A short heavy middle-aged woman clomped into the room. Her face was round, red, over-made-up, tiny lips and tiny eyes florid, the orange curly hair bobbed like Harpo Marx. Seeing David and Sam, blinking back fresh tears, her short fat arms opened, she shuffled quickly toward David.

"Aw, honey, I'm so sorry, so sorry." Ruth Sheehan's flaccid body slammed into David. He let her press him close, her damp purple tent dress sticking to his hands. Called Sister Ruth, she lived in a trailer on the road out of town that led to David's homeplace, eking a starveling existence from "auras" and palms. David had known her nearly all of his life. She was a good woman and a friend of his father. David had always liked her in spite of the small-town reputation as queer and forbidding. Townsfolk joked about her publicly but David knew many of them secretly visited her.

"You pore baby." She rubbed his head.

Her thick fetid motherly embrace brought back childhood superstitions. Her deodorant and raw flowery perfume were overwhelming.

She whispered in his ear: "Your daddy . . . he was brave and good. David . . . more than you can guess, son."

He extracted himself from her arms. She and Sam stared. They looked curiously at him and glanced uncomfortably at each other like accomplices in an unsuccessful conspiracy. He frowned. Then he thought, You're back in the country, man, down here where God and Jesus and the devil are real and believed. Where people live more by faith than by fact. Be tolerant, they love you. If they know anything you should know, you'll find out soon enough.

"Hi, Sam," Ruth smiled. She put out her hand. Sam took it in both of his and patted it. "Don't he favor his daddy more and more?" She smiled weakly, showing bad teeth between orange lips.

Sam nodded gravely. Their eyes exchanged something understood.

A thin-bodied but baby-faced bald man in a black suit with hard creases appeared in the doorway to the second room. Hands clasped piously on his chest, he smiled with exaggerated sympathy, not parting his lips. David turned to look at Ron Phelps, the mortician.

He detached himself from Sam and Ruth.

"Can we go in there and talk a minute?"

David had, like every other kid in Bickford, feared and avoided this shrewish, ageless little profiteer in death. The holdover came now in spite of adulthood and knowledge of medicine. Phelps nodded meekly. David followed into a smaller room.

They sat on a tufted velvet couch. More pictures of Jesus gazed serenely down as David began, steeling himself with a kind of protective detachment.

"I take it the—casket can't be open?"

"No, I'm afraid not, David."

David winced. "I mean, the physical damage was, um, too severe?"

"I'm afraid so. I tried my best. The bullet did a lot. Too much. Will services be held tomorrow, as tentatively scheduled? I took the liberty of making arrangements with Reverend Shackleford, but of course, if tomorrow isn't convenient—" Phelps' eyes blinked, birdlike.

David nodded. He swallowed a thick edge building high in his throat. "What time?"

"Ten o'clock if that's suitable. We'll have proper words here at the home, then move him into the hearse for the cortege. Drive on out to your home."

David frowned. "Out to the plantation?"

Phelps lifted his brow in affirmation.

Phelps sighed patiently. "Your daddy's lawyer, Barksdale, has already handled the private grave permit through county offices. Your daddy stipulated in his will that he be buried in you-all's private family cemetery near the river bluff. Didn't you know that? I assumed . . ."

David shook his head. The old plot on the plantation held generations of Rawlings, but not since his grandfather had passed on had anyone been put to rest there.

"His wish was to be laid away in the crypt," mused Phelps soothingly, blinking. "Sam has already prepared it at Barksdale's instructions. It was all clear in your father's will. I understand he made the request only a week or so before he—well, before—"

"I understand," David muttered. The atmosphere of the little room, the closeness to the mortician, seemed stifling. His breath felt thick and labored, his body hot and sluggish.

He stood. "I'll see you tomorrow, then."

He moved suddenly from the room. Sam and Ruth stood by the casket. He avoided their eyes and went quickly to the doors, feeling the weight of their gaze on his back but unable to speak further.

In the sunlight again, crossing the immaculate Bermuda grass to the yellow Scout where Melanie and Sandra and Streak watched him approach, he tried to free his face from the stiffening mask he knew must appear obscenely dark and afraid, and yet afraid of what, he could not have said. Perhaps it was only himself.

Five

David slid into the Scout. His palms, slick with sweat, kneaded the steering wheel. On the back seat Melanie teased Streak with the rubber ball, giggling impishly. He closed his eyes and sighed. Sandra's fingers brushed his cheek in silent communication—take the pain out of you into myself, love. In that instant he forgot fear and death in a furious surge of love for his small family. He opened his eyes and saw the narrow road ahead. The bucolic little river town of Bickford, Mississippi, where he had gone to school and laughed and cried and learned about becoming an adult. The blue sky, birds wheeling above old uncut oaks lining the street. Fresh white old houses. A knot of boys whooping on bicycles. His father dead. Tomorrow to be put into the ground. Forever.

But these hours belonged to the living. The fear in Sam's eyes was not a good thing. Nor his own inexplicable unsettling dread.

"Let's not spend the night in Bickford," he said.

"Anywhere you say," replied Sandra comfortingly.

Melanie grabbed the front seat. "That Holiday Inn we passed off the expressway—it's got a pool! Daddy, please?"

He smiled. It felt crooked and stiff, breaking through his grimness. He rubbed Melanie's silky head.

"Whatever you say, chief," he grinned, feeling the smoothness of her young cheek with the back of his adult hand.

David U-turned back through Bickford toward the expressway. He slowed and pulled in at the incongruous Exxon sign to fill up. The Scout crossed an air-line, a bell dinged—so much about the old town disturbed David with little tugs of nostalgia. Seeing the old converted house, its warped clapboard. The tobacco signs and ancient Coke machine, the rusty hubcaps nailed over the garage doors, he remembered old Sammy Crowe, gaunt happy drunk who used to pump gas, always a whiff of corn whisky on his breath, always a joke. But some things had changed. From the garage darkness, wiping greasy hands, sauntered a man in his late twenties. Long stringy hair. *ZZ TOP* sweatshirt. A thin dirty beard not hiding pimples but emphasizing eyes too close together.

"Regular," David said. He climbed out and shut the door.

The attendant eyed the Tennessee plates, picking his nose furtively. "Y'awl from Memphis?"

"Used to live here, though."

"You not—Dave Rawlings, are you?" Suspicious smile showing yellow strong teeth.

David nodded defensively.

"Do I know you?"

"I'm Woody Sheehan, Ruth's son. Must be ten years."

David smiled with recognition. "You've changed." He realized the irony of the long hair—ten years ago a longhair uninformed enough to wander near Mississippi was in danger of castration. Now it was the style. Ruth's boy, Woody—always in some kind of petty trouble, never making it to school. A decent type, happy-go-lucky, a prankster.

"Fill 'er up?" Woody asked.

"You aren't still watering it down these days?" joked David.

Woody grabbed the pump nozzle and grinned. "Old Sammy used to water it some, I reckon. I don't, though. Ruin my own car if I was to."

Woody grabbed the stiff black hose toward the Scout. Streak lunged abruptly from a window, snarling, baring long white fangs, his almond eyes slitted in anger.

"Whoa!" cried Woody, leaping back.

David whirled with surprise. Not like Streak at all. He reached to stuff Streak's head back in the window. But the Doberman kept snarling, threatening Woody.

"Get him, Melanie," scolded Sandra.

Melanie tugged the big dog back inside. "Bad boy! What's the matter with you?"

Woody made tentative moves toward the gas cap. Streak lunged again. The weight of his shoulders cracked the rear glass. With a backward leap Woody dropped the gas nozzle. The big dog snarled raggedly, watching him.

"Christ!" Irritated, puzzled, David picked up the nozzle and unscrewed the gas cap and plugged in the nozzle himself, shaking his head. He clocked the feed on automatic. Again Melanie tugged Streak's head back into the Scout.

On the other side of the pumps, Woody wiped beads of sweat from his face with trembling filthy hands, adding streaks of black grease to those already there.

"Sorry," David sighed. "Guess we're all of us out of sorts today."

Woody glowered. His eyes were locked with Streak's. "I don't like them Dobermans, man, y'awl keep him away. Hate to have to run and get my scatter gun."

David felt brief revulsion. "That won't be necessary. I don't know what's got into him."

Woody rubbed his thighs. He glared at the Scout. Speaking without facing David. "Guess you're burying your daddy tomorrow."

"Yes," David mouthed through brittle lips. He glanced down the road away from Ruth's ugly son.

"Momma told me all about it. They was good friends. My momma and your daddy. Too bad. Some bad things happened in Bickford this year."

Stiffening, David watched the spinning numbers on the face of the pump, wanting them to hurry. Sandra opened her door. She crossed the lot toward the archaic Coke machine. Woody stared appraisingly. David watched him with disgust.

"Want one?" Sandra called to David.

He nodded.

"Me, too!" cried Melanie from the back seat.

The pump clicked off. David replaced the cap and handed a ten to Woody. Woody made change from a filthy jeans pocket. The bills felt limp and warm in David's hand. In the back seat with Melanie, Streak still snarled, low and rumbling. David had never heard the dog make a sound remotely like that. It was the kind of warning he might have imagined had that old man in the old apartments been near.

"Mean sombitch, ain't he?" Woody muttered. "Anyway I was sorry about your daddy."

David gave a false smile and climbed into the Scout. Sandra climbed in the other side and handed him a wet chilly glass-bottled Coke.

"Ten cents. In a bottle instead of a can. I'm not believing this town of yours, David. Every time we've come here it's been like The Land Time Forgot or something."

"Yeah," David agreed softly. He put the Scout in gear and pulled out onto the narrow roadway.

Melanie released Streak's slip-chain as the Scout took speed. The Doberman lunged immediately at the window, his head glaring back at the station where Woody stood wiping his hands by the pumps, growing smaller and smaller.

The Scout took speed. Sunlight strobed through overhanging trees. Then they were out of town, passing the farms again. Melanie watched the stock animals, rubbing Streak with one hand, glad he was settling down.

"Can we ever live in the country, daddy, ever—ever?"

"Maybe someday." *You had that chance,* he thought.

"Because I want a horse. Could I ever have one?"

"Sure," he shrugged.

Melanie grabbed the front seatrest and threw smooth arms around his neck, nearly choking him, smothering his cheek with wet warm kisses.

"Hey!" warned Sandra. She pushed her daughter. "Want us upside-down in the ditch?"

"No way," grinned David. "I'm the Great White Driver."

"Well, just watch the road, okay?" Sandra hated cars. She hated all road trips. The night of her Senior Prom, her drunken date—in a macho rage after being refused the intimacy of her breasts—had raced his Stingray over a dangerous crooked road east of Memphis. She had seen the tree coming at them. With incredible suddenness the next thing she saw was the hospital. Awakening, lights phasing in and out. The face of her mother weeping by the bed. The awful sting of her face, encrusted with bandages. Tubes violating her numb body. Cars were things of necessity, never taken lightly. David had had to learn to drive more carefully after he met her. But he understood her fear, like he seemed to understand everything.

Miles passed. Sandra and Melanie sang—*Sergeant Pepper's Lonely Hearts Club Band, we hope you will enjoy the show*—a song from one of Sandra's favorite old albums. Even David joined in. And then Streak began to howl. They broke up with laughter but kept up the tempo. Sandra scooted close to David on the front seat.

An hour later, a bloated red sun hung low over the blackening western horizon of jagged trees, a Holiday Inn sign appeared in the distance, blinking its message of no surprises.

At half past six David laid stretched out on an aluminum lounge chair by the Holiday Inn's small oval pool. Below him in the water a preteen nymph backstroked. He could hardly believe she was Melanie. Her streamlined contours moved hypnotically. In the lounger beside him Sandra read a historical romance. He shivered. The first evening breezes freshed his water-beaded chest and face and limbs. His eyes kept going to Melanie. Purple and orange sunset-flecked water moved with her. A dark streak of hair trailed her head. Her leotard-tight navy blue tank suit showed the first budding of breasts. She plunged under the surface. His heart quickened, his vision sharpening involuntarily. Her shadow almost disappeared under the reflected sunset. He sat up but she surfaced, spewing water happily, treading and waving for him to come back in. Giggling, she splashed water at Sandra. Sandra sat up quickly with a little cry, then laughed.

God, I love them, thought David.

With a sudden spring he was up on his feet. Melanie squealed with delight, paddling away. He bent and leaped out into the air over the water, arms tucking legs, landing on the gentle surface in a huge cannonball splash that shattered the ripple of sunset colors.

As David laughed and trod water, watching Melanie brush water-slick hair from her smooth forehead, it all came back—lazy afternoons as a boy, Johnson's Mill Pond, swinging far out over the green warm smooth water on the rough wet hemp rope, letting go at the apex of a high arc, falling forever before the water came up to cover him with the roar of his plunge into iron-cold dark, then the rise through black then green and sunlight again, the bold sunlight that was always waiting at the surface above the dark cold belly of the pond.

David and Melanie sat exhausted by swimming and laughing on the tiled edge of the pool, drying off with thick soothing towels. Melanie rubbed her hair. An unusually serious expression crossed her delicate brow and lips.

"Daddy?" she questioned softly.

He felt fantastic. "Hmm?"

"Is there really a . . . hell?"

David felt the good mood sink. He stared away as the sun disappeared under the blackening tops of nearby trees. He swept the dark pause away and faced her.

"I don't know," he admitted, at a loss for truth.

"I mean . . . if there is . . . Granddaddy Chester, he doesn't have to go there, docs he? Because of the way . . . he died?"

David shut his eyes. Suicides go to hell—*I don't believe in heaven or hell. In fairy tales or myths or superstition.* I was taught it in church as a kid but I'm grown now and I know that *what I see is all that is real.*

"I'm sorry," Melanie said gently. Her hand was on his arm, the thin soft kind fingers of a child.

He looked at her and smiled.

"It's all right. I was just thinking. No, he doesn't have to go there. Nobody does. Not unless . . . maybe not unless they believe in it." He wondered why he had said that.

But she nodded, seeming satisfied.

Melanie thought, looking away from her daddy at the sunset, But *what if granddaddy did believe* and that's where he had to go?

Sandra snapped her paperback shut. "Come on, aquapeople, let's put on the feedbag."

David stood up. "Hungry?"

"Ravenous," Sandra grinned. She picked up the suntan oil and extra towels and urged Melanie along with a wet slap on her small round buttocks.

Six

The plastic atmosphere of the Holiday Inn restaurant was ironically soothing to Sandra. She despised Muzak, found gilded plaster coats of arms ridiculous, was repelled by the clammy plastic booths. But it was all somehow like being back in the city.

Food came—seafood platter for Melanie, rib-eye steaks for David and Sandra, relatively cheap but probably good. No wine on the menu. Cokes would have to do.

"Everything all right?" force-smiled the red-faced old waitress whose hair shone like blue steel in the indirect light.

David nodded falsely, wincing at the Roquefort, mostly mayonnaise. Little old lady waitresses always had an advantage on him—he felt sorry to see grandmothers hustling dishes for strangers.

"Watch out for bones," he told Melanie.

"Scallops don't have bones, daddy."

Melanie ate one portion of the dish at a time, devouring the platter with a relish David could hardly remember. Her vitality made him grin.

"Don't choke yourself," warned Sandra.

She threw David an understanding smile. As Melanie had grown, so had their relationship. Their initial body-love had borne fruit and now their love was intertwined with love for the child. Shared moments of communal love. Not even when they were alone in bed, with the fervent bodily search of passion, was Melanie far away.

Catching Sandra's smile, David winked. Her smile deepened

and suddenly he wanted her tonight. The impossibility of having her alone in the motel room made him want her more. Her sensual smile seemed to know all that. His eyes took her in deeply, sending back a rakish promissory grin. Under the table, provokingly, she scolded and taunted with a stroking gesture of fingers, her smile growing even more sensual. To David at this moment she was more beautiful and desirable than any woman had the right to be.

"What are you two grinning about?" teased Melanie.

David and Sandra laughed simultaneously. David's toe brushed Sandra's calf under the table. They laughed again. People at the other tables stared. Sandra averted her face. David made faces back at them, sending Melanie into giggles of delight.

"Some dessert?" The waitress was suddenly at the edge of the booth, pinch-lipped, matronly.

"Can I have a banana split, daddy? Please?"

"You're gonna pop," chided Sandra.

David grinned. "Bananas flying everywhere."

"One banana split," Sandra said, her eyes probing David's again. They laughed together.

The waitress hurried away in a huff. David knew she thought they were laughing at her. He watched her sad flat bottom shuffle away, then, Sandra's eyes, and again they laughed in unspoken communication.

"You two are weird sometimes," mused Melanie, frowning thoughtfully.

Still laughing, Sandra rubbed her daughter's head with love.

The artificial light of the Holiday Inn was dull against the night. From the distant expressway linking Memphis to Jackson whines and faint thunder of high-speed traffic bled through the walls and windows of no-surprises room sixty-four.

Melanie watched the odd turret-necked motel television; she sat on the floor rubbing Streak's throat, then his shoulder blades where his claws and fangs could not reach, then the base of each ear. She had sneaked him in from the Scout after dinner—Sandra had kept watch for the motel manager—no pets allowed.

Sandra lay on her back on one of the hard double beds, reading the historical romance in a rim of yellow lamplight. A dark handsome stranger pursued a lovely forlorn maiden.

David lay on the other bed watching his wife and child in alternation. His vision strayed over the television. Bionic woman. Moving in slow motion. Featherweight fake boulder flying through the air. Cartoon villains in jump suits scattering, open-mouthed in astonishment. Melanie shouted encouragement to the sleek heroine leaping unconvincingly over a cyclone fence. In his mind, the world tilted.

His father was dead.

Daddy is dead.

His whole body tensed. In this unlikely suspended moment the truth at last took him. The man who loved him was no more. Ceased. Cancelled. Gone forever. It was tragically clear. Never again those calm reassuring eyes. The gentle pressure of his powerful hand. No more chance to heal the wide rift of separation. His father lay in Bickford in a steel box. *Remains.* What was there beyond *remains*? What was gone, that the residue should be described as *remains*? Will granddaddy Chester have to *go to hell*, daddy?

David rose stiffly from the bed. He went into the bathroom and shut the door before they saw what was happening to his face. He stood on the tiles alone. Stripping quickly, holding deep in his chest a choking rise of heat, he turned on the shower and stepped into hard cold water.

It crashed over him. He wept in silent rasping bitterness. Tomorrow the remains lowered into the ground forever. Forever. *Forever.*

And where were *you* when he had need? When it was happening—whatever it was, driving him crazy? Making him want to do that to end himself? Was it pride, wanting to be a doctor, not caring that he wanted you to stay on the homeplace and work the plantation to continue the work of generations? And then mother dying, leaving him alone? Where were you?

He ground both fists into his eye sockets. Water as cold as the black bottom of springs smashed full into his face from the shower head.

Oh God, no. Not my fault.

He remembered the night eleven years ago when he had gone into the study to tell Chester he was going to study medicine; to tell, not ask for advice. Mother thinks it's good. I don't want to live here all my life. I don't want that, daddy. Can't you see? It's what I've always wanted. I want to help people, to heal. If you won't help me, I'll do it on my own. I don't need you.

There had been a vicious fight.

He had left, left most of his clothes behind, his old TR–3, even his dog.

And then later, in Memphis, the small checks had come. At first he had sent them back. Then with Sandra and soon with Melanie on the way, he had begun cashing them, wincing in guilt and prideful hurt but spending the money in great need with belated unspoken thankfulness. Help had never really been that far away. Nor love. He had taken Sandra and Melanie down to visit, thinking to heal some of the old wounds. He remembered their first talk together alone in the moonlight on the veranda on the back of the manor, watching the river. Did you know your mother is sick? They give her a year, maybe more. She'll have to go up to a hospital in Memphis soon. We'll see more of you then I suppose, if you want. No matter what, *I love you, son.*

The unbearable weight pressed him against the shower wall. Cold water rained in his face. He saw his mother ghastly against white hospital sheets and tubes. Her personality fading in drugged agony, a travesty through which she reappeared with the light of love shining through unspeakable pain in dying eyes. Chester watched her go bit by bit.

And now it was all blindingly clear. He knew why his father had committed self-destruction. Facing it alone, eroding away inside, sanity fading night after night of torturous pining until he put an end to it.

If I had been with him—instead of going my own way—

He heard a rapping on the bathroom door.

"David? It's Sandy."

He coughed. "Yeah?" he croaked.

Outside the door Sandra stared at the painted wooden panel as if she could see him suffering within.

With a sigh she sank into a plastic motel chair. Melanie prepared for bed, brushing her teeth. Hair in a bow, Melanie stripped in a dark corner by the beds. Her slender naked body shone in the last sudden whiteness as Sandra got up and switched off the television.

Sandra went to the drapes and tightened them though they were firmly drawn.

Turning, she saw Melanie slipping into her flower granny gown. Statuesque, her arms held the gown high over her head for an instant, her legs together, no dark hint of pubic hair between them. Then the gown fell over her like drapery. Snuggling into the wide motel bed, Melanie patted the covers for Streak to join her. Streak hopped on the foot of the bed and curled fetally with a grunt of satisfaction. Sandra cocked her head, grinned, and let them be.

In the privacy of her mind Melanie felt the oncoming of

sleep. Her parents had never taught her to mouth prayers before bed. No blessing was ever said at their table. But as she always did, alone in the rising blackness behind her lids, drifting on a surface in swirling motes of light, she sought the pleasant gentleness—the peace—thinking the words. *now i lay me down to sleep, i pray the Lord my soul to keep, if i should die before i wake, i pray the Lord my soul to take.* . . . please help daddy's hurt. . . . please help granddaddy find his way to the good place. . . . don't hold the bad thing against him, *i bet he's sorry,* okay?

As it would, an answer seemed to come.

Sandra lay on the other bed watching her daughter fall asleep with a sweet curl of lips. Wish I could fall asleep that easily, she thought. Thank God we're kids first. At least it's easy for a while.

She glanced toward the bathroom door. It was opening. David came out in pajama bottoms, rubbing his face with a motel towel. He moved toward the bed with his face averted, in the towel.

She lifted the covers back.

He slid in beside her. She switched off the light and felt for him and was astonished at his sudden arms and the depth of his need as she held him like a forlorn baby in her arms.

In the long-since converted kitchen of his funeral home, Ron Phelps stood over a stainless-steel table. Grooved with drains. A Kool in a fake-ivory holder dangled from his lips. The fresh arrival on his mortuary table was a great-great-grandmother in her nineties. He fretted, meeting the difficulties of draining an age-tightened vascular system to refill it with embalming fluid. The drainage done, he smiled and did something special for her—mixing a full ounce of perfume into the formaldehyde, a scent brought by the infrequent Avon Lady from Jackson; one of his wife's discarded fragrances that she didn't like after purchasing it.

Body work done, he began to create her face. He wished as always that the art could somehow be improved by some method of leaving the eyes open, perhaps by removing the death-glazed eyeballs and substituting glass eyes exactly matching the subject's in life. He sighed. Bowing to tradition he invisibly stretched the lids shut lest they pop open and cause screams during the services.

Parchmentlike skin crackled under his cosmetic brush. He stepped back to admire his work.

Phelps turned suddenly, hearing a whisper of movement. From where? The other rooms in front. A late visitor? No—the front was locked. Or had he forgotten again? Phelps opened the embalming room door. He peeked out with care, keeping his body in the crack of the opening, the contents of this room inviolate. But he saw nothing.

He stepped into the small room where so much grief had spent itself, closing the door quietly behind him. He advanced with studied reverence to the open door of the main room. Nothing, no one here. Flowers had been arriving all day. The dim room was thick with perfume and shadowy colors.

Was the wreath slightly out of place on the Rawlings casket?

Phelps moved to the bier. He did not look up at the thing watching outside the gauzily curtained windows, yet he felt a stirring unease, like the first chill of a meat locker. It was late, he thought, it was the need for sleep.

Meekly but without reservation, Phelps licked his lips and opened the casket to check the cadaver of Chester Rawlings.

Strange. It caught his eye at once—the right arm twisted slightly, the hand no longer arranged in serene composure, stiff fingers twisted as if reaching to cover the stony death-dry face. Phelps replaced the hand with a tongue-cluck of regret. Really too bad the bullet shattered the forehead that way. If the bullet had only destroyed the back of the skull or even both temples, he might have done something very nice with Marvel Wax and a wig. But the broken skull was too much even for his artifices. He smiled warmly at the copper-lined coffin, his very best, its purpose to protect and to aid in preservation of the body. Phelps wondered again whether he should clothe the huge mute body. He decided again that since the casket would never again be open it was a silly waste of a burial suit, and a saving of nearly fifty dollars. He ran an admiring finger over his neat whipstitching V on the abdomen. Then he reclosed the heavy lid of the container upon the abject shell of a man once a pillar of the community, its vascular system and body cavities full of formaldehyde scented with four ounces of English Leather cologne.

He locked the casket and flicked the switch for the blue neon cross over the front porch.

Outside, Sam Johnson stood hidden in the shadows of an evergreen. His eyes were fixed wildly upon the tall dark thing that moved on the porch. His heart hammered. His fists tensed on the shotgun he held as tightly as a drowning man clutches a broken board.

A scatter of rain fell from gathering clouds.

Sam heard the thing hiss. He half-raised the shotgun, shivering.

Rain blew across the porch. The thing there flinched and hissed. It seemed to strain and stretch. Then suddenly it was gliding away.

Sam stared insanely as it melted into deeper shadows across the lawn. He felt a gust of wind, like a sweep of wings in the night, and knew, maddened, that it was gone.

Seven

Morning.

The funeral home was stifling and humid. David sat between Melanie and Sandra on a hard slick pew, Melanie's soft warm hand in his left, Sandra's long cool fingers in his right. On the other pews in three ranks sat various people of Bickford. Ruth, Sam, old ladies, workmen, Barksdale, a scattering of kids. Faces remembered. Sincere and curious. Still, the taste of forgotten boyhood, of returning. His eyes ranged over the ranks of flowers, their mingled fragrances dizzying now as his eyes settled upon Reverend Shacklcford's flushed liver-spotted face and full wide lips. David hardly heard the litany of regret and fulfillment. . . .

"Lord, help these who have loved to always remember their lost one in all his wonderful strength and his honesty and his love of God and of them. . . ."

David had done his crying last night. Now his face was harsh, brittle on the outer surfaces. The white-haired preacher went on. . . .

"God, we know you hear us and feel our words, we know that in thy divine wisdom thou seest into our hearts where we grieve for this man who was loved and who loved us. . . ."

The words rang on but David hardly listened. He was a doctor. Proximity to death and mourning was nothing new. It was his turn now. He faced it materially, rationally. The casket contained dead flesh. There was no spirit to flee magically to some higher place. There was no mystery. Only tragedy. He listened, wincing, tolerating the funeral ceremony, most ancient ritual of man. He and Sandra and Melanie wore black. The incomprehensible words of the wide-lipped preacher were lulling him. Then, like an edge cutting and waking, the words ceased.

All heads bowed in silent prayer.

Melanie peeked, struck by the simple devotion of the mourners. It was something so special, she would always remember. All the flowers, the majestic words said so importantly, the minister sounding like he never doubted a single thing he said.

Sandra steeled herself as the service went on. Annoyed by morbidity, irritated at the overlong eulogy, she nevertheless kept a soft reverent face of proper grief. There might be long hours now, helping David cope. She had plenty on her hands. More than anything she strove not to relate this funeral to that of her own father. Not to bring back that agony and that dread of loss that had haunted all her childhood, making the nights lonely and terrible before meeting David, who had filled that hollowness with the passion of his body and the hope of his love.

The service ended.

Shackleford stepped down from the altar beside the bier. Like waking manikins, mourners rose slowly. David was up shaking hands, nodding gravely. Then Sam was there.

In Sam's arms he almost broke down again, yielding to a flood of compassion from the man who had helped him grow from boyhood. Again, the guilt came hard—*I wasn't there when my father needed me.*

Outside, the sun was bright. Under the weight of the right front of the casket David marched with other men through doors to a waiting six-year-old Cadillac hearse. Its rear door hung wide like a black steel mouth. The breath of the other bearers rasped in David's ears. The brass handle was cold in his grip. Through the handle he felt the dead weight inside the long ornate box. Stiffly, he lowered his end. The casket slid in as he stepped clumsily out of the way.

The cortege was forming. Sam gestured for David to join Sandra and Melanie in the Scout just behind the hearse. For an instant David felt a drop in space. He teetered. Then his legs were moving robotlike.

In the Scout, Sandra's and Melanie's hands reached for him. He climbed in with them.

"David?" asked Sandra.

"It's okay, Sandy . . . I'm fine." He was numb.

"I love you, daddy." Melanie whispered, bending across to

kiss him. David felt a remarkable strength in the small loving grip of her hand.

A bird sang outside the Scout and it began to move.

The cortege passed slowly through Bickford. It was less than twenty vehicles long. David's father had been well known and respected. The small town felt its loss; a small Mississippi town where anything lost was a tragedy to all. Though only close friends and distant relatives participated in the funeral itself, here and there a black band of cloth hung across a front door.

The narrow road wound into the country toward Whitewood, the plantation manor where David had been born in an upstairs bedroom and grew into manhood. In the Scout, he watched the passing farms with a strong sense of unreality. He had come down this road with his father so many times. Now—the last time.

The cortege passed the ruins of an antebellum manor.

"Whose house was that one, daddy?"

"Family named Houston." David astonished himself with the calm clarity of his voice. "But they were gone before I was born. There's another bigger mansion a few miles ahead, the DeBois place, before we get to Whitewood." Whitewood, the ancestral home built by his great-grandfather. He felt quick pride and pursuing guilt. He had left it.

The cortege passed Ruth Sheehan's trailer—high weeds and a tall hand-shaped sign by the road: *SISTER RUTH* ADVICE AND CONSULTATION*. The old house trailer looked like a long fading 1950 jukebox. David smiled bleakly. Melanie turned in her seat to look back at it.

"Can she really do anything weird, daddy . . . like tell the future and stuff?"

Sandra patted her daughter's hand. "Not now, honey, okay?"

The cortege wound on slowly. The two-lane blacktop shimmered in the rising heat of morning. A passing car pulled over in respect as the cortege went by. Twelve miles from Bickford, still a mile from Whitewood, David tapped Melanie's shoulder.

"This manor just ahead, around those trees, was pretty famous once. The DeBois family owned it but they went away and sold it after World War Two. Built in 1858, I think. There's a marble stairway carved in Italy. Of course, it's falling down now. . . ."

David stopped talking as the Scout rounded the curve. The DeBois mansion stood in completely restored splendor. He gaped. Its octagonal dome was no longer green, gleaming polished now in the sunlight. Carved veranda moldings shone with fresh white paint. The brickwork was clean and solid. The lawns immaculate. The sudden effect of seeing it in its original state for the first time ever was weird, ghostly, as if the great house had returned from the dead.

Sandra hissed in admiration.

Melanie twisted on the seat. "Wow, neat!"

"Who restored it?" David asked Sam.

Sam spoke slow, huskily. "Man name of Sprague. Came to town last year." Sam didn't look at the manor as the Scout drove past.

"The man must have spent a fortune," prodded Sandra.

Sam nodded mutely.

The curve hid the restored mansion from view. Moments later, on the left, David saw the gables of Whitewood rising from the moss-draped cordon of ancient water oaks. He swallowed. Pride again, and guilt and dread. The burial was minutes away.

Headed by the black hearse the multicolored train of cars snaked off the highway onto the long uneven time-smoothed brick drive of Whitewood.

A smile of further pride curled unawares over David's face. The mansion was in full view now through aged handsome oaks. It was grand as ever, unchanged except for ivy trained up its walls. Whitewood was a strong example of Greek Revival adaptation. Its simple entrance and wide upper porch sheltered behind six towering white columns thicker than a man. Tall oak doors were set into pleasant broad white clapboard walls. Narrow black shutters braced tall full windows. David frowned—that ivy. How had it grown up in so short a time? Hardly more than a year since he had last visited.

The cortege reached the mansion. David saw the old stone gargoyle on the front lawn where he used to play. No weeds around it. Sam had kept the place up. Lawns cut, shrubs trimmed, no flaking paint. But glancing left he saw the western fields—unplowed, unplanted. Not like daddy one bit. Neither was suicide. The guilty weight that was on him almost made him laugh in sudden rebellion, too heavy.

As always, Sandra hissed involuntarily, catching sight of the manor and grounds. Melanie, in awe of grandeur, gripped David's arm.

"Can we live *here* now, daddy?"

"Hush!" whispered Sandra.

But David half-smiled, facing the innocence of his child. He braced himself against dark seeds of self-doubt and guilt.

The hearse halted at the end of the drive beside the manor. Sam braked the Scout. Streak, in the hatch area, skittered in a tight circle, waiting to leap when the door opened.

"Want to stay here with Streak?" David asked Melanie.

She looked at her mother. Sandra put a hand on her wrist and nodded, "Why don't you wait here, honey. Unless you—"

"Okay," Melanie shrugged, half-glad yet half-disappointed at missing the majesty of the service.

Opening his door, David could see the stones of the old family cemetery through grape arbors a hundred yards behind the manor. Past that he knew was the river bluff. Rawlings land bordered the river. Between the western fields and the manor stood a garage, then a tennis court. An old riding stable was farther on, with its fenced jumping course unused since David's childhood, when his mother had been a horsewoman.

People dismounted their cars. Phelps opened the hearse rear doors. David moved automatically.

Melanie waited in the front seat of the Scout. Head near the window, she listened to the distant chant of the burial service.

On the back seat Streak was suddenly alert. His bobbed ears pricked up like horns. A low deep snarl erupted in his throat. Melanie turned to look. Streak was staring through the back window toward the garage and tennis court. A scattering of shrubs held shadow. That's where he seemed to be staring. He bristled, snarls growing ragged, savage, his white fangs extending against black curling jowls.

"Streak!" Melanie popped his muzzle. "Hush!"

He didn't hear her at all. Something in the high shrubs had his attention. Suddenly he barked. The booming loudness echoed in the Scout. Melanie grabbed his neck. She looked off at the trees. Now she thought she saw something where he stared—a dark shape merged in shadow, its profile toward the burial service as if watching. Streak barked deafeningly.

"Hush, Streak! Quit it!"

But he barked again and again. His nails clawed the door panel. He strained against the front door thrusting his head out the window, raging.

David stood on the mossy ground of the cemetery among the mourners. The Mississippi River was a vast brown slow-moving lake below the bluff. The crypt was very old. An arch of protective putti angels hovered above its marble mouth, the sealing slab ready nearby. Sparse clusters of headstones gleamed like old teeth grown up from the sun-dappled shade. Sandy held David's hand. Ruth Sheehan sobbed softly. Sam was a tall bent figure of head-lowered grief.

As David watched the casket slide into its vault, Streak began to bark. Mourners turned frowning faces to the distant noise. David tried to ignore it. The minister droned on. Streak's barking grew louder.

David turned an angry face, *what the hell's the matter with that damn dog?*

In the Scout, Melanie saw something dark in the shrubs. It merged suddenly back into deeper shadow. Streak ceased barking. Low snarls gurgled in his chest. Melanie saw a raven rise from the shrub line, circle, and fly away. Streak whined. He settled back against Melanie and licked the side of her face belatedly. She tapped his long nose.

"You're a bad dog, daddy'll be so mad!"

At the crypt, the casket was in place. The final words of the preacher.

"And we beseech our Lord Jesus, protector against the evil one who incites evil, take this loved one unto him forever. . . . Amen."

David recognized the discreet reference to suicide. For an instant he hated the minister, hated the posturing of the service. Then it was over.

Mourners drifted away. Some brushed against David with hands and condolences. He watched Sam kneel at the mouth of the crypt. The heavy marble slab was set in place. Sam had a trowel, a tray of mortar. His broad back bulged a cheap shiny suitcoat. The trowel scraped. David imagined a sealing out of light forever. And some fragment of the nightmare flitted beyond his reach.

Grady Barksdale waited for David and Sandra at the end of the brick drive. His face was heavy-jowled. Long hair from the side of his head was combed over the central bald spot. He wore a good linen suit. His short legs stiffened as David looked up and saw him. They had shared the school experience of boyhood. Football and hunting buddies. Fishing trips with Chester. Obsolete memories, null and void. Barksdale licked his lips and reached out a hand to David. They shook halfheartedly.

David took a breath. "Grady this is Sandra, Sandra, Grady Barksdale."

Barksdale smiled forcibly. "I don't guess there's any good

time or place to say I'm sorry. Wouldn't do any good. But I want to tell you anyway."

David said he was grateful.

"Are you spending the night here, at the manor house?" asked Barksdale.

Sandra glanced at David.

"Hadn't thought about it," David lied, shrugging. He looked up wistfully at the great old manor.

"I wish you would," suggested Barksdale. He stared down at his shoes, then at David's forehead, avoiding the leaden hurt of David's eyes. "Why don't you?" he added.

"What difference?" asked Sandra.

Barksdale cleared his throat. "Well, when the will is read . . . you'll see why." He flashed a stern courtroom smile.

David's eyes passed over the big left face of the manor. Its broad white clapboard surfaces were trained with ivy. Serene it seemed, having seen generations come and grow and fade and disappear with the cries of new children. Men died, but the house lived on. He felt returning traces of comfort, staring at the solid walls and trimmed shrubs, at white fluted columns standing strongly like pillars of faith.

"I think we will stay here tonight. Yes, I think we will."

Barksdale seemed relieved. "Can you come into Bickford tomorrow for the reading? Or would it be better if. . . ."

"It's okay," David said, "tomorrow's fine, Grady."

"I'm real sorry, David, you know I am."

David grinned brokenly. He slapped Barksdale's shoulder with abrupt warmth. "You old sombitch. Good to see you again."

Barksdale beamed. He gripped David's outstretched hand, then turned and walked down the drive toward his Buick.

"Wonder why he wanted us to stay here tonight?" mused Sandra.

"Grady?" David had hardly heard her. He was staring past the house toward the little cemetery.

No, Sandra thought, I meant your father, *the will*. Turning to the house she felt the impact of its grandeur. Looking up at its high gables and columns made her sigh. Terrific old house. Fine and splendidly huge. Every touch a mark of skilled artisans and craftsmen, from the capitaled columns to the broad white faces of the walls. The great oaks rising about it seemed to guard it from all outer-world harm.

Sam finished sealing the marble face stone of the crypt,

which was flanked by multicolored masses of roses and gladiola. Sam's finger smoothed the seam of grout, examined it approvingly, then stood on creaking knees.

Of the mourners only Ruth remained. Sam looked at her and shook his head. She bit her lip with yellow crooked teeth. She stepped to the crypt and knelt, grunting. Under the arch of weathered angels she removed a long silver-tipped pin from her hair. Sam fingered the crusty trowel. Uneasily, he watched Ruth prick her right index finger with the pin. He stared as she drew a cross on the face slab in her blood.

The thick woman rose with a disturbed gaze toward the western fields and trees. Beyond them stood the restored DeBois manor.

Sam wiped nervous sweat from his brow. His eyes met the woman's. Their eyes shared fear. Then, without a word, Ruth shuffled heavily away.

Eight

It was midafternoon. From the house, only the bright glimmer of flowers at the old cemetery gave any hint of a morning funeral.

Sam helped David bring the weekend luggage into the manor. On the front lawn, Melanie played with Streak under the oaks. They ran through irregular patches of sunlight, Streak chasing his gnawed rubber ball.

Within Whitewood, afternoon light shafted down through high windows of archaic undulant glass. Flickering rectangles moved on thick carpets as heavy limbs outside the windows fluttered in a light breeze. Sandra moved through the rooms in awe of their furnishings. She hardly dared to step on the Oriental carpets. Others were equally fine, sculptured, French or English, in patterns of roses or fronds and intertwining vines. Walls held dark paneling or rich paper. The furniture would have filled several very good antique shops.

More than a year ago, when they had visited last, she had endured the house as forbidding, too rich, discomforting. But now she was seeing it all through new eyes. She wondered—will we have to sell it? Of course they couldn't maintain such a place. And David's career—what is there, really, for a specialist in pediatrics in rural Mississippi, a doctor who in Memphis could attain six figures yearly within a decade?

But she was fascinated. She moved slowly under chandeliers, over polished dark floors, staring up at fourteen-foot ceilings, smiling at little putti cherubs on the dining room walls. And the library—so many books, most bound in leather.

She was frankly agog. Then in the central hall she stopped and laughed aloud at herself—*you silly greedy bitch!* Glancing at her image in a tall gilt-edged mirror she posed self-mockingly, patting ludicrously at her hair, pursing lips to lewd imaginary lipstick. She broke up laughing at herself, one hand to her mouth.

David rounded a hall corner. He smiled, seeing her laugh. It made him feel less lonely somehow, being back in the old house, seeing Sandra laughing, hearing distant joyful cries of Melanie mingling with Streak's playful barks. A kind of painlessness was settling in that he did not resist.

"Some old house, isn't it?"

Sandra turned and saw him. His unexpected smile made her open her arms to hold him close.

David held her. His mouth invaded hers, tasting her. The embrace felt savagely clean. He realized how much he had missed her passion and her body these last two wretched days of pain and guilt. Her breasts pressed him warmly, softly. He felt the firm strength of her hips against him where his own heart heat was building. He tasted her more deeply now, sending hands low around her warm waist, letting them feel upward to her breasts. The twinned roundness filled his palms. Her nipples pressed through the thin fabric of her blouse. He shivered and breathed deeply, her passionate contact intoxicating.

Sandra felt a need to devour him. She took his tongue deeply, as if she were starving. Her delicate hands kneaded the hard muscles of his back.

For David she was vital, imperative, a clean white wave sweeping out of him every dark anxiety.

Arm in arm they slipped silently upstairs on the wide curving staircase. The newel post was carved with a fox's head, the risers with oak leaves and acorns. Down the long hall they reached his old bedroom. Posters and prints still covered the walls. Tartan bedcovers remained on the brass bed. The hooked rug, the clipper ship model, everything was the same. David paused in the doorway. Nostalgia flowed with the warm light through thick rough curtains. He felt strange to be here but then Sandra was in his arms again. He was pressing her toward the bed, their bodies tight and close and impatient.

Twenty minutes later their naked damply scented bodies lay close together on the sprawl of twisted sheets.

"I ought to check on Melanie," sighed Sandra.

David moaned. He watched window-splintered light play across the ceiling.

"Like going back in time, Sandy, being in this house."

"For you, maybe. Growing up in apartments makes this

house awesome. But I think I'm crazy about it, David." She knew she was.

"Crazy enough to spend your life in it?"

"Doubtful."

He let out a deep breath. "I don't know what I'll do about it. Don't know if I could bring myself to sell it. A hundred years of Rawlings."

"How much is it worth, do you think?"

"Who knows? A million, including the land. Two, maybe three. I couldn't guess."

She was up on one elbow, not believing it yet. "I'm really sorry, darling . . . about . . . you know."

"Yeah," he nodded. "Me, too." He rummaged in a night-table drawer, found a dry pack of Camels that he knew had to be ten years old. That's how long ago he had quit. He found a match folder—TREFLAN HERBICIDE— He shook a stiff cigarette from the pack and lit it. Sandra didn't interfere.

"Not going to warn me not to? What's the matter, don't you love me?" He grinned and drew smoke deeply.

Nicotine exploded in his chest cavity. Triphammer blows rocked his chest. The leaden high climbed quivering neck muscles into his brain.

Sandra ignored the cigarette. Anything that helped him feel better she would allow, now.

"Your body felt fantastic." She brushed his thigh with long fingers.

"Ditto." He coughed smoke. It rose brownish, catching the window light in grained swirls.

"Tell me about the house," she asked.

"What, specifically?"

"I don't know. Any horse-thieving uncles?"

David laughed. "A Rawlings? You're kidding. During the Civil War I had an ancestor, only other doctor in the family, who turned it into a hospital. Union soldiers shot him on the back veranda, took him for a smartass, I guess. Feds took it over so at least it didn't get burned. Since then a long line of planters. Except yours truly."

"I'm sorry. I'm so stupid." She felt like an ass.

"It's okay." It was, for now. He sat up on the edge of the bed.

"We better check on Melanie," Sandra said.

* * *

Late that afternoon the sun began to set over the river.

Long shadows reached across the lawns from arbors and trees and from the great house itself. Nocturnal insects cried prematurely in the close-cropped grass.

Finishing a long stroll with Melanie, David led her into the kitchen by the back veranda.

"You stay outside," he told Streak.

Within, his ears told him that Sandra had discovered the Steinway baby grand in the study—his mother's instrument, always in perfect tune in the past but now audibly dissonant. Quick and fairly unsloppy chords of a Beethoven sonata came through the front rooms of the house.

He rubbed his daughter's head. "You'll find a shower at either end of the upstairs hall, little miss, two bathrooms, take your pick."

She looked up, wrinkling her nose seductively.

"Aw, daddy—do I *have* to?"

"Sure do."

"Can't Streak come? Please? He's trained, you know, daddy."

David relented. He opened the door. Streak bounded in. Grinning impishly, Melanie jogged through the hall. Streak ran after her. David heard them reach the stairs, skipping steps to the top. Sandra's playing intensified. He smiled—her taste was eclectic. She broke into Bartók, or was it Milhaud? Some Rolling Stones would sound good, David thought with a grin at the incongruity of British R&B in Whitewood.

He went through the hall and found himself standing at the library door looking in at the snug leather sofa and chair. His gaze ranged over Oriental carpets, walls covered with generations of books, dark rich paneling. Was this where his father had done it? Yes. It would have been here, in his favorite room. David seemed to feel the hours and hours of his father's presence here. As if the man and years had soaked into the books and walls and floors. He entered the room.

Stains seemed recently cleaned off the carpet by the heavy Victorian desk. A trace of darkness deep in the weave. Death residue—clean and freshly scrubbed around its edges.

He passed by the book-covered walls, his eyes wandering over the titles. Suddenly, frowning, he paused.

There was an entirely new section. *Satan in the Old Testament. Occult Research Techniques. Goetry.*

Goetry? Puzzled, he took *Webster's* from its nook by a window. "Goetry (gō′ e-trē)—the summoning of spirits from the abyss by calling the name of the demon desired; sorcery; conjuring, usually by one skilled in the art of sorcery; Gr."

With a frown of disgust he snapped the dictionary shut and reshelved it. Then he noticed something else. The library broom closet was padlocked. New hasp and oversized Master laminated lock.

He rattled the lock with his hand. Curiosity piqued, he went to the desk but found no keys in the drawers. In the forbidden top drawer of his childhood, the gun was there, a revolver. He touched it with knowing revulsion. He fingered through copies of *Southern Farmer* piled on the desktop, then Agriculture Department reports. Among seed and herbicide catalogs he found an old volume of Herodotus printed in the original Greek. Examining it he grinned, remembering his father's intellect. Not many people in Bickford or the surrounding farms would have guessed that Chester had graduated *magna cum laude* from Vandy: Latin and Greek, ancient history, cultures of the past. And David sensed again the profound and bitter tragedy—that a ten-cent lead slug could destroy the fine brain of a belatedly brilliant man.

He turned the book to set it down. A key slipped from the back pages, clattering on an open space of desk glass.

He picked it up and was about to toss it into a drawer. Then his fist closed on the key. He went to the closet, eyeing the section of new occult titles curiously as he passed the bookshelves.

The key turned in the padlock. The tumblers clicked. The steel U fell open in David's hand. He pulled the lock free, hesitated, then opened the door.

A scream rose suddenly in his throat. His teeth clinched, stifling the cry. He stood back from the open door, catching his breath, gaping at the lurid fanged mouth and fierce shell eyes that glared from the closet shadows at him.

The African mask hung at eye level in the closet like a Picasso face in three dimensions. With a short embarrassed laugh, he touched the smooth carven wood. Below it was a squat gray floor safe. David knelt and studied it curiously. Combination unknown—he had never seen it before. He twirled the timeworn dial and stood. On one wall in the deepest closet shadow a shelf held half-a-dozen antique leather-bound volumes.

Discours des sorciers.

Leather-bound with rusting iron hinges, it felt worm-eaten against his palms, clammy and slick. It fell open in his hands at the inserted sheet of paper. A foul odor rose darkly from the pages. His face twitched in disgust. He peered closer. The hand-penned text was French.

On the left page was a large uneven woodcut—a sorcerer? He decided that it was. A wizard stood with lifted invoking arms in a chalked pentagram, a raven perched on his shoulder. A young girl lay nude in altar shadows. Above her reared the obscene, a hideous horned beast, materializing from a whirlwind of crosshatching. David grunted, shuddering in revulsion. His spine tingled with surprised pity and disgust.

Daddy, he thought, my poor daddy. . .is *that* what happened in your mind? Did *fantasies* kill you? Don't you know that one real cigarette is more evil than all that silly occult shit put together?

Turning the inserted sheet of paper, he saw it was in his father's hand, apparently copied from some archaic text:

"Known verily by few and nonetheless attestable, it is fact that the will of a dead sorcerer hath claim upon its dead body, and by means of its familiar can raise its corpse up from the tomb and continue such actions as were unfulfilled in previous life. Particularly be this the case when said sorcerer hath been slain. Such a resurrection is indeed rebirth in the case of one of extreme powers, and invariably for the continuance of malevolent deeds and of revenge.

"The excelling will of the most powerful wizard hath power to return his body into its former state, regardless of decay.

"If a sorcerer be slain, the body of the slayer must be acquired by his familiar, who most readily will perform this deed, acted upon both by the will of its master and by its hatred of the void, to which it must return should it long remain matterless on earth."

The last paragraph was heavily underlined. David shook his head, sadly bemused.

He snapped the massive old volume shut. A foulness clung to his hands from the cloying leather. In the light the stretched hide looked almost like human epidermis. He frowned, hastening to return it to the closet, a bitter taste rising oddly in his mouth.

With a last glance at the grotesque ritual mask and the inscrutable floor safe, David shut the door and replaced its padlock. He left the room with a sadness tainted by revulsion. Never would he have dreamed his father—of all people—would have sought solace or refuge in an area so degrading in its vulgar absurdity. The foulness of the ironbound book felt ugly on his hands. Rubbing them together, he hurried toward the kitchen for soap and water.

Nine

Night fell across the vast slick swath of the river. The last twilight glimmered rosily. Upon the high bluff, Whitewood's gables were strongly etched against faintly appearing stars. Yellow light came through its old high windows, showing life within.

Sandra had not had to prepare dinner. The huge tile-floored and brick-walled kitchen was crammed with goodies sent by folk sympathetic to tragedy, many of whom David's father had helped in his lifetime. Pies, cakes, hams and basted fowl overflowed the kitchen's ample stainless steel food lockers. David had asked Sam to stay for dinner. Both men were anxious to renew their old acquaintance. Now, Sam helped Sandra set the long walnut dining room table. Instead of dining buffet-style in the kitchen, she thought it would be terrific to use the richly furnished dining room, to eat properly on a long table beneath a looming multiglittering chandelier. Since they were staying the night, she earlier had freshened the upstairs master bedroom. It had eastern exposure for dawn light.

She wanted to take every advantage of the great house so long as she was destined to spend any time here. And she already knew she loved it. You're already spoiled rotten, she thought.

It would be a definite comedown to return to the new Memphis apartment, no matter how much better it was than what had sufficed before—the ugly image of that old man in the old apartments flickered leeringly across her mental screen, his gnarled hands reaching out for Melanie. She set sliced ham on the table, pushing the unwelcome obscenity back into the darkness of repression.

They ate in relative silence, David at one end of the table, Sandra at the other, Sam and Melanie facing one another across the middle.

David chewed slowly, gazing up at the handsome portrait of his mother. It hung on the prominent end wall of the dining room, its predominant hues golden in the chandelier light. A small brass plate on the gilt frame was engraved, simply, *LEAH*. She was young and very beautiful, he reflected, Sandra's age when Chester had commissioned it, engaging Haskell, a then-renowned Southern painter from New Orleans.

"This tastes super," said Melanie, chewing.

"Don't talk with your mouth full," Sandra scolded.

Sam grinned.

David was struck with it all—so much like dinners of other times, his father holding his mother's chair, maybe a friend or two joining them—strange sensations of the permanence of what had gone before. Of course, Sam had never sat here, not in forty years.

David's eyes wandered. The chandelier cast myriad sparkles over ornate damasked walls, the portrait, color-warming the food and the lovely faces of Sandra and Melanie, throwing into relief Sam's mute face. His dark skin lined with age like polished wood.

"So nice to have real beauty in this old house again," murmured Sam.

David lifted his eyes, caught a strong wink from the old man. Sandra blushed. Melanie glanced worshipfully at her mother, young face aglow with mellow light. Sandra smiled—Mommy's so pretty, she knew her daughter was thinking, the innocent child completely unaware of her own stunning loveliness.

"*Two* lovely ladies," amended Sam.

Startled, Melanie looked up from her plate and smiled sheepishly.

"David," Sam grinned gently, "in a few years you'll need you a stick to keep boys away from your door."

"Heck," growled Melanie, embarrassed. "I don't like boys, anyway."

She slipped a furtive piece of white meat under the table. Streak hid near her legs. She felt the tender nibble of his lips and a tentative nip of incisors, careful not to harm her generous fingertips. "I'll be too busy studying to be a doctor, like daddy," she added boldly.

Amused, Sandra and David smiled. Sam nodded, pleased. The old man was obviously flattered to sit with them, David saw. The fact was oddly embarrassing. No old friend should be flattered; David was warmed by Sam's nearness.

The soft click of utensils continued. Sam ate slowly, more watchful than he seemed, feeling sadness low in his thick chest and belly—David had lost his mother, now his daddy. I won't let nothing else happen. Get them away from this place in the morning. Something is out there. I know it is. I'll stand between it and them. Because I know what it is. I seen it, when it was too late to help Chester.

Whitewood's wide rear veranda was ten feet above the wide lawn. Arbors of grape and roses went off toward the bluff a hundred yards distant. Veranda stairs led to a mossy brick terrace. The house shone in the pallor of a rising moon. Fireflies swirled blinking against tree-shapes darker than the night. Frogs drummed and crickets sang countless dissonant night songs. A hundred yards from the back of the great house the tombstones and the shoulders of the crypt glimmered. Below the bluff a half-mile vastness of river ran silvery with moonlight, as wild as the unconquered night itself.

Smoking a pipe, Sam sat upright in a wicker chair on the veranda. His feet were not propped on the rail. The white clean paint shone bluish in the illusive night pallor. His pipe held straight Turkish, the good tobacco Chester gave him every Christmas. The bowl of his pipe flared as he sucked. Its reddish glow illuminated rough features, his eyes deeply embedded in his head, two gleams that stared steadily out into the night depths toward the old cemetery where Chester lay sealed behind marble.

Beside Sam on a wicker table in the shadow of a potted fern, rested an Eveready flashlight and an obsolete but workable .32 top-break Smith and Wesson. The old man smoked without haste, his deep eyes fixed with distance. The kitchen door to the veranda opened. A flood of yellow light violated the darkness.

Sam closed one eye to preserve his night vision. With the other he saw David step onto the veranda with a bottle of whiskey in one hand and two shot glasses pinched in the other. David's foot eased the door shut. Darkness rushed back over the veranda.

David moved down the veranda and sank into a wicker chair beside Sam. Glasses clinked in his hand.

"How about some liquid refreshment?"

Sam smiled without taking his eyes from the crypt. "I could stand a shot or two."

David's eyes adjusted to the darkness. He opened the bottle and poured whiskey, splashing twice into shot glasses.

Sam took one and threw it back neat. David did the same, feeling the scalding rush then the slow sweet progress of fire through his entrails, vital and welcome. He refilled the glasses and sat back exhaling alcohol-rich breath.

"There's a time for drinking," he said thoughtfully. Sam grunted affirmative.

They sat without speaking. The nearness of this strong old figure from his childhood fortified David as much as the whiskey. He did not sense the tension and awareness coiled in Samson Johnson like a Stone-Age man lying in fearful but deadly ambush for an inevitably stalking tiger. David poured again. Sam refused this round. David tossed his back neat, swallowing harshly.

While Melanie watched television in the den, Sandra perused the book-laden walls of the library. She wondered briefly at a section of occult material—all new books.

Then she found what she was half-looking for. A thick leather picture album. Tintypes of the oldest generations imprinted with the names of Memphis or Jackson picture studios. Turn-of-the-century visitors in Paris, Eiffel Tower behind them. A Memphis Cotton Carnival. Holiday voyages on a riverboat. She came to the modern snaps. An impatient boy in Sunday clothes standing impatiently between father and mother. Chester and Leah looking no older than David and herself. The boy already showing signs of handsomeness, his dark hair and bright eyes. She smiled and rubbed the boy's face with a finger.

"You little rascal. . .Christ, I love you."

The photos progressed through David's boyhood. Boy with rifle. Boy in football uniform. Boy with date for prom, giving Sandra a twinge of jealousy against the doll-faced girl beside him in her stiff satin and net gown. Then a Polaroid snap of David and herself, Melanie a baby in David's arms—the photo they sent years ago, here carefully preserved in the center of a page by itself.

Sandra smiled and shook her head. She stared wistfully at the page, unseeing. Her own father had died when she was so young. Industrial salesman; a car wreck on a lonely road. She never really knew him, not really, yet she had images of his big face above her, of heavy and damp night-night kisses. Those jolting rides on his towering shoulders when the world looked a mile below. His booming laugh that always startled her. The night the phone call came and mother cried, his car, the bridge abutment, the whispered drunkenness. Then the terrifying funeral, coffin going down—fresh scent of earth and mother's squeezing hot hand.

Sandra stared at the picture of herself and David. He had filled that long-building hollowness her father had left in her. An emptiness she had never come to grips with until the first night alone with David, when tentative caresses had deepened into wild sexual reality. They had loved and they had given themselves.

Eyes damp, she closed the scrapbook. Feeling a deep bittersweetness, she went into the study and sat down on the piano bench. Her long white fingers poised above the yellowed keys of the old Steinway. They descended. Chopin's "Berceuse," slow and mellow, suitable to Whitewood, filled the rooms and halls of the fine old house.

Outside on the veranda, Chopin came faintly. David threw back another shot and refilled Sam's glass. Sam set the glass down beside his chair without drinking.

David cleared his throat.

"This stuff is poison, you know that, Sam?"

"I reckon so. Maybe it takes poison sometimes to kill a bad thing."

"To make it easier on the brain we rot our liver and kidneys. What the hell. He threw back another shot, wanting to talk to Sam but not knowing what to say. The rich scent of Sam's tobacco came to him mixed with fragrances of the arbors—rose, grape, azalea, verbena. The whisky was softening brittle edges. He felt a growing intimacy here; it was nearness to his boyhood, to Sam, to the very paint and wood of the veranda, the permanent patterns of the arbors and even the cemetery, to the river, that everlasting wide river beyond and below the high bluff where he had so often played.

Suddenly a thought made him laugh.

"Hey, Sam. . .you remember when I was, about ten I guess, and we were in that john boat on the edge of the river? You were catfishing and I had that old single-barrel twelve gauge?"

"Which time?" Sam's eyes were fixed upon distance.

"We went under those trees that grew out over the water,"

David chuckled, remembering as he spoke, "and this big snake must have been sunning on a branch. . . .It fell right into the damn boat!"

Sam grinned, grunted, hissed with amusement.

David howled a short laugh. "And *BOOM!* I was so scared I blew a hole right in the bottom of the boat. The boat went down like a rock with muddy water coming over us and you cussing like hell and me flopping, thinking I was gonna drown."

Sam allowed his own small laugh. It tickled him, thinking about it now. He laughed louder.

"Thing you didn't know was that damn old snake scared me too! Even if you hadn't of blowed out the bottom of that boat, I expect I would have jumped right out into the river. Never was no snake handler, son."

David chuckled. "Never knew you were scared of snakes."

"Well, I am," Sam sighed.

"Always thought of you like a kind of John Wayne," kidded David, pursuing his delight in joshing his old friend.

"Black John Wayne." Sam snorted, grinning. He tossed his shot of whisky back neat and refocused his vision upon the moonlight vista below them. The moon had moved. The crypt was in shadow now like a black hump against the flat pale sheen of water that stretched so far its far shore was visible beyond the bluff.

David leaned forward with hands and chin on the veranda rail. It felt cool and smooth. He glanced up along the roof-line above his head and saw a bank of six floodlights. They looked new.

"Sam? When were those lights put up?"

"Your daddy had it done."

David frowned. "Chester afraid of the dark?"

"He wanted them put up and I saw it was done," Sam said flatly.

David lifted his brow. He rubbed his face, wondering how severely his father had changed. "You said he sent you away?"

"About three months ago, he did." Sam's voice was steeled, like one recalling unwelcome pain.

"Why?" pursued David. "I can't remember a time without you here."

Sam sighed. "Said it was for my own good. Don't know why."

David caught the reticence, the withdrawal in Sam's voice. He shrugged, his body pleasant with whiskey, his mind clear-er than it had been in days. Unformed questions teased his thoughts. Sam seemed to keep staring at the crypt. He seemed to be watching it or something.

David looked up at the broad moonlit walls of Whitewood.

"What about all this ivy, Sam? It usually takes years for ivy to grow like that. Wasn't there last time we came down."

Sam didn't answer, as if he had not heard. Then he grunted. "Your daddy got a package one day, full of sprigs. I saw the label—all the way from Hong Kong. I set them all around the house like he said, all around that tomb, too. Damn stuff grew right up the walls in the summer last year."

"Around the *crypt*?" frowned David.

Sam nodded slowly.

David touched the arm of the tall old man. "Why would he have wanted it around the crypt, unless he was. . . ."

Sam stared out into the night. "Planning to die? I don't know. David, look. It hurts me to answer these kind of questions right now. I don't mean no harm. You know that, son. But maybe there's some things you ought not to get into. You just buried you daddy today. Don't dwell on it no more."

David winced at the graveness of Sam's voice. For a moment he felt a tragic surge. He wanted the old man to hold him. He believed now that his father had planned to die. Putting ivy around the crypt months before the final act. Insanity. Occult texts. Floodlights where there were no prowlers. Yet—prowlers of the mind, in that darkness where there is no escape.

Sam spoke, relenting. "That ivy and the lights, it was after they found that young banker in town. Butler was his name. Had his head stuck in a microwave oven with his fingers locked on the switch. They found his wife half-naked in the living room. All bloody like she tore at herself, family snapshots lying all around her. Sent her off to Whitworth in Jackson.

David gasped. "Butler? Was his wife named Holly?"

"The same girl you used to date," Sam acknowledged grimly.

David could hardly believe it. "Holly. At Whitworth. My God." Whitworth was the state mental hospital. He had taken Holly to the prom. Dated steadily. Then they had gone to separate colleges and made separate lives.

"They had a little girl," said Sam, voice thickened, "About Melanie's age. I saw her once, pretty little girl." She wasn't in the house. They never found her, not one trace. FBI came up from Jackson. Didn't find nothing. Your daddy wasn't right after that. Maybe he acted . . . well, different—hard to put your finger on."

David tensed. "What do you mean, Sam? Surely, you don't think he. . . ."

Sam looked at David, his deep-set eyes twin gleams in the pallor. "That he had something to do with that little girl?" Sam's tone was edged with anger and something more, something dark that David could not fathom, a haunted sharpness like dread.

"Of course not. . . . I just. . . ."

They sat in silence for a while. Torn contact. Fatigue and unanswered questions rose through David unnervingly. He took another shot of whiskey. Sam lit a new bowl of tobacco.

Still wanting to talk, David turned the subject in another direction.

"Noticed the old DeBois place has been restored."

"Uumm," nodded Sam, puffing, face red in the flare. "Somebody laid out lots of jack on that one."

"Man named Sprague, I hear." Sam's voice was cold now, measured and hard. David barely recognized it. "Never met him. They say he's blind. From New York and rich as sin. Came here to retire, I reckon. Spread lots of cash on the masons and carpenters and the town liked that. Needed it. Name of Philip Sprague." Sam said the name with clipped harshness.

"You've never seen him? How come?"

In the pallor of frayed moonlight David saw the old man's tensed posture, his pipe gripped savagely immobile in his jaw and hand, his deep eyes never moving from their fixation upon the sweep of the night beyond.

"No, I never seen him," Sam said finally through clenched teeth.

David remembered how vacant the restored mansion had seemed in spite of its fresh reincarnation. No sign of humanity. No animals. No gardener on the lawns. Almost like a huge lifeless picture pasted with incredible reality on the side of the road, with an illusion of depth.

Sam's voice came edgily. "Don't stay too long around this place, son."

"What do you mean?"

"People in Bickford, some claim pets are disappearing. Some say we got a ha'nt in the woods. Others talk about UFOs. Me . . . I seen strange enough things in my own time but I never needed to know why of it. Seen a two-headed water snake once but I killed it. Didn't need to save it for show. Put it out of this world. Didn't ask how it got that way. Twice last year and not long ago I seen a raven killing bluebirds. Used my shotgun the last time but it just flew away. Knowed I hit it square. You see, point is that when a place is going bad, you stay away from it. Don't ask why. Don't look inside. Maybe there's a lot of things in this world nobody is expected to understand."

David loathed superstition. He wanted to fight against this backwoods crap making Sam seem less than he should. But he was too weary, too drunk now to pursue his feelings or Sam's words.

With creaking joints, he stood. He patted Sam's shoulder. "Night, Sam."

Sam took his eyes from the night and looked up at the young white oval face of a boy grown into a man. And as he watched David go into the house with a suddenness of yellow light from the door, Sam thought how little David had learned in the city. How little anybody knows or can know from books. David could save a body now but never a soul. Whatever was out there waiting, no man should have to face.

Get away from here, boy, Sam thought.

And he stared into the night where the crypt was sunk in shadow, clouds scudding over the pale face of the moon. He watched as the clouds thickened. The night insects sang louder, shrill and plangent.

With the first sprinkles of rain Sam's strong dark face broke in leathery smiling creases, and his whole being relaxed as the rain fell.

Ten

He lay stiff in the darkness and he heard it. Scratching, wanting to get in. Wanting him. Nails, clawing. Hideous malignant titter. He tried to see. All black. No stars. No moon. Blacker than blindness. But it could hear him trying to see, it knew where he was. And it was coming, scratching the protective stone, clawing its way in. His arms would not move. Legs frozen. Trapped. Helpless. Now it was reaching in. Its claws reaching in. Its obscene eyes peering in. . . .

Sandra woke beside David. His body was twisted fetally. His limbs quivered spasmodically, shaking the four-poster, neck muscles corded in a pathetic effort to scream. Cries choked through his clenched teeth.

She reached across the bed. Her hands touched his shoulders and his mouth opened in a bestial cry. He was sitting up suddenly on the bed, shaking, his eyes open now but not yet seeing. She rubbed his face.

"David! David! It's okay! Wake up, David!"

David's head rang with dissolving images of horror. He felt the throb of last night's whiskey. He realized he was in a bed at Whitewood with Sandy. He had escaped a nightmare he could not now remember.

Sandra rubbed David's tanned shoulders skilfully, keeping close attention to his mood. "You okay now?"

He turned blinking and kissed her gratefully. He shivered at the unremembered horror, knowing it was like the nightmare suffered in Memphis, unable to recall its details, not even wanting to.

"You okay?" she asked again, seriously.

He grinned, sighed. "You sweet thing." He kissed her again.

She pouted coyly. "That's all I mean to you, a toy."

With a lewd comic grin he grabbed for her across the bed. Her nude arms evaded his fingers.

"Hands off my pure body," she teased, just out of reach.

Leering with dramatic villainy he bounded across the middle of the bed. "I must possess you!"

Sandra jumped up with a laugh. Naked, striking a hip-cocked pose, she tilted her head and licked the corner of her mouth with the tip of her pink tongue, then lost the pose with a giggle.

"I'm saving my purity for somebody better than you, Bart," she said in surprisingly good cockney, " 'ee's a doctor, a proper gennulman, 'ee is."

Struck by her beauty, he paused, staring. Her long dark hair clung to smooth shoulders and curving white breasts. His eyes moved down the contours of her belly and hips toward long parted legs. The windows shone behind her, haloing her body like a model in some art photography magazine.

Sandra watched David's comic mask dissolve. Not rising, he reached out sensually with his arms and hands. She came back to the bed.

Breakfast was thick-sliced country bacon, French toast with sorghum molasses, eggs sunny-side up, prepared by Sam. David ate voraciously. Food seemed to smother a hangover.

The morning-filled dining room windows offered entertainment—bluebirds nesting in a handsome homemade birdhouse built like a little Whitewood manor. The view took in the tennis court, the old stable and jumping course, and the western shelterbelt of woods beyond which the DeBois land lay, now owned by the man Sam had called Sprague.

"If birds didn't nest, could they still have babies?" asked Melanie through a mouthful of French toast.

"Don't talk with your mouth open," Sandra said with a furtive wink at David.

Melanie was serious. Her brows knitted together with anxiety. "You think they mind us watching?"

"They don't know we're watching," Sam suggested, amused.

David noticed Sam's red eyes—had he slept at all?

"Would they fly away if they knew?" persisted Melanie.

Sam lifted his heavy brow in thought. "I expect they would. Things don't like to be watched by other things stronger than they are, that could hurt them whenever they took a mind to."

"But we wouldn't hurt them," Melanie protested. "Daddy can't I take a picture, please?"

David smiled. "Camera's on the hall table."

Melanie bounced up and returned with David's battered Pentax. Chewing his last precious piece of French toast with homemade muscadine preserves, he set the exposure for her. She took the Pentax carefully to the window. David looked at Sam.

"Could you watch Melanie a couple of hours? Sandra and I have to go into Bickford." The will had to be read.

Sam nodded. "Be glad to."

Sandra took a last sip of coffee and stood. Looking at the old man and Melanie, she felt a shiver of horror, remembering another old man, one with ugly hands and hungry obscene eyes. Yet she sensed how different, how good Sam was.

Suddenly there was a banging at the windows. Melanie shrieked. Sandra dropped her cup with a crash on the table. David whirled toward the windows.

He caught a glimpse of something dark diving past the birdhouse. Both bluebirds flapped frantically, feathers flying, wings plummeting against the windows, banging the glass. The birdhouse careened, twisting on its wire. The dark thing dove again. David saw a huge black raven, wings gleaming like burnished black steel. Sam cursed thickly, strangely. The raven struck the defending male bluebird. Melanie screamed. Sam was running through the hall toward the kitchen door. David saw the male bluebird flutter to the ground with its neck wobbling, its wings fluttering feebly in a shower of broken feathers. Its mate was inside the tiny Whitewood miniature, her head trying to defend against the attacking raven. It was three times her size. Ruthlessly the raven thrust its long beak at her.

Sandra's screams joined Melanie's.

Then David saw Sam running outside, raising a shotgun. The raven saw, too. It soared skyward at once. Sam fired three quick blasts.

Then it was over. The female, alive but terrified, stayed within the birdhouse.

They all went outside.

"I knowed I hit it," Sam swore to David. "But it was just like I didn't."

Melanie was crying, Sandra comforting her. David buried the dead male bird. He thought of the raven in the woodcut, perched on the sorcerer's shoulder.

"I hit him," Sam muttered, staring off at the western shelterbelt of woods. "But it was like it couldn't hurt him."

David and Sandra drove into Bickford. Passing the restored DeBois manor—"*Sprague*" on the wrought-iron mailbox—both of them turned to stare.

"Someone with money and sensitivity did that," Sandra commented, "a rare combination."

"Maybe wanting a showplace," David said.

"Always the cynic. No, you're not, really. But it doesn't *look* like whoever it is wants a showplace—nobody around at all."

"Sam told me a rich New Yorker came down to retire. Blind, he's heard, though he hasn't seen the man himself. Apparently something of a recluse."

"I'd love to meet whoever it is," Sandra said earnestly.

David smiled. "Social climber."

She pinched his arm with a grin.

He tried the new C-B radio. Nothing on most of the channels.

Then came two twanging thick voices: "Don't know about this town no more, Cotton Chopper, that banker and now that planter, and all them pets disappearing here and yonder."

David winced.

"Well, Lightfooter, you know how folks in a little town like we got, they jump at any kind of bad thing to have something to talk about. Still, I kind of knowed that planter, Rawlings, *did* some plowing and bush-hogging for him from time to time, couldn't meet a nicer old boy, pretty much of a gentleman-type, you'd never thought he'd—"

David switched off the radio. He swallowed thickly. Sandra's face was averted, the wind in the open window blowing her dark long hair.

They passed Ruth Sheehan's mobile home where a bird dog rummaged through tall weeds. Sandra squinted at the palm sign reading SISTER RUTH.

"Has Ruth known your family long?" she asked.

David nodded. "Her folks were poor and my mother's had money, guess that was the main difference, but they used to be friends. But mother was no snob. You know all those muscadine preserves?"

"Yumm, you bet."

"Ruth made them. Always visiting, something good to say about everybody. I guess she could be quite a gossip if she was prone, plenty of secrets whispered in that old jukebox of a trailer. But not Ruth. Always smiling." Except at the funeral, he thought.

The outskirts of Bickford appeared. At the end of the main drag, Barksdale's office was a converted old brick building with a cheap new facade shared with a State Farm agent.

The yellow Scout nosed into the curb. David and Sandra stepped into the sunlight. David walked around the Scout as Sandra smoothed her pale blue linen dress and removed her sunglasses, tucking them into a simple canvas shoulder bag.

They looked at each other, then at Barksdale's office door, and resolutely went toward it. David opened it for Sandra. She went ahead, lips pressed together.

The neutral air-conditioned interior reminded David of the Holiday Inn. In the single large room Barksdale sat behind a wide metal desk, reaching for a law volume from a bookcase. Above him on a paneled wall were framed degrees and a stuffed bass. He turned with a grin as they entered.

"David!" he grinned, rising heavily with an outstretched hand.

David gripped the fat palm. It pumped his arm. The rotund lawyer smiled, taking Sandra's slim hand with a clumsy mannerism of gentility. He waved toward two plastic contour chairs.

"Y'awl sit down, make yourself at home, please."

David gestured toward one. Sandra sat primly, crossing long smooth legs. Barksdale's eyes flicked past them as he returned to his desk chair. David sat stoically in the chair beside Sandra. He did not expect this to be pleasant.

"Well," smiled Barksdale, "guess you wonder how I ever made it through law school." His thumbs twiddled on the desk glass.

"Maybe you wonder how I made it through medical school," shrugged David equitably.

Barksdale snorted. "Un-uh, boy, you always had brains. Me, I needed help. Know who gave it to me? Your daddy. That's right. Lent me the money and the confidence to make it through Ole Miss. I reckon Bickford is as good a place as any for an old boy like me. Where you gonna practice medicine, anyway?"

David shrugged again. He wanted Barksdale to cut the small talk.

"Memphis," said Sandra.

David winced. The decision whether to practice in a small comfortable scenic community or to make scads of money in Memphis was a sore point between himself and Sandra, one not pressed upon too often. He grinned back at Barksdale, remembering the loud-farting beer-drinking high school boy. And he was glad Chester had helped him.

Barksdale winked at Sandra. "David and me, we was—were I should say—on the high school champion football team for Hatchie county. That ole husband of yours was our champion quarterback. Man, how those girls went after him."

Sandra gave David a friendly accusatory smile. Remembering the doll-faced girl in the prom snapshot. He blushed slightly. The fat-cheeked lawyer chuckled. David thought of Holly, who had been cocaptain of the cheerleaders that championship year . . . now in Whitworth. He made a mental note to ask about her when this was over.

Barksdale's jovial grin was stiffening, darkening. He obviously had something difficult to do. His fat rosy fingers adjusted his tie, making it more crooked.

David squirmed in his chair, curiosity building as he remembered Grady's comments after the burial yesterday asking them to spend the night at Whitewood. Were there strange provisions in the will? Something more difficult to deal with now than all he had so far endured?

"Let's get on with it, Grady," he suggested.

"Yes," agreed Sandra, "please."

Barksdale nodded. Smile fading, growing brittle, he opened a desk drawer and extracted a manila folder. He opened it on the green blotter in the center of his desk. He cleared his throat and looked up at them separately.

"Before I start reading I want you both to know something. I had the utmost respect for Chester. To my mind, when he brought me this will in a couple of weeks ago—"

"He changed it a couple of weeks ago?" interrupted David.

The lawyer nodded. "Affirmative. But, David, to my mind he was as rational as you could want. Yes, he looked tired. I'll give you that. He looked like he might of aged ten years since I'd seen him last, like a man with combat fatigue. But his eyes and his hands were steady. That same old fire he always had."

David fought a heat that rose behind his eyes as Barksdale lifted the first page, coughed twice, and began.

"I'll skip the sound of mind business and get into specifics. Let's see. . . . 'I leave a fund of thirty thousand dollars to help rebuild the Bickford Baptist Church. To Samson Johnson, good friend and companion, the sum of five thousand a year for the rest of his life. I thank him from the bottom of my heart for all he has given of himself to me and my son over the years. I bequeath a trust of two hundred thousand dollars, to be drawn from bonds and securities, to establish a yearly scholarship for the one most promising student of Hatchie County High School, to aid him or her in the study of medicine. . . .' "

Barksdale's voice droned through details of the scholarship trust administration and selection. David felt light in his arms and legs. His eyes burned drily. With lower lip between his teeth he felt his father reaching out to close the gap torn between them. He could almost hear the gentle yet stern voice saying, *It's all right you left the land, I wanted continuity of generations but I realize now how important your own life is, that you are worthy, I should have helped you more to become a doctor and I'm proud you made it on your own. . . .See, I've set up this scholarship, don't hold the years of what you took for indifference against me, son. . . .*

David realized Barksdale had stopped.

"Are you okay?" the pudgy lawyer asked softly.

David nodded. Sandra's hand touched his. Barksdale went on.

"So, as sole survivor, you'll receive the balance of the estate, David. I estimate roughly over a million in securities and the shares of the two Memphis firms. Naturally, Whitewood with its properties. But now. . . ." The plump boyish face wrinkled, reddening. Barksdale lit a Camel and puffed hard in obvious discomfort. He nibbled his right index finger with yellow uneven teeth. "The next part is a little—different."

Sandra waited calmly. But David tensed, ready for almost anything. Almost. Anything but what he was about to hear.

Barksdale frowned at the folder in his hands. He read: " 'David, I ask only one thing of you. This is my last request of my son, the only person on earth I feel I can trust completely. Sam is a good friend, but blood binds you and me. I know that you will grant me one last thing. Please think deeply before you answer. Then do as your heart requires.' "

Barksdale paused, looked up at them both and sighed. He frowned at the folder, blushing, embarrassed at what he was required to read.

" 'I ask that you stay on at Whitewood for seven weeks, never leaving for a single night. Check the seal on the crypt daily. Tend the ivy around the manor and my crypt. I am sure that Sam will stay on with you. If there is any trouble, ask his advice. I pray merciful God I am not putting you in harm's way, and I ask him for rain in this rainy season. I give you premature thanks, David. Never forget that your mother and I loved you. I am only sorry that the rift between us was never properly healed. I hope it is now. Be loving to those who love you. Good-bye.' "

With the last words Barksdale's voice had hurried, thickening. Now with lowered eyes, he sighed and reverently closed the sheaf of papers. Sandra sat sharply forward in her chair. Perplexed, she wanted to trade puzzled glances with David. He was gazing at the sunlit window. Leaf shadows danced on the panes.

"But that's unreasonable," Sandra protested when David said nothing.

The rosy-cheeked lawyer shrugged uncomfortably.

"We can't do that, of course," Sandra half-smiled, half-grimaced. "Such a gap would set David's career back two years. At least. He might even have to start his work over again. Are those provisions binding?"

Barksdale tried to smile. "It's up to you both, naturally. I personally don't consider the last part legally binding, not in the context of the will as stated."

David rose stiffly from the chair. He lifted a hand for Sandra.

"I'll let you know, Grady. Thanks."

The lawyer watched their disturbed faces. He handed David a Xerox copy of the will and stood while they walked out.

In the Scout, neither David nor Sandra spoke at once as the road led out of Bickford.

Sandra felt the rush of warm wind through the hair of her arm resting in the open window, sunlight was hot on her skin. She stared ahead at the country road, glancing aside now to discern David's emotions. His profile was rapt with obvious struggle, and that troubled her. His decision should be quite simple.

"Of course, it's totally unreasonable," she said. David said nothing, seemed not to hear her at all.

She toyed with her sunglasses frame, aware of the little marks left on the bridge of her nose. At moments like this, torn between conflicting emotions—hurting for the man she loved but scared of what he might want to do—little things obsessed her. The bumps of the old country road making her breasts ache slightly. The mild irritating whine of the Scout's tires. The wild sometimes-ugly, sometimes-gorgeous scenery of the country that seemed to mock all cities and places where she was comfortable and secure. The old trailer where that Ruth woman lived—hag seeress or whatever she was supposed to be. Scrawny old dog foraging the ditch beside the road, threatening to step in front of the Scout. No, she didn't like the country. She knew she should like it but didn't at all. Something deranged about its untidiness, the anarchistic growth of life in too many unpredictable forms. The lack of man's control. Nights unlit by public electricity. Houses far apart. As if civilization had lost battles here and gone elsewhere.

She cleared her throat before speaking again. That will was absurd. David's silence was threatening.

"Of course we couldn't stay seven weeks, your career, Melanie, and some of my piano students begged me to teach summer school. . . ."

Staring ahead, David heard Sandra. He didn't know how to answer. She wanted argument, to dissuade any inclination. He might have to obey his father's will. It would be hard for her to accept what he had already decided—that his father's last request, no matter how odd or inconvenient, was inviolate. At this moment he was enjoying a kind of strained relief from guilt. His father had asked. He would comply. If it were penance, he would serve that penance. His father was gone now. Forever. If he had been with his father there would have been no suicide. He owed his father a lifetime. Seven weeks was nothing compared to that. He would live in his father's house—*his* house, now—give up his life pattern for a short while. Even if the will had said seven years he knew he would have done it. Let the arguing come later, he thought, enjoying the relief of a question that could be answered—Son, will you do this for me? Yes. Your crypt and your crazy ivy. Whatever it is, I will do it.

The yellow Scout hummed past the massive DeBois manor. Its restored walls shone against sunlight, darkness held within high windows. Fresh finish and immaculate lawns belied any sign of life.

Sandra turned her head instinctively to look. She did not see the dark immobile figure that watched from tree shadows, motionless as a photograph, its malevolent eyes catching the reflected scout in twin images as the yellow machine sped past.

She shuddered without knowing why, and touched the frame of her sunglasses.

Eleven

In patched jeans, faded cowboy shirt, and favorite resoled cowboy boots, Melanie stood on the crest of the high bluff looking out over the vast panorama of the Mississippi River. Sam had let her play outside. Whitewood was behind her, the cemetery back on her left, shadowy in its copse of birch, oak, and magnolia.

The river moved a hundred feet below the edge of the bluff. The red eroded wall where she stood was thick with kudzu. Its broad leaves rattled in the wind rising to her from the sweep of the water, the brown moving surface a half-mile wide at this point. Streak whined behind her. He would not approach the edge. Her hair trailed from her smooth face in the warm wind. She shook her head with a smile at the wonder of space and stretched dimensions, tempted for an instant to spread her wings and sail forever like a great free bird.

A river tug appeared on her left. Pushing a long train of barges upriver toward Memphis, it looked like a toy. Fascinated, she stood for a long time until it had wound its way across her vista, gone around the far bend, leaving muddy waves lapping far below her against the reddish kudzu-choked shoreline.

"I love it here." She turned smiling at Streak. He rested sphinxlike. Head between his paws, he never took his eyes from her, giving an intermittent whine. She giggled.

"You silly. Come on, let's play."

She ran past him. Leaping up, he ran frolicking beside her, nipping at her thighs like a puppy.

She pulled his ball from her jeans pocket and threw it hard. It bounced across the uneven ground toward the graves. Streak chased it into shadow.

The child found nothing frightening about old mossy stones with archaic inscriptions. Her mother had taken special care to explain that people passed away when they were too tired, that everybody did it, and then they rested forever. It was shady and pleasant among the mossy graves. Faint rabbit paths crisscrossed between the plots. Sunlight dappled down through overhanging branches that creaked gently with each wind from the river. Birds nested above the graves, singing sourceless songs that she took for laughter. It was a happy restful place, a special cared-for place. She walked among the stones and read their inscriptions:

IN MEMORIAM—SUSAN RAWLINGS, WIFE OF PETER.
JOHN TAYLOR RAWLINGS—HE IS NOT DEAD
BUT SLEEPETH.
IN MEMORY OF GEORGE RAWLINGS, INFANT SON
OF THOMAS AND ELIZABETH.

She was deeply touched. All of them with the same name as her own. *Rawlings*. Her daddy's family.

She came to the crypt and paused. The little angels carved in the stone arch smiled at her. But she was aware of something unlikeable here. Like something afraid, something not right. She noticed a mark on the marble sealing slab and knelt, peering at it. A cross, darkly scrawled. She rubbed at it with a finger. The stone was smooth and cold. A trace of stain came off on her fingertip. She scowled and thrust her finger in the grass.

Suddenly, behind her, Streak barked. She spun around. Streak stood a few yards away with his back and buttocks to her. He snarled at something on the ground.

Melanie frowned. She stepped across a grave to see. "What did you find, silly?"

Something dark and quick scuttered between two graves. Melanie squealed, leaping back.

Streak did not attack at once. He snarled, remaining in place between Melanie and whatever had moved. His eyes were bright and hard. His long lean body quivered, a foreleg slowly outstretched, ready to snap into action, jowls curling back in black folds that revealed the forward inch-and-a-half long fangs dripping now with anxious drool.

"What is it, boy?" whispered Melanie, as unmoving as he.

Something large darted on her left. Melanie whirled in an arm-flailing arc.

Perched atop the tombstone nearest her hissed a huge rat. It reared on thick hind legs, tiny eyes gleaming, needlelike fangs barred.

Streak attacked even as Melanie screamed. The huge rat leapt. With a cry, Melanie fell on her back. She hit the ground and rolled, lashing out frantically with her hands. Streak was already there. She saw him beside her, a black dodging motion of long legs and white blurred fangs. She saw the hugest rat she'd ever imagined. It was on its hind legs, feinting and attacking, trying to get past the dog. Melanie squealed, kicking her feet, bumping in a backward panic on hands and buttocks.

The rat ran past Streak, charging. But Streak was just as fast. His jaws caught its thick back with lightning speed.

For an instant Melanie glimpsed Streak's head slinging the pinned hissing rodent back and forth like a rag. She heard tiny bones crack. Blood erupted in droplets on the air. She was up on shaky feet quivering as Streak slung the huge rat aside. It landed a few feet away. Its brown bloody corpse was twisted, broken. She was shaking with horror. Then she squealed again. The broken animal was suddenly not dead at all. It leapt up, hissed on rearing-back legs, and disappeared through the shadows of the tombs.

Streak leapt savagely in pursuit. Abruptly he stopped short. Looking left and right, he gave a confused whine. The rat was gone. Melanie sank onto a mossy hump. She rubbed her fingers through her hair.

"Wow," she half-grinned, scared for Streak now that her own danger was past. "Streaky? Come here, honey."

Streak trotted to her.

She grabbed him around the neck and hugged. "My good big boy, my brave boy. What a dirty big old rat." She giggled, nuzzling Streak, "You sure saved me, you big boy."

She stood and brushed herself off. Her legs were rubbery. Looking at the place where she had first seen the rat, she frowned—a rectangle of fresh earth was mostly covered by leaves, as if someobdy had scraped them over it for camouflage. She hadn't noticed it before. Streak whined for her to come away. His head pushed at her hand. She fondled his velvety muzzle, wondering at the fresh length of dirt. Streak nudged her hand nervously.

"Okay, okay." She looked around with a shrug and broke

into a run, laughing, Streak bolting to catch up with her as they ran from shadows into fresh burning sunlight.

David and Sandra had returned. They sat in the study. Sam stood just inside the kitchen door listening to their argument echoing through the hall. His head was lowered intently, the leathery fingers of his big right hand worrying the serious folds of his brow.

"I know how you must feel," Sandra was saying. "You know how sorry I am about all you're going through, God knows I am. But seven weeks?"

"We'll have to work it out, Sandy."

"I think you're feeling guilty right now, honey. You feel like you let him down. Now you get a second chance. Is that it?"

"That's exactly it."

"Davie, don't you see? You're guilty of nothing. It's so totally baseless." Sandra's voice was controlled but with a rising hint of panic. David's was calm and gentle and decided, but earnest for her to understand.

"He wanted me to do something and I'll see it done. We can work out the details. The hospital or whatever."

Listening, Sam bit his lower lip and shook his head, staring at the kitchen wall, stiffening at David's insistence.

"Sam can stay and watch everything," pleaded Sandra.

"I'm sure I can get leave from the chief of surgery. School is over so you and Melanie have no problem there. In seven weeks we'll go back to Memphis if you want. Or you both can go back and I'll stay here."

In the drawing room Sandra sat on the white sofa beside David. A long silent look at him showed she had used all her arguments. She put belated arms on his shoulders.

"David, David. . . . If this is what you want, you know I'll try to help."

A smile of thankfulness crept across his lips and eyes. "God knows we could use a vacation, anyway," she said. Looking into his eyes she realized suddenly that if she had had a father, one she had been lucky enough to have known and to have loved, she would do exactly what David felt he had to. She sighed, bending close to kiss him. Her practical mind was working now. "I'll go back to Memphis tomorrow, pay a couple of months' rent, phone, and utilities—try to make peace at school and the hospital—write me a letter for your boss, and phone him, too."

"Tell them it's family," David said, caressing the hair from her forehead, "part of my legacy."

"I need a drink," sighed Sandra, standing.

In the kitchen Sam grunted. He shook his head miserably, fearfully.

Melanie lay on the lawn. A warm breeze moved slowly through Whitewood's corridor of moss-draped water oaks. Their thick age-twisted limbs towered dark and strong above her, holding shadows and coolness on the front lawn. Melanie watched Streak dart after another squirrel. They were too small and too quick. The squirrel got away up an oak like the others and she was glad. She stared upward through the branches, watching clear patches of blue sky and white clouds. Her head rolled aside. The old stone gargoyle stood a few yards behind her. She got up to look it over—a funny old thing with its demon's face but kind of like a bunny-rabbit, too, gray-soft-looking though it was hard stone.

She crawled up the coarse slant of its back. Perched astride its neckless shoulders, she prodded its grainy ribs with the heels of her cowboy boots, watching Streak chase back and forth eight feet below her on the lawn. She loved this place. She was sure of that already. It was far away from Memphis, from that old man in the old apartments, his stinking breath and fat wet lips and tongue on her face, bony hands under her clothes, the hurt of her fists hitting him, and the look in daddy's and mommy's faces when she told them through tears what had happened. That was long ago. It was far off in Memphis. Here everything was so different. Birds singing instead of cars grinding. Whisper of the breeze instead of jets roaring overhead from the airport. Only that rat—but Streak sure took care of him. And that mean black bird.

She prodded the ribs of the stone beast, letting her head fall back so she could watch the clouds moving slowly across the blue patches through high branches. A squirrel peeked at her from draping gray moss. She giggled happily.

"I wish we could stay here forever," she sighed drowsily, her smooth white face trailing long gleaming hair in the warm sluggish breeze.

Piano music came distantly from the manor. Melanie smiled—mommy likes it here, too.

Within Whitewood, Sandra sat on the piano bench in the study. Her long fingers moved contemplatively on the keyboard of David's mother's baby-grand Steinway. Chopin. Her eyes moved toward the sun-hazed windows. Through gently lifting sheer curtains she saw David walk across the grass, making Melanie climb down from the gargoyle. She took a deep breath. A harsh introspection suddenly struck her—was she jealous, bitter because she never had a father? Was that closer to the truth of why she fought against staying, to make the idea sound so absurd to David, to try and make it sound like nonsense? She winced, remembering long-repressed taunts of childhood—*hey, little girl, where's your daddy? better run!*

Sandra shut her eyes, shoving back ugliness. Then it struck her with stunning force—she was rich. She had not even realized how the will affected her personally. She was literally filthy rich. Things rushed crazily at her. Travel. The best schools for Melanie. A new car. Almost any house anywhere. Even a big old nine-foot Steinway for herself. Maybe a real master to teach her classic pianoforte pieces that until now she had only muddled through. She could have a career, play in concert in a few years, do anything within her own innate limits.

Sandra shook her head in a daze. What had she been arguing about, for Christ's sake? David never once used the most obvious argument. He had given her time to understand.

She flushed with shame at her sudden greed. David had lost his father and she was thinking suddenly of what she could get out of it, and was suddenly more than willing to stay here as long as he wanted.

Biting her lip guiltily, Sandra rose from the piano bench. At the window she watched David and Melanie playing keep-away with Streak's ball, the beautiful Doberman leaping into the air as they tossed it back and forth, laughing. Love for her small family rushed through her furiously. Her eyes became hot, wet through her smile. You're a very lucky lady, and don't you ever forget it . . . *don't you ever.*

She heard something and turned with a start. Sam was standing in the study doorway watching her. She wondered how long he had been there. She almost cried out.

"You-all are staying on, aren't you?" He asked with a strange fatalism.

She nodded uncomfortably.

His eyes were dark with strange emotions she could not fathom. Saying nothing, he turned and was gone.

It was late afternoon when Ruth Sheehan's pink '55 DeSoto came trailing smoke up the long brick drive. Whitewood itself projected an immense shadow through the oaks. The sun was still above the horizon in the west, above the river that lay like a vast gold band in the distance behind the manor.

David was sipping a gin and tonic alone on the front veranda. Seeing Ruth's car, he smiled. He descended the steps and walked to the drive.

With a grinding of metal, the DeSoto halted near the manor. It chugged and died with a fit of pre-ignition, jetting blue smoke from a broken tailpipe. A door squawked open. Ruth climbed out and the heavy pink door crashed shut.

She came at David with open arms, thick face puffy from crying and lurid with covering makeup, large breasts drooping in a muu-muu with orange and red flowers.

"Poor baby," she grunted, throwing hot meaty arms around him.

She kissed his cheeks hard. David was overpowered by her thick perfume and sweat but glad to share her warmth, knowing it was sincere. He led her to the veranda. They sat in wicker chairs.

"Just passing, thought I'd drop in a sec," her bad teeth smiled between lips painted an iridescent orange.

"Want a drink?"

"No, no thanks." She glanced at the massive front doors. "Is your folks inside? Don't bother them. Let's just you and I talk a minute. Oh, this wicker feels fine. Nothing so restful."

"Want me to call Sam, tell him you're here? He'd be glad to see you."

The big woman patted David's wrist. "No, no son, don't bother any of them. This is between you and Sister Ruth."

Watching the lengthening shadows of the lawn grow from the manor, from the mossy-hung oaks, David steeled himself, expected difficult words of consolation for the loss of his father. He wanted none, but Ruth was too old a friend to offend. He liked her and had liked her as a boy.

She rubbed her flabby neck with a heavy green scarf. "You always was a mature boy, David. Like you understood a lot of things. I think you were one of those kids wise before their years. I don't mean to flatter so don't go getting that idea. What I was just wondering was—you intending to take up where your daddy left off?" She peered at him with questioning tiny eyes.

"In what way do you mean exactly? Planting and so forth?"

"Are y'awl gonna stay on here for seven weeks?" she asked.

David was surprised. "You always know everything, don't you?"

The big woman shrugged. She gazed out into lengthening shadows of trees and shrubs and the great blue bulk of the house shadow. From within Whitewood came playful sounds. David recognized Melanie's voice teasing and a short bark came from Streak.

"You know, don't you," Ruth said, "you've got a lovely sweet little girl."

David smiled, "Thanks."

She was not looking at him now, staring off through the shadows. "I was sick to my heart when I heard about the awful thing that happened a few months ago in town. That poor Holly crazy, her young husband dead that way. And they never found a single trace of the little girl. She was pretty, too, you know. Almost pretty as yours."

David stiffened. His fist squeezed the empty glass.

"Sam mentioned it last night. I used to date Holly. What do you know about it?"

Ruth grunted. Her index finger circled sadly at her temple.

David waited for her to speak but she was staring off into the shadows toward the road. He was about to invite her inside when she spoke quickly, startling him.

"Why don't you just pack up right now, David? Get away from here—before tonight." Her fat hand was heavy on his wrist, a hot damp weight. "You don't want to be here . . . with such memories."

"Ruth, you must know I'm staying seven weeks. How'd you find out, anyway?" He looked at her, trying to catch her eyes.

Her hand jerked from his. "It wasn't Grady if that's what you're thinking. I knew about the will before he did. You know, your daddy often confided in me, son. I always wanted the best for you-all, you know that."

David shook his head. "So you think we should leave, even knowing what my father wanted me to do?"

She turned now, abruptly fixing his eyes with hers. "Why do you think he wanted you here, son?"

David stared back keenly. "Why do *you* think he wanted me here, Ruth?"

"I don't know." She frowned and shivered, looking off into the shadows again. He was sure she had more to say but seemed afraid to say it.

"You're being even more inscrutable than usual," David frowned, puzzled.

The large woman nervously rumbled in a tiny sequin-covered bag. She found a Pall Mall and lit it with a solid gold lighter emblazoned with a cloisonné winged insignia of the Army Air Corps. She exhaled smoke and seemed on the verge of speaking. Then her thick head turned sharply.

David saw the raven come gliding in under the lower shadowy boughs of the oaks. Birds burst from the trees. The raven opened wide black wings, braking, its talons gripping a thick tree branch. It perched there staring at them soundlessly.

David stood and cursed it, remembering breakfast. He turned and saw Ruth staring stupidly up at the raven.

"Ruth?" he said.

Ruth blinked as if waking. Rising heavily, she laughed, brittle and overdone. "Just a silly old woman passing the time. Guess I'm not all together anymore. . . ." She tapped her temple depreciatingly.

"Come on, you were very emphatic." David frowned, annoyed. He glanced up at the raven. It squatted immobile on the limb, not preening, not calling. It was as still as something on a snapshot. "That damn bird killed a bluebird this morning. Big, isn't it? Sam shot at it."

Ruth shook her head. She moved to the steps. "Listen, I got to go, son. Got to get back to the trailer for the night folks. They'll all be getting off work soon, you know. Wanting to know about their love lives and chances of profits and so on."

"Wait a minute." David followed her chubby wriggling hips down the porch steps onto the lawn.

"I really got to be moving." She waddled swiftly toward the drive.

Nonplussed, he watched her duck into the old pink DeSoto and wave once with a brittle smile. Her engine started with a cough. The old car luched. She was backing suddenly out of the drive, the DeSoto making S-patterns in reverse, almost weaving off the driveway on both sides until it reached the road. She was gone in a cloud of blue exhaust.

He rubbed his face. "Crazy old biddy."

He turned and looked up into the tree. The raven was in exactly the same spot, immobile, seeming to stare down upon him. Its eyes were pinpoints in its blackness. David picked up a bedding stone from the roots of a shrub. He pitched his arm back to throw. His motion ceased in midstroke.

Arm back, stone in hand, he saw that there was no raven on the branch at all. He glanced left and right to see where it had flown. There was no sign of the large black bird. It was as if it had simply disappeared.

Twelve

David ate cold fried chicken in bemused silence.

The dining room was again elegant. Its chandelier tinkled in a gentle window breeze. David glanced at his wife and daughter, and then at Sam. Sandra ate with characteristically graceful gestures. Her smooth face was lovely in the candlelight, a white oval enhanced by dark shining hair. You've got a lovely little girl, Ruth had said. It was so true. David watched his daughter's dark yet bright eyes, her long neck and sleek graceful arms. He saw her innocence obvious in every gesture of eating, even the way she held her fork and the way she opened her mouth so wide to take a bite. He tried to catch Sam's eyes but Sam was staring inward as if torn by some secret foreboding. Melanie's hand snuck furtively under the table. David heard Streak smack on a morsel. The dog peeked over the edge of the table for more and Melanie stuffed his broad black head back down. After the funeral he had asked Sam about Chester's bird dog, sad to hear the dog had been found dead the morning Chester had been found.

"I bet you think I've been starving these two, Sam," Sandra grinned, winking.

Sam looked up with a polite smile. He obviously had not heard.

"We don't know what real cooking is," admitted Sandra. "Don't have time."

"I cook Pop-Tarts some mornings!" protested Melanie.

David and Sandra laughed.

Sam shook his head. "Well, down here folks can at least

eat well, even if we can't get good TV reception from Memphis or Jackson."

Sandra nodded at Melanie. "Speaking of city people, you and I are driving back up to Memphis in the morning, little woman."

Melanie crinkled her brow. "We're leaving?"

"There's rent and utilities to be paid, and explanations to be made, and when that's all done we're coming back."

Melanie looked vastly relieved. David glanced smiling at Sam and saw a dark mood distorting the old man's good-natured eyes and mouth.

"Can't I have a horse to ride?" begged Melanie.

David shrugged. "Sam might find you one." He grinned and winked at Sandra. Sam had not heard. He stared at the blue gathering darkness framed in the high casements on the long wall of the dining room.

"Sam, can I?" pleaded Melanie. She got up and ran around the table to grab Sam's thick strong hand.

The old man's age-lined face turned with surprise, softening in a strange mix of love and fear that weakened further into simple resignation.

He stroked her hair. "Why sure you can, honey, anything you want I can do you can have."

"We don't want you getting a broken neck or leg," Sandra warned.

Melanie kissed Sam's rough dark cheek. She ran to David with a kiss and then to her mother. Streak ran beside her from person to person, snuffling her hand for hidden goodies.

David saw Sam looking at them the way he had seen countless visitors at the hospital gazing longingly and mutely upon their endangered loved ones.

Night fell densely over the river. The moon glimmered through gathering clouds like a flashlight through a dark blanket. On its bluff, Whitewood stood as it had stood for a century, yellow-lit windows bright against the night.

On the back veranda Sam sat in his wicker chair, staring out at the crypt. Beyond the crypt the far side of the river was the spoiled color of dark milk. Crickets and cicadas sang dissonances and fireflies blinked erratically against jagged black treelines.

David came onto the veranda and sat in a chair beside Sam. The flap of the screen door was a profane loudness quickly smothered by the denseness of night.

"The rain song?" asked David.

Sam's head turned without comprehension.

David grinned. "The crickets and cicadas. Way they're singing now. When I was a kid you used to call it their rain song."

Sam half-smiled. He stared out into the darkly shining pallor of illusive shapes and lines.

"You remember good."

David filled a shot glass. "Want a drink?"

"Not tonight. You hitting that stuff kind of heavy, son."

"For medicinal effect only."

"Does it help that much?"

"Only on occasion." David threw the shot back neat. He never drank that much but whiskey seemed to go with these nights. The fiery chemical stream traced the interior of his upper gastric canal like a graph.

"You plan to sit out here every night, Sam?"

"I reckon I might, for a while." Sam shifted nervously in the wicker chair; its old frame creaked.

"Still think I shouldn't spend a few weeks down here?"

"You do what you think is right, son. That's all I know." Sam's tone was now noncommittal, fatalistic.

David nodded. It was what his father had always said—decide what you think is right and stick to it. He searched for traces of irony in the way Sam had said it and found none.

"Ruth came by this afternoon. Looks like she's of about the same opinion as you were."

Sam sat still and silent for so long that David thought the old man hadn't heard. A firefly blinked nearby in the dark, making Sam's narrow eyes gleam like green lights going on and off.

"What did Ruth say this afternoon, David?" Sam asked slowly.

"Nothing much. We saw that damned raven again."

Sam looked at David suddenly. "It went away?"

David nodded. Sam stared back toward the crypt.

"What about this Sprague person?" David asked.

Sam seemed to tense. "What about him?"

"I was thinking of going over to meet him tomorrow or the next day," David said, pouring another shot of whiskey.

Abruptly, Sam's hand reached David's wrist. It gripped him with amazing strength. Startled, David almost dropped the shot glass. Sam's voice came thick and hoarse with unexpected emotion.

"David—don't go messing in things where you might not be wanted. Why don't you go on back to Memphis? I'll be staying along here. I'll taken care of things. Go on, go with them in the morning. You can phone me from time to time."

David tried to pull his hand away. Sam's grip was fierce. "What the hell, Sam?" David hissed.

Sam's fist relaxed. The old man seemed to sag, his emotion draining away as suddenly as it had come.

"I don't know, son. Don't pay me no attention. I'm getting old and spooked, I reckon. . . . It's just . . . there's things I don't understand my own self. Seems to me like everything was going along all right till that man Sprague came to the country. No, I ain't saying he's done anything, except. . . ."

David watched the old man as his words tapered off. Sam gazed into the night like a sentry with eyes fixed in a thousand-yard stare. Was it senility? Or the impact of Chester's death? A delayed trauma effect?

"Don't pay me no attention," Sam repeated. He knocked ashes from his pipe and repacked the bowl from a zipper bag. As he relit it, puffing, his face glowed orange with each draw.

David touched Sam's shoulder. "Get a hold on yourself. You're letting things run away with your mind. Why do you sit here night after night this way?"

Sam puffed intently. He did not answer. A rift in the thickening night clouds sent brief moonlight across his worn and archaic profile. His old head was cut from the shadows like something hewn from wood, his gray hair frizzy, his forehead and chin as strong and rough as eroded granite. David felt deep love for the old man and was worried.

"When was your last checkup, Sam?"

Sam shrugged.

"I'm giving you a routine physical tomorrow. Got my bag in the Scout. Hypertension is indicated, I'd say."

Sam shook his head in his noncommittal way.

Quick gusts of wind blew a sudden mist across the veranda. David felt its soothing coolness on his face and hands. The mist turned to drizzle. David realized Sam was humming some old blues song. The old man was humming happily, David realized in astonishment.

Lightning flashed. Sam was grinning. Rain lashed down abruptly in hard sheets.

Some recent thought lingered in David's subconscious—he tried to remember, and it came, his father's odd remark in the will—"thank merciful God it's the rainy season."

"You always hated rain," David said. "Now you're grinning like hell."

Sam nodded. "Some things in this world, they can't cross

free-running water. And that sho' is free-running all out of the sky."

Shaking his head in concern for the old man, David watched Sam staring out into the gray slanting rain, the rugged profile lit again and again by dull radiant lightning.

Suddenly David saw the situation clearly.

It stunned him. Sam was watching his father—*he's watching over Chester, for Christ's sake, and he's glad it's raining. . . .*

What the hell's going on down here? Ruth, Sam, Chester's will. . . ?

Shaking his head, David left Sam on the porch and staggered into the house to bed.

On the veranda, Sam watched the rain. He stared out into the night. Mist rose over the bluff from the river, making him shiver. He remembered another night not long ago, before the funeral. A drunken night of grieving for Chester. A night of seeing something move in the graveyard shadows. He had crouched, drunken, listening, not knowing whether what he saw was real or illusion. Among the dark arbors he had crouched, watching a shape gliding among the graves. Sprawled across its arms had been a long gray cat. The old man had thought the cat was dead. He wanted to rise up and shout bravely but horror held him where he squatted, froze his muscles, his limbs.

The dark shape had halted. A patch of moonlight rayed down through overhanging branches of trees that shadowed the graves. It silhouetted the black shape and gleamed upon the sleek gray fur of the lifeless cat.

The old man had stared in increasing disbelief and horror as the thing bent over the prostrate animal in its arms. For long moments the scene was suspended. Suddenly the cat shrieked into life. It writhed, twisted but not escaping as if staked in fire. Its babylike howls pierced the night shade where the old man cowered, tears of horror and cowardice streaking his weathered cheeks. The ground shuddered. A rectangle of earth ruptured in front of the shape and the screaming animal. Clods flew up into the rays of moonlight. The earth burst open. And the old man shook at what he knew he could not be seeing. That twitching, squirming corpse floating up from the broken ground. The cat ceasing to struggle. The trembling corpse floating up to the waist-level of the dark shape. The thing placing the now-still body of the cat upon the hideous chest of the floating squirming corpse, taking them both in its arms, turning like a robot on a pivot and gliding off toward the western shelterbelt of trees that separated the Rawlings land from the restored manor of the DeBois.

For an hour the old man had dared not move. His clothing was befouled. Sweat stung his eyes. He squatted alone in shivering terror in the primeval dark.

Now, watching the rain, Sam remembered. And he watched the crypt, struggling with fear, not knowing whether he would find the courage to protect it when its time was at hand.

Thirteen

Dawn came with damp cool air through the master bedroom windows. The rain had ceased. David rolled on the bed toward Sandra. He woke her with kisses, wanting her again before she left for Memphis.

His hand slipped down warm familiar curves, gently probing. She moaned and stirred and nestled to him.

In no other phase of their life together did they seek perfection so fervently. The ultimate goal was consistent mutual pleasure. Through the years the sensitivity of their bodies had increased. Lovemaking had grown both more heated and more subtle with years of searching one another's passion on the common ground of their bodies. When it worked, David forgot himself, lost all personality in the pure escape into Sandra's being. With every new experiment, Sandra enjoyed a wild and wanton guiltlessness. The delirium of giving and of being possessed set her mind and body free. In youth she had feared sex, felt disgust at the whispered ritual of coupled lust and orifices. Her first experience with a boy in college had been ugly. He had been thoughtless, greedy, and crude in his grasping. She had disavowed sex until David. His patience and tenderness had astonished her at first. The intensity of their ultimate act had erased adolescent revulsion. With David she had realized how a woman could feel with a man—not being violated, not conquered, but loved.

Sandra turned into David's arms now with delicious passivity. They kissed away the languor of dawn sleep. Sandra's blood quickened as David readied and took her. A slow breeze wafted over them from the windows.

They moved together, were one, then lay apart with the breeze still freshening their damp bodies.

"You're fantastic," whispered Sandra.

"Had to wake you up somehow."

David's body twitched as her nails dug playfully into his back. Grinning, he rolled against her. Her smile was sprightly, devilish, and sleepy.

"Don't go visiting any ole boyfriends while you're in Memphis," he jibed.

"You know I have to keep in touch." She traced a cool fingertip over his lips.

He kissed her eyelids, his mouth wandering over her nose and lips, moving down along her throat to one of his favorite places, the hollow of her throat where he buried his face when their bodies moved in unison.

"Wish I didn't have to go," she pouted.

He raised himself on an elbow. "Only for a day or so. Clear things up and come right back."

"Have you written that letter?"

David snapped his fingers. The chief of surgery. He sat up on the bed. "I've got to do that right now."

She watched him grab a pair of jeans and underwear. She sat up and hugged herself, savoring the warm tingle that hummed like a sweet song through her belly and her limbs.

At half past nine David and Sam stood by the brick drive in the sunlight. The Scout idled. Sandra lifted one hand from the steering wheel and touched David's face. He leaned into the driver's window and kissed her, then Melanie, catching an errant lick from Streak.

"See you tomorrow afternoon," Sandra sighed, adjusting her sunglasses reluctantly.

"Be careful on the road," David said sternly.

"Hi-ho," Sandra quipped. She put the Scout in gear. With a final wave she pulled away.

David and Sam watched the Scout back down the long smooth brick drive. It reached the highway. Sandra and Melanie waved from opposite windows. David and Sam waved back. The yellow vehicle accelerated with a buzz, tiny before it was finally hidden by trees.

David spent most of the morning working on the lawns. In cutoff jeans he sweated, pushing the big Snapper lawnmower growling over the grass on its archaic bicycle wheels. He worked barechested. The sun blazed on his back and legs and arms. He welcomed the mind-healing fatigue, trimming shrubs with clippers, pruning the weeds from budding arbors and plant beds. Sam didn't come out of the house. Probably asleep, David thought, up all night with his crazy obsession. Chester's mental sickness might have somehow infected Sam. He would have to watch the old man closely. Too many of these all-night vigils could break his health. Maybe a tranquilizer prescription for a few days—ten milligrams of Valium or perhaps Thorazine. Sam's blood pressure had checked slightly high but within range for his age. The tension was not merely physical.

David labored until noon, pouring sweat. It felt terrific. He was hosing himself off beside the old garage on the far side of the drive, shivering and whooshing, and he remembered something that made him shout. Throwing the hose down without even shutting off the water, he trotted around the garage and untied the thin chain on the rusty hasp of the double doors.

There it still sat. Covered with dust. One flat tire. His old green TR–3. Exactly where he'd left it almost ten years ago.

He moved toward it slowly, the car Chester had given him on his sixteenth birthday. Left there when he went to Memphis. Deserted because of their argument. Unwanted because it would constantly have reminded him of all he owed. A figment of the past waiting here for him to reclaim it after all these years.

He grinned nostalgically and palmed a layer of thick yellow dust off a fender. What an ass I was, he thought.

Quickly he snatched off the old tonneau, taking care not to let heavy rolls of dust fall onto the seats and dash. He opened the driver's door and dislodged a dirt-dauber's clay nest from the doorjamb.

He sat behind the wheel, staring through thick windshield dust. Too proud to take it with him. Doing his own thing. Not taking it to show his father that he didn't need him.

"Christ," he grunted, with a nostalgic shake of his head.

He tried the clutch and brake pedals. Clutch okay. Hydraulic assist probably still good. Brakes down. Maybe just fluid low. The old brass key was still in the ignition.

"Thought I never come back, huh? Thought you'd get to sit here and rest the rest of your life? Hope you're not all stuck inside."

He spent the next hour changing the oil and draining the

gas tank. No water came out first, so he knew the lines were okay. He hit the front-end grease joints with a hand lube gun. The spare was still up. He put it on. All the tires were okay—no dry rot to speak of—old iron-durable Michelin radials. No way to tell if the battery would take a charge. He opened the trunk, found the manual starter handle, fitted it through the hole in the grille, and cranked it over six times. It hit on the seventh. He stood back amazed.

The old Triumph sat there chugging smoke which soon turned to clear exhaust, its valves and rings reseating as the engine warmed.

David got in and pulled out into the sunlight with a lurch, having forgotten to add brake fluid. He had to snatch the emergency brake lever to stop it. He got out again and grinned. The ammeter showed the generator charging. The car would live again.

A half-hour later, after a thorough wash job, he stood admiring the forest-green paint and wire wheels. He got in and drove up the drive. The exhaust crackled as he entered the road. He turned left, away from town. Going through the gears on the old country two-lane took him back through the years. His life seemed telescoped into the buzzing open car that had been brought to him by a grinning proud father a lifetime ago. He went through the hot asphalt S's, wind tearing through his damp hair and T-shirt. Insects veered off the windshield.

He passed the old abandoned cotton gin.

Tarpaper shacks. Edifices of another era.

Marches of oaks and sycamores along a swamp.

He U-turned and gunned it back toward Whitewood, toward Bickford. The same scenery came back faster. He let the old car out a little now, sixty, sixty-five. Tight through S's. Passing a dilapidated smoky pickup, he waved and was waved to. He felt like a damn kid again and loved it. Warm air washed his face. Hot sun glittered on the hood.

There was Whitewood again, coming up on the right, its grand corridor of moss-hung oaks, its white pillars strong, its face the proud architecture of another age. Slowing to make the drive, he changed his mind and downshifted, speeding on, not wanting it to end, as if he were a kid again with his mother and father still alive in the great house. He passed the restored DeBois manor, taking speed.

The curves and S's made him grin. He let the speed climb, regaining confidence in the old machine, whipping past Sister Ruth's doing eighty-five.

Half a mile out of Bickford the red needle wiggled between ninety and ninety-five on a straightaway. He glimpsed the telltale grilled-and-blue roof-lights of a cruiser hidden off the road in high weeds.

"Shit!"

He braked, cutting speed hard, but knowing he was passing through a radar trap.

The cruiser appeared in the rear-view mirror. Blue lights flashing, grille looming. David bitched at himself. He pulled the roadster to the shoulder, the cruiser right on his tail. He turned in the bucket seat.

A tall paunchy officer with thumbs tucked in khaki belt loops strode weightily toward him. Man-with-no-eyes sunglasses. Hard line on a meaty jaw.

"Get out of that car, boy," the officer drawled, half-growling.

David sighed. He opened the door and hoisted himself out.

Quick enormous hands suddenly impacted his shoulders. He found himself flopping across the hot sheet metal of the Triumph's hood, looking up into his own reflection in mirror sunglasses. The smell of bacon and eggs came down from the huge close face with bared teeth. He could see every pit and hair in the rough skin.

"What you mean, tearing down my road thataway, boy? What I'm gonna do now is kick yore God damn ass."

David shoved impulsively against the uncalled-for brutality. Too quick for the grabbing hands, he dodged back along the roadster, the big cop stomping after him.

"Hey, what're you doing, man, wait a minute!" David had his hands up, open-palmed but ready.

The officer halted. Hands cocked on khaki hips, he belly-laughed and ripped off the reflecting sunglasses. David's mouth dropped open—Dewey Pounds, the biggest, dumbest best-natured old boy on the Hatchie County football team stood there chuckling at him.

"Dewey?"

Pounds slapped David's arm and let out a howl. "Hey, boy, when you was quarterback I saved your ass from many a mean linesman."

Grinning, blushing, David grabbed the offered hamlike hand and pumped it. "You big bastard, you scared the hell out of me."

Pounds tapped the Triumph's fender, "That thing'll still hit ninety, after all these years."

"Sorry, guess I was letting it out."

"Not to worry, boy. Hey, listen, I had to be over in Jackson day of your daddy's funeral. Couldn't make it but sure meant to."

"You're Bickford's sheriff? Got a quiet county, anyway." David had always liked Dewey, who never let cornfed plowboys break through the line before a pass.

Pounds rubbed his groin wearily. "Ain't so quiet in Bickford. You probably heard our young banker killed hisself, yeah, his wife's still nuts and their little girl ain't never turned up. And we got these damn pets missing. People bitching about lost pets. Some of these little ole ladies really love their animals. Cats and no-count dogs probably getting run over or run off but everybody says we got us a pet-snatcher weirdo or some kind of spook. Ain't as quiet as all that, David."

They small-talked about football days and agreed to get together soon.

David drove on into Bickford. He parked between two pickups in front of Davis Variety and Grocery.

Rawboned old men grinned at him on the porch. He smiled back, their tobacco-stained jaws and shrunken toothless maws reminding him of times long past. He walked up the steps into the cool dim store. Cloth and new tires on the right, groceries on the left.

White-haired old man Davis was behind his counter, short and wryly methodical, checking every price three times. David nodded hello.

The spry old man waved him over. His false teeth clicked as he chattered. "Sorry to hear about your daddy. So many things happening now, I just don't know what to think. Them young folks awhile back, too. Bad things run in spurts, I reckon."

David wandered through the shelves picking up necessary things. Near the back of the store he overheard three old men in overalls hunched around the air-conditioner.

"It's cats more than dogs," one was insisting.

"I say a panther come across the river, that's what's getting them all," another retorted, spitting into an empty coffee can.

"No tracks. Nobody seen any sign of panthers noway."

"One of them UFOs done set down in the woods, I say. Looking for samples of what's living here. Be catching one of us directly."

Amused, David carried his armload to the counter. Old

man Davis checked and rechecked the prices, peering over the top rim of gold-framed spectacles.

Then David was on the road out of Bickford again, letting the speed climb, enjoying wind and sun and speed. Sister Ruth's trailer passed.

Farther on, the restored DeBois manor loomed through scattered trees. David let off the accelerator. His right foot trod the brake gently.

He suddenly wanted to meet the man called Sprague, the blind man from New York with so much money he could have restored such a place; the man his father must have known or at least met; the man Sam didn't want to talk about.

David stopped the Triumph at the old DeBois drive. He sat up in the bucket seat, amazed, surveying the restoration.

From the drive it seemed weird, ghostly somehow now that its high octagonal pleasure dome was clean and glinting brassily like some fairy-tale wizard's minaret. The balustrades and brickwork were like new. The house itself was four stories. Its cupola-dome rose two more above the center. An absolute masterpiece, David marveled.

He remembered playing here, stalking through huge shadowy interiors via a loose window, the others long nailed shut. It was frightening then as a shell. It was more awesome now in its sudden newness, surrounded by cropped lawns, its great magnolias the only thing unchanged. The view of the river was even wider now, he reflected, only a mile or less from Whitewood along the river bluff. The two plantations were separated by a thick belt of woods where Chester and Sam used to take him hunting. He'd never known the DeBois family. They were gone before his time but in the old days the Rawlingses and DeBoises had been good neighbors. Great parties Chester had spoken of years ago. Dove shoots, dances under the moon where silk gowns sashayed, lit by breeze-flickering candelabra. But the last DeBois had sold out and gone to New Orleans after the Depression. A few share-croppers had worked the land for a bank. The great manor house went to seed like so many others.

But now it was like new again. David was deeply impressed. In no more than a year a man from New York—rich and blind according to Sam—had been able to restore the grandeur of the place. Yet there was something negative about the fresh windows, like a watchfulness prickling David's neck and spine. Maybe it was the total lack of human or animal activity. A stillness almost deathlike against the newness.

David put the car in gear. He idled up the drive. Somebody was keeping the place up. There was somebody here for sure.

At the loop of the drive beside the towering corner of the house he parked and got out.

Hardly a bird singing. Only a restless breeze troubling manicured shrubs and lilting through magnolias and the gray Spanish moss that hung from gnarled oaks. He stood at the edge of the lawn and felt the strongest sensation of not being wanted here. Of being watched.

Shivering with an uneasy laugh at himself, he crossed the stone path toward the front veranda. His shoes scraped the stone steps. At the tall carven oak doors he studied the heavy, heavy bronze knocker, put fingers on the polished face, and let the knocker fall. It made a startling boom.

No one answered. He looked at the tall doors and let the knocker fall booming again. Nothing. He shrugged, descended the stone steps and gazed up at the towering masonry. Something seemed to stare back down upon him. Giving off a massive silence. Making him feel threatened, vulnerable, and alone.

Then he saw the black bird perched with steely wings on an eave by the huge brassy rising of the cupola.

It stared down at him as immobile as a metallic shape sculpted from the eave itself. He had flinched involuntarily, caught off guard. He was angered by the staring thing.

"What are you looking at?" he demanded, calling upward with a clap of his hands.

His human sound faded. The large bird did not move, peering down malevolently and as coldly unreal as the newness of the house.

David gave it the finger and strode nervously toward the drive. At the corner of the house he glanced up. The raven was gone.

He walked along the side of the house toward the back lawns, admiring flawlessly tended azaleas. But there was something wrong. He couldn't put his finger on it.

The restoration of the rear gardens and portico was as fine as anything in front. Attention to detail in every respect. Far off on the river a tug horn sounded, coming faintly. But the old gardens were silent. Then he knew what was bothering him. No buzzing bees around the flowers. No birds in the oaks or magnolias. No squirrels. As if insects and animals instinctively avoided this place. Insecticide? Hidden traps to keep animals from digging and tunneling?

He felt suddenly very alone.

"Hello?" he called insistently at the back of the house. He felt ridiculous, scanning the upper windows for a face that did not appear, irritated at the absurd sensation of being watched, determined to meet the man Chester must have known this past year.

There was no sound from behind that startled him. Yet he knew suddenly that he was no longer alone. Something was close behind him.

He whirled awkwardly with a stifled cry, face-to-face with a man who stood lean and darkly inscrutable, black eyes glittering arrogantly into his. The immobile face seemed faintly Oriental but mirthless, somehow inhuman. The black eyes held no trace of human warmth. David was at a total loss. He felt absurdly like bolting in a run.

"I was looking for a Mr. Philip Sprague," he managed to say. "We're neighbors. . . ."

The strange man stood mutely immobile and unchanging, as frozen as a dark figure on a photograph, the expressionless eyes without wit or expression, staring into David's.

"I'm Dave Rawlings, I live on the next plantation, through those trees. Is Mr. Sprague home today?" He had to avoid those black gleaming eyes, their inhuman immobility. "Listen, I'm not intruding. Or am I?"

The man did not move a muscle. Was he mute? David wondered. Sprague was supposed to be blind and old so this could not be him. The black eyes kept piercing his like a dark assault of will. Finally moving himself suddenly, David strode toward the drive. His back crawled with being watched from behind. He struggled not to hurry his pace and at the corner of the house he glanced back.

Nothing. No one there.

Beside his car he glanced up again at the house.

"Nice neighbors," he growled and slipped behind the wheel.

It started quickly. He backed out the long smooth drive, glowering, disturbed. And as he backed onto the road and gunned the Triumph toward Whitewood, he knew that he had been afraid.

On the road again with sunlight and speed the sensation of having been caught intruding upon a dangerous situation fretted in his manhood, gnawing there as if he had faced a dark will stronger than his own morality.

"Chester wasn't friends with anybody there," he muttered aloud as Whitewood came magnificently into view.

Fourteen

For an hour at the end of the brick drive beside the house he savagely compounded the old roadster until it gleamed and his anger was worked out in a drench of sweat. Still, he could not forget that immobile staring, that expression of almost inhuman arrogance and contempt.

In the house he had a ham sandwich with an icy Coke. Sam was snoring on the back sun-porch divan. Smiling, David watched the old man for a moment. A dazzling shaft of sunlight was creeping across Sam's face. David lowered the window blind a little before going back inside.

There was plenty to do. In the old days Whitewood had required a bevy of retainers to keep it up. David knew that Sam was too old to try. He pulled crabgrass from the azaleas and verbena. He wire-brushed the moss off the old stone gargoyle, rubbing its nose affectionately. He worked the lawns until long purplish shadows were falling. The green arbors and lawn turned blue with the sun low on the horizon across the wide sweep of river.

His stomach was growling. He passed the kitchen windows, heard frying, smelled pork chops, and grinned. Before he went inside he stood at the back veranda steps. Gazing over the darkening lawn, past the arbors to the old cemetery, he felt a shiver as the sun was cut in half by the black horizon across the river.

David ate with Sam at the drop-leaf kitchen table.

"This old house has been a lonesome place these past

years," Sam said, chewing. "Worse after Miss Leah passed on."

David sighed. Eating in the kitchen made him nostalgic, lonely. Memories lingered everywhere in the house. Kitchen memories of coming in after hunting, after school, after swimming, catching a quick bite of good supper at this same walnut drop-leaf table with the cutting boards hanging there on the brick wall above, the two big inset stainless-steel ovens, the same yellow light on the sinks and brown tile floor, the rising nightsongs of crickets and cicadas coming through the dark blue windows, the smell of fried food and dressing, and the drip of a faucet. If Streak had been there now to walk through the room it would have been complete —the ticky-tack-ticky-tack of a bird dog's nails padding toward the door, scolded and banished from the house by his mother.

"How did Chester's bird dog die?" David asked.

Sam tensed, staring into his plate. "He was lying beside your daddy. His neck was broke."

"How? Neck broke?"

Not answering, Sam finished his tea, ice cubes rattling against his front teeth. David shook his head. Too many things made no sense at all.

"You ought to get on away from here," Sam muttered gravely, looking down into his tea glass. "Take your young family and go back where you made a place for yourself."

David reached across and touched Sam's thick grizzled wrist, mahogany leather flecked with white hair. He scrutinized the old man. Sitting out there every night, watching, talking about how some things can't cross water, hoping for rain—

"Sam—I'm worried about you. It's hard for me to say this—"

It was hard, very hard. David swallowed. "But I know Chester must have gone . . . well, ill of mind. A man has to be sick to do a bad thing to his own person. I'll be damned if I'll let you go off into fantasies. Your imagination is strained by his death, don't you think?"

Silent, Sam stared away toward the windows.

"What is it you're scared of, Sam?" persisted David.

"I ain't scared of nothing."

"Then you sleep in the house tonight. I'm worried about your health. You need regular rest."

Sam got up and took his plate to the sink to wash it.

David shook his head and got up. "Okay . . . okay, but if you don't take it easy I'll put you on tranks and I mean it."

Sam looked around, puzzled.

"Tranquilizers," explained David.

The old man nodded.

David saw that Sam was acting. A veil drawn between them. Just like boyhood times when David had fired his gun too soon, or handled a horse the wrong way, or tangled up his fishing line in a wasp nest or shot the hole in that boat, the same veil of exasperation and confusion drawn between them. Disturbed, David rose to wash his own plate.

A half-hour later he followed Sam out to the back veranda again. The moon was bright blue on shadow-hunched arbors. The flat stretch of lawn stopped in the shadows of the cemetery. The far silvery glimmer of the Mississippi moved in a silver sheen, so slowly it seemed motionless. Fireflies appeared in intermittent greenish winkings. Sam sucked his pipe. David wanted to make the old man go inside to bed. But his arguments did no good. Sam's main virtue was persistence, and he was just as stubborn. He searched for some way to help his old friend who sat like a great quiet tree beside him.

His obsession of watching Chester's crypt was potentially dangerous, as was any obsession. And David wondered—why had Chester sent this strong old man away instead of leaning on him? Had Chester been afraid he might harm Sam somehow?

Sam coughed. "They says if you sleep under the moon without a rag over your face you go moon-crazy. That the moon got blood on it and it'll come down and get in your head."

David grinned. "I never heard that one."

"Lots of things I never told you when you was little. Things men don't half believe but are scared of just the same. Sometimes that moon is red as blood. I seen it a thousand times that way. It don't do to take chances with things you don't know nothing about."

"Trying to scare me?" David chuckled.

"They say that falling stars is lost souls being cast out from heaven," Sam continued fervently. Tremors of emotion shook his voice now. "You see them burnt up before they hits the ground. The earth, it's Satan's territory. The heaven belongs to God. It's up to us down here to fight. Devil wants to destroy human folks. That's his job. And he does it good, I reckon."

David shook his head. He believed in a life force. Some

kind of regenerating physical energy that scientists had yet to discover. But not myth or heaven or hell or God or Satan. He wondered if that were a clue to the old man's obsession with Chester's death.

"The nighttime," Sam's voice labored, "is when the devil does his best work. Dark, it belongs to him. We got these electric lights and such trying to keep him back. But things ain't changed much except for that. Satan wouldn't like nothing better than for weak folks to convince ourselves he ain't out there. But I know he is."

David wanted a drink. Sam's superstitions grated on his tolerance for the old friend.

"Is this Sprague guy kind of short and dark and oriental-looking?" he asked Sam abruptly.

Sam stiffened, turned sharply in the wicker chair, making the wood shriek. "Why you asking me that?"

David tensed, startled at Sam's sudden intensity.

"Don't get so upset, Sam. Christ. I drove by the DeBois place this afternoon. Couldn't stir up anybody, then when I was just standing there out back and turned around and this weird guy was looking at me, not moving a muscle."

"Don't you never go there again, boy!" hissed Sam's moon-lined face, teeth bared and gleaming faintly.

"Sam? For Christ's sake. . . ."

Sam turned back to stare off the veranda in silence.

"Sam, you're acting crazy. . . ."

Sam said nothing. David shivered, reacting. Resisting anger, he rose and went into the house, to bed.

On the porch alone, Sam began to nod. The last vision he had before dozing off was the eroded brightness of the moon blurred against ragged black foliage above the tiny ancestral graveyard. Sleep took the tired old man unaware.

Sam opened his eyes.

It was still night. Stunned, he realized he had slept. His eyes widened in fear.

He thought he saw something move.

The moon shone through fleeting patches of cloud. The arbors and black trees hulked about the old cemetery seemed to move as the pale celestial light came and went.

The old man hissed. He saw, beyond the arbors, a flitting shadow blacker than the tree shapes that darkened the cemetery and bluff. It glided through the trees toward the graves, moving along the bluff, coming from the shelterbelt of trees that separated the DeBois and Rawlings estates.

Quivering, Sam tried to shake himself into action.

"God help me," he whispered, panting.

He picked up his flashlight and the old hammerless .32 from the wicker table. He crept over the faintly creaking veranda boards and down the steps into the moonlight.

With mincing steps he stalked toward the arbors, flinching once to stare behind his neck, then moving slowly again forward, his wide shoulders trembling. He forced himself forward.

In the arbor shadows he peered into the darkness ahead. The graves were limned in patches of moonlight that shafted down hazily. His lips mouthed a silent prayer. Scanning left and right, his eyes watered with fear.

He stepped forward, keeping low, moving among the first graves. Brush crackled faintly underfoot.

He felt it watching him suddenly.

He clicked on the flashlight. The penetrating five-cell beam lashed out through the thick layers of shadow. Something hissed. Sam whirled left. He played the beam frantically, pistol wavering in his right hand, the tombstones and the crypt casting bone-white pallor.

With reptilian suddeness a shadow left the black trunk of a tree. Sam whirled. His beam flashed wildly. Its yellow glare passed something and went back. The thing that stared at him made his mouth open in a childish scream. Cradled in the thing's arms, a body in rotting clothes squirmed. It was not the corpse of Chester Rawlings nor was it wholly dead.

Sam gaped. His body refused to move, his jaw slack, the pistol and flashlight almost falling from his hands. The thing stood in the yellow-coned end of his flashlight beam. He couldn't tear his eyes from the earth-smeared corpse, its dangling arms quivering, its teeth chattering in the drooping head, its whole length twitching obscenely as the light struck it.

In a spasm of horror, Sam fired. Three rapid ear-shattering reports sent smoke across the shaky flashlight beam. The thing moved. Sam flinched back with a cry. Then he seemed to be alone. The thing was gone. He remembered the floodlights with regret, wishing he had turned them on.

Warily, panting, the frightened old man crept forward between the graves. A river mist was settling in the hollows.

His foot struck something large and rubbery. He looked down, grunting in fear. His light shone on mold-circled red eyes glaring up from a moldering putrefied face.

"Sprague!" rasped Sam. He had seen the body raised, now

it had returned. He stood between it and the crypt where Chester lay.

Its ragged voice came sputtering from putrid lips. "Fool! You dare protect him who slew and buried me? Why, then, join your master."

Sanity shaken, Sam made a convulsive move to run. Something large slithered. Brush rattled.

Sam cried out miserably, dropping flashlight and gun, screaming and slapping at ropelike loopings around his ankles. His feet went out from under him. He fell with arms flailing. His face hit the ground and his heart pounded, hammered in his mind like cathedral bells as he felt broad metallic scales sliding over the skin of his hands and ankles and throat. Disbelievingly, in a glimmer of moonlight, he glimpsed a scaly head swaying near his face. Its glassy eyes reflected two floating moons. Its long forked tongue darted at him, the flickering touch like a brand on his pulse-hammering forehead. He had no breath to scream. One of his arms was still free.

Outstretched, the hand groped, fingers clawing and opening, stiffly erect. The night was still. There were no sounds but the crushing and sliding of scales upon scales. In a last blurred vision Sam saw the twitching corpse struggling upon knees and elbows, dragging itself across the ground toward him and the crypt. Thick loops covered Sam's eyes but in the red twilight of his last moments on earth he felt something brush his outstretched hand. His writhing fist clutched at it with a last desperate strength from his trapped body. He felt something like twigs snapping in his hand. Then the black waves crashed through his last defenses. The silver cord of his life stretched taut and broke into a black howling infinity.

David awoke. Sitting up in bed he knew he had heard gunfire. Three quick successive shots. He sat listening. "Sam?"

He ran into the hall and down the stairs, grabbing the newel post and spinning into the hall, hurrying down it through the kitchen and out onto the veranda. Straining his vision into the moonlight sprawl of arbors and lawn, he caught a glow of yellow light. It was a flashlight a hundred yards off among the graves.

He switched on the floodlights. Six white beams lanced into the night. Peering, David gasped. Among the pale reflecting tombstones lay a twisted body.

David ran down the veranda steps, sprinted through the arbors. He came to a panting halt.

The old man lay with arms hugging himself, legs twisted together, his once-fine features contorted in an obscenely comic leer. David had seen the effects of agony a thousand, ten thousand times, but it never lost its edge. And this was Sam. Wincing, he knelt to examine the old man.

"Aw, Sam . . . Christ."

Turning Sam's face gently aside, David did not see the dark shapes merge into the dimly fog-shrouded shelterbelt of trees to the west. The moon was out again but David's eyes stared down at Sam.

He tried to be clinical. A bloody foam oozed from the forever-flared nostrils, blackish in the blue floodlight. Blood trickled from the dirt-flecked ears. Sam's eyes gaped blood-red, pupils deep black spots like punched holes. David grimaced. He lifted the old man's head and held it against his side, stroking the crinkly hair. Cause of death? Obviously a stroke. A classic textbook stroke. Most massive he had even seen firsthand.

Sam, he thought. God, now it was Sam. He was thankful Sandra and Melanie weren't here to see this.

He laid the old man down. Bloody foam reached the grizzled chin and rolled down the leathery throat. The arms were stiff. David folded them with difficulty over the broad still chest. Sam's dead eyes gazed up bloodily at him as if beseeching somehow, almost questioningly, almost in fear.

David rubbed his face. First Chester, now Sam.

People get old, he told himself. Everyone dies.

But that made it worse. Guilt ebbed back from where he had hidden it. He should have been watching the old man. He knew Sam had an obsession. He should have used tranks. He should have made him leave.

Sam's fists were clenched. David tried to unclutch them but could not. He brushed a palm gravely over Sam's eyelids. They wouldn't close. Every muscle in Sam's frame or at the surface of his body was stiff and hard.

David picked up the flashlight and wearily stood. A long streak of shadow from the arbors had kept half the cemetery dark. The river fog was thickest there. David's flashlight beam played toward the crypt.

He gave a short cry of rage and disbelief.

The marble sealing slab lay aside. One corner was broken. Long white marks scarred its face as if someone had torn at it with a sharp multipronged tool. The dark mouth gaped mockingly at the end of the quivering flashlight beam.

David moved quickly and bent to point the flashlight inside.

The new coffin lay on one end of its shelf. The lid was thrown open. Its fleecy white interior was empty and softly glowing.

Fifteen

David stalked through the floodlit arbors toward the house. The image of the white lining of the casket seared deeper than Sam's hemorrhaging face.

Sam knew it was going to happen.

What lousy fucking bastards would have done that? Sam *knew*. Did someone have a grudge against them? Chester knew it, too. They *knew* and I laughed.

He climbed the veranda and entered the kitchen. Day-old coffee was hot in the percolator. He mixed a cup with whiskey and drank it scaldingly down.

Shakily dialing the kitchen wall phone he reached the operator.

"Sheriff Dewey Pounds, please." He sat on a wobbly stool. His legs quivered like plastic tubes of jello.

"Is this an emergency?"

"Yes."

"I'll connect you with the deputy at his office."

"No. Give me his home."

"Moment please."

The number rang four times. Dewey's deep groggy voice boomed irritably on the line.

"Pounds talking."

David identified himself and told what had happened.

"Holy shit," grunted Pounds. "You'll need an ambulance."

David nodded as if Pounds were there. "Dewey, I want those God damn vandals. I mean, man, I *want* them."

"We'll find out what assholes done this. I cain't believe it, Gawd."

David allowed a grim smile. His hands doubled into fists. He wanted to see Pounds when they caught whoever it was. He wanted to have a piece of them himself.

"Pore old Sam," Pounds said. "Reckon they scared him. I call that murder. If he hit one of them I'll catch 'em at Doc's."

"Keep me in touch."

"I'll be by directly."

Pounds hung up. David sat on the wobbly stool, seething. Obscene comic visions popped up irresistibly. He tried not to see his father's pitiful stolen remains propped up somewhere by pranksters, the shattered skull attracting flies. On the side of a road or in the middle of it. Hung upside down from a tree. Put against a road sign like some grotesque hitchhiker.

Maybe it was a bunch of kids who somehow heard about the will—violating a crypt, for Christ sake—the drunken fun of punks.

He hoped with all his heart that Sam had hit one of them. Considering vital organs that Sam's bullet might have passed through, he grinned fiercely. Tears came. Tears of rage as much as sorrow.

The first red slashes of dawn crossed a gray eastern horizon as David met the ambulance on the drive. White-suited attendants stepped from their vehicle, seedy and sleepy, a short gaunt white one and a tall pudgy black one. David realized the state had come a long way. Years ago no black was allowed intimacy with a white victim in an ambulance.

"Where've you been?" he asked. David's limbs were stiff and cold and his face showed dark mixed emotions.

"Ever try to find a place in the country you ain't never seen?" demanded the white one. A polka-dot collar peeked from his ambulance whites.

"Where's the customer?" inquired the fat black attendant.

Minutes later, stretcher rollers squealed to the rear doors of the ambulance. David had loaded Sam onto it himself, heavy rigid body, the bloody eyes that once held laughter, compassion, wisdom, and friendship. Grunting, the attendants trundled it up into their vehicle. David stood back and they slammed the doors. The finality of that sound was like a fist in David's chest.

David glowered, speechless. He stood there watching them

slam the doors and drive away. Red and white lights flashed as the ambulance turned onto the two-lane blacktop.

It was half past nine when Sandra pulled the Scout into Whitewood's long brick drive. The sun was long up. She was happy. They would see David very soon. Leaving Memphis in predawn blackness had been frightening but now she was glad.

Beside the manor, Melanie shoved her door open. She grabbed her hair dryer and vanity mirror and jumped out. Streak bounded across the lawn, stretching his legs from the long drive.

When David met them on the front veranda, Sandra saw from his eyes and the hard line of his mouth that something was very wrong.

"You two have a good trip?" he asked.

They hugged.

"We sang songs and played with the C-B," Melanie smiled.

David felt Streak's head nuzzle under his hand. Sandra's eyes probed his. His hand fondled the Doberman's sleek head.

"Did Streak behave?" he asked. He wanted to be alone with Sandra before telling her what had happened.

Sandra knelt and roughed the Doberman's jaws with both hands. "An absolute angel. Never felt safer."

David helped them finish unloading. Melanie ran onto the front lawn, teasing Streak with the gnawed rubber ball, making him leap for it like a circus dog.

"Haggerty was very warm and understanding," Sandra informed him. Haggerty was chief of surgery at the hospital. "Taking everything into account, I think he has quite a bit of respect for you. Said if you're not back to work with him in a couple of months he'll take you by the ear."

David smiled bleakly.

"What is it?" asked Sandra. "What's wrong?"

"Sam's dead, Sandy. Stroke. They took him away a couple of hours ago." He listened to his own words as if someone else were speaking. Sam dead. Gone like Chester.

She hugged him. "Oh, David. God, I'm sorry."

He told her haltingly about the vandalized crypt. Her eyes widened in revulsion. Then, in sympathy for him, she was almost in tears. On the lawn, Melanie giggled, teasing Streak.

It was almost noon when David met Pounds at the driveway. The big man climbed out of his Dodge cruiser with tight lips and a shake of his sweaty neckless head. Big dark wet patches blotched the armpits and back of his khaki uniform shirt.

"Ain't found nothing, Dave. My ass is been all over this county since you called."

David grunted in ironic relief. At least if Dewey Pounds hadn't found anything, the body hadn't been conspicuously abused—yet. His fists knotted, opening and closing. "When we find out who it was, I want a couple of minutes with them, Dewey. For old times' sake."

Nodding, Pounds hitched up his khaki trousers. "Let's see where the damage was done."

The husky sheriff followed David around the house. The arbors still sparkled with dew in the warming sunlight. They stood at the crypt. Its open mouth gaped darkly. David could hardly stand to look. Daylight lanced in upon the white fleecy casket lining.

"Shit." Pounds licked sweat from his lips. "Shouldn't let y'awl move Sam's body. Where exactly was he lying?"

David pointed out the crushed patch of grass. The big man knelt, feeling the ground with huge hands.

"They as much as murdered Sam," said David. "Stroke or not."

Pounds stood. "As a doctor, you're satisfied it was a stroke?"

"Classic." David wanted to lie, say it was murder, a blow to the head, a bullet through the chest. But he knew the county M.E. would examine the body as a matter of course.

Sam's pistol lay on the ground. Pounds picked up the old top-break revolver gingerly with a twig through its trigger guard.

"All I can say right now, Dave, is if Sam hit one we might match up the slugs. I can say it must of been more than one, the way that marble is ripped open like it is."

David looked at the scorings on the slab.

"Look at them tool marks," Pounds said.

"What do you think they used?"

Pounds grunted, perplexed. "Like something with prongs? Don't rightly know. Strong bastard, whoever it was. Funny though—"

David stepped closer. "What's funny?"

Kneeling, Pounds ran his free hand over the scars on the marble. "I seen a barn wall once where a big cat tore his way inside. Like claw marks, ain't it? But no cat in this world could scratch marble like that."

"It wasn't any animal," snapped David.

Pounds heaved himself with a grunt. "No, I don't reckon so. No unusual tracks at all on the soft ground." He frowned, gazing over the tombs. "No man-tracks either is another funny thing. Except where Sam came up to where you found him."

That *was* strange, David realized. The weight of his father's corpse—even lessened to 40 percent by embalming—would have weighted the vandal's tracks carrying it away.

Pounds went to the bluff and peered over, studying the shoreline below. David had already done that but he waited patiently. Dewey was slow but he usually finished whatever he started.

They walked together in a widening circle among the graves until the last arc took them outside the plot.

"I don't guess there's anything more here," admitted Pounds.

They returned to the drive. David invited Pounds in for coffee. The big man declined.

"Got my work cut out for me. You know, a lot of things around Bickford just don't make no sense. Pets disappearing. That little girl missing still. Her daddy doing that to himself. His wife Holly gone nuts. You used to date her? She was a pretty cheerleader."

David nodded, felt a twinge of sadness for a sweet girl.

"Then your daddy," Pounds went on. "And now Sam. All this shit happening to me. So close together, seems like."

"You think they're related?"

Pounds shook his head. "Don't think nothing without fact. But when everything's all peaceful and a bunch of stuff starts going on, it makes me wonder. It don't make good sense."

Pounds opened his cruiser door and placed Sam's pistol and flashlight carefully on the back seat. Nestling his big body in behind the wheel, he fitted his mirror sunglasses to the thick bridge of his sweat-slick nose.

"I'll see what I can stir up around town. It's a sad state of affairs, Dave. I can't say how sorry I am."

David managed a bleak smile through the anger that made his face livid. He watched the cruiser until it had gone down the long drive and up the highway.

David went back into the house for coffee and a shower. Sandra met him upstairs. His naked chest glistened with water from the shower. Her hair was tied sleekly back with a pale blue ribbon. Her dark eyes met his tenderly. Her hands stroked the damp sides of his torso.

"Poor baby." She kissed his mouth.

David held her at arm's length. "I've got to drive into town, see about arrangements for Sam."

She sighed. "You know how sorry I am." She was sorry but frightened, too. "David? You think we're safe here? I mean, if people were out there last night. . . ."

"I didn't want to bring this up right now, but I think you and Melanie ought to go back to Memphis."

"Without you?"

"I'm staying here to see this thing out."

"Well, we are too, then. You know we're not leaving without you." She saw bitterness and anger in his eyes. Then they softened. He smiled and kissed her.

Downstairs, she watched him go out the door. She slumped into a chair, bewildered. So much happening so fast. No way she could take another funeral. She wouldn't. Nor Melanie. But no matter what happened, she wasn't going to leave David here alone. He was so stubborn. If she couldn't convince him to leave, they would see it through together. Sticking together was the one thing she could always rely on.

David drove the Triumph into Bickford. Passing the restored DeBois manor he stared—deserted, it almost seemed. The blind windows. Perfect lawns. Have to find out more about this Sprague, he thought. Things around Bickford seemed to have deteriorated since the man moved here. David shook his head, accelerating toward town, finding the idea absurd that a blind man could cause anyone harm.

He stood waiting in the floral reception room of the funeral home. Phelps, the mortician, strolled out with a greeting but condolent smile, a white carnation pinned on a black polyester lapel. David shook the limply offered hand, feeling revulsion.

"Terrible, terrible," said Phelps.

"Yes," agreed David.

"What are your wishes?" Phelps found it odd that a black man lay in his embalming salon. He had a reputation to uphold. Yet he did not wish to offend a powerful landowner, which David now was.

"Detail expenses to Barksdale's office. Has the medical examiner been here?"

Phelps wrinkled his nose. "Left an hour ago. Messy individual."

"Stroke?" asked David quietly.

"Worst he said he ever saw." Phelps plucked an envelope from his jacket and smiled inquiringly. "Say, was old Sam digging in the graves or was somebody playing a crummy joke on you folks out there last night?"

Phelps wiggled a finger for David to follow him to an alcove. Irritated, David followed. Phelps handed him the envelope. David opened it. He flinched—two human fingers, dirt-streaked, fell onto his palm. Each detached at the second joint, obviously in an early stage of decay. They seemed to flex slightly at the touch of his skin. He glared at the mortician in a flush of abrupt anger.

"What do you mean by this?"

Phelps' eyes widened. "Don't blame me," he whispered. "Got them out of Sam's right hand. Wasn't easy, neither. Really had a grip on them."

Stunned, at an utter loss, David shook his head. He studied the digits more closely. Their state of decay was strange. The outer skin was hardened and thin, yet the interior tissue, visible at the joints, was red and almost fresh, as if buried but resisting decomposition. Incredibly, the marrow was still reddish-white. And the nails were long and sharp.

"Listen," whispered Phelps confidentially, "I want you to know that it don't make one bit of difference to me that Sam was a nigra. Not to me. But I don't know how it might affect the reputation of my place if the word got around about them fingers."

David stared at Phelps. "You're not playing some stupid practical joke, are you?"

Phelps stuttered a protest. David realized the man was sincere, even afraid. And he realized that Phelps did not want services held here for a black man. He knew he could force the issue but did not want Sam where he wasn't wanted. He instructed Phelps to send the body to Pordrey, a nearby town where Sam had relatives.

Immensely relieved, Phelps reassured David about the fingers. "I seen a lot of odd stuff come through here, I can tell you, but it never gets past my front door."

"I'm taking these with me," David said, waiting for argument. There was none. Phelps shrugged.

David walked out and climbed into the Triumph. Shuddering, he put the envelope in the glove box. Its grisly contents could well prove to be important material evidence of some kind. It would require delicate handling, however, lest word spread through Bickford, causing wild rumors and embarrassing unanswerable questions.

He drove to Pounds' office. A bony young deputy, chewing gum with rotten teeth, said that the sheriff was out somewhere in the county.

Not leaving the envelope to the deputy's questionable discretion, David drove out of town.

Passing Ruth's trailer he slowed the car. With a decisive U-turn he sped back and pulled into the weedy trace of her drive. Yellow-winged grasshoppers buzzed into the warm air.

He put the envelope in his pocket and climbed out of his car. The antique streamlined trailer flaked greenish faded enamel. Half in the shade of a chinaberry tree it sagged, one end resting on blocks, weeds choking up from underneath. Sun-bleached curtains with little crescent moons hung in oval age-fogged porthole windows. Ruth's broad red face peeked out the door window curtain as David walked up through the weeds under the chinaberry tree.

The trailer door squeaked open. Ruth grinned, her tent dress voluminous in the doorway.

"David! Come on in, son!"

David's legs swished through high grass. He mounted wobbly concrete blocks. Ruth hugged him and led him inside by the hand. It was cool and dark and littered.

Zodiac posters and star charts covered uneven walls. Ruth's black-clothed consulting table filled one end of the living room. A black tomcat slunk into another room as David entered. He smelled boiled greens and sour cat litter.

Ruth pulled a folding chair from a newspaper-stacked corner. "Sit down, make yourself to home. Get you something to drink? Coffee? Coke? Bourbon?"

"Coke, thanks." He took the chair.

She brought two Cokes from the kitchen and sat heavily in a protesting wicker rocker.

She patted his hands, obviously glad to see him.

"I was such a bad guest the other day, son. Sorry I had to leave so sudden-like. You know, this old body plays tricks. I cain't believe it, you're a doctor now. With yore own family."

Lamely, David returned her small talk. He watched her bare feet. They were blue-veined, huge toenails painted orange, wriggling as she chattered. At a pause, she reached for a can of air-freshener on a litter-packed table and swished the cheaply sweet mist in overhead circles. David saw the black cat peeking around the kitchen door.

Edgewise, interrupting, David told her about Sam and the vandalism of last night.

Ruth stiffened. She sat forward in the chair as he told

of the crypt. Her eyes flicked at each window as if she were being spied on. The red tip of her tongue licked wide orange lips. Beads of sweat popped out on the heavy ridge of her brow, gathering on the twin pencil lines where hair was plucked. David watched her teeth sink into her bottom lip and he had the queasy sensation that he was confirming some horror she had long dreaded.

"Ruth . . . if you know something about this, I want you to tell me. You would, wouldn't you?" The Coke was fetid in his hands, the bottle slippery, warm.

The big woman rose grunting and waddled to a window, pulling its stringy curtain aside. "Know something? Lord, how would I know about something so damn awful, son? Course if I did, you'd be the first to know. Lord, must have been some wild kids, I reckon." She left the window and went to another to peer out.

"Look at this, Ruth." Revulsed, David pulled the mortician's envelope from his pocket and handed it toward her.

Frowning, Ruth approached him and took it. Her fat fingers tugged the white flap. She peered inside and her tiny eyes opened wide. Her orange lips wriggled on her face. Her hands flew apart. The envelope fell to the floor, fingers tumbling hideously on the dim surface.

The cat hissed and raced into the room. David snatched the fingers from the floor an instant before the animal would have reached them. Shrieking, it leaped at his hands. He cried in pain and surprise as foreclaws snagged the back of his left hand.

Ruth screamed. She slapped the big tomcat aside. It rolled and was up again, baleful green eyes glaring at David's hand, at the fingers. With a low curdling snarl it turned, hackles raised. It poised again but Ruth slapped it back. With a hiss it slunk from the room once more, looking back at David before disappearing.

Shakily David replaced the envelope in his pocket. Blood trickled across the back of his hand from four perfect needle-like punctures.

"Let me see to that, hon," apologized the big woman. She touched his hand but her eyes were on his jeans pocket.

"It's okay." He rubbed the back of the bleeding hand. He could not be certain Ruth knew anything but he remembered that moment of shock when her face had frozen and gaped at the fingers. He had known her all his life and he knew when she was holding back. "Let's talk a little more before I go."

With a glance at the windows, she shivered. "I don't know what got into him," she said unconvincingly.

Yet he had the sharpest sensation that she *did* know. His hand stung, losing numbness. He rubbed it.

"Where did you find those ugly things, anyway?" Ruth eyed him now intensely from wary slits.

He told her, warning her against rumors.

She regarded him seriously. "Hon, why don't you take yore family and go on back to Memphis? Get on away from the bad memories. You don't have nothing to hang around for now." She spoke sweetly but her words seemed sharp with warning.

He sat forward toward her, "You told me that the other day, Ruth. I'm asking you why?"

"Get away from bad memories, son." She was inscrutable now.

He stood. "You know there's no way I can leave until I get this thing straight."

She shook her head slowly, sadly. Her wide veined hands rose to her face regretfully. She looked at him, meeting his eyes now as if ready to speak.

Abruptly her eyes snatched toward the windows. One by one she stared at them. He watched her as she seemed to listen to unheard voices. An act, or something genuine? He couldn't tell. But when she looked at him again she was smiling from a more brittle mask. She looked like a novice in a play.

Ruth slapped fat knees. "I'm just a crazy old woman, son. You know everybody thinks so. Don't pay no attention to me."

She rose and went to open the door. "If there is anything I can do for y'awl. . . ."

Passing her as he went out the door, David paused and stared directly into her face. She gave a forced wink, orange lips pressed tightly together. Then she stepped back and closed the door so that he had to step down onto the wobbly blocks.

For a moment he stood at the bottom step in the weeds looking up at the trailer door. Frowning, he turned and went to the Triumph. He drove back to Whitewood, four pricks of blood congealing on the back of his hand.

Sunlight almost seemed to stop at the western shelterbelt of aged trees. A shallow darkness was held within the half-mile woods that separated the DeBois and Rawlings plantations.

Melanie walked along the edge of the shade. She stopped, gazing into the shadows cast by dark and monolithic trunks. Sandra had warned her not to wander out of sight. Streak whimpered beside her, nipped her thigh playfully. But the woods looked so cool, so secret, so ripe for exploring.

The child advanced into bordering thickets with a sense of wonder and awe. She stepped into an opening of giant old trees—even bigger than the oaks in front of the manor. Weak rays of sunlight struggled down feebly through boughs a hundred feet overhead. Gray moss hung down like the beards of wise old men. There were pleasant scents, mint and dead leaves. Thick growth stood so darkly green it was almost black.

Almost at once she found a treasure. An old piece of wood etched by an engraver worm. She walked farther into the trees.

Streak stalked beside the child faithfully, eyes casting left and right. He whined nervously as she foraged deeper into the sourceless twilight.

Melanie knelt over a mossy patch, tracing childish white hands over the coiling roots of an enormous towering cypress.

Somewhere, unseen and secret yet very close, the beat of a large bird's wings rattled. The beating ceased as if something heavy had swooped and landed.

Streak stood stiffly alert. Melanie turned as the Doberman began to snarl. His hackles were up, jowls curling back from bared white fangs.

Melanie tried to see through the thickets of holly and cane where the animal was staring. She stroked his quivering head. "What you getting mad about, boy, huh?"

Brushing forest-floor debris from her bare legs and shorts, she suddenly felt very alone. She wondered how far she had strayed. And though she heard nothing, saw nothing unusual except the huge trees going away in all directions, she felt an instinctual crawling horror of being watched by someone she could not see.

Melanie stepped away from the tree. She cried out, the back of her hand covering her open mouth. A dark tall man stood not ten feet away.

His face was strange, raceless. He stared into her eyes, his own dark eyes glinting and yet perfectly still. His eyes held hers with depthless vicious force and in them she tasted horror she had known once before. Years sprawled backward. Evil came from her repressed memories like red lights rising in a black pool—*that old man's eyes before his hands touched me in the old apartments.*

Streak stepped in front of the girl. Every muscle in his back and legs was corded under the sleek black hide. His bared fangs slathered, tense eyes locked on the dark intruder, long limbs quivering with stiffening rage.

Melanie stared into those deep glittering eyes. They did not move at all. But she felt them like hands on the open throat of her loose blouse, like cold fingers moving over her chest and down her stomach like that old man—*don't touch me there, don't.* He stared immobile like something made of metal and darkly vibrant, livid with evil. She glanced at Streak and looking back at the man she saw he was closer though she hadn't seen him move.

A terrible fear shuddered through her limbs. All at once, with a panicky cry, she broke and fled.

Girl and dog raced through the trees.

Streak ran beside Melanie, head turning back again and again snarling and whining as he loped. Melanie fell through a mound of rotted leaves and scampered to her feet. She saw the man immobile on her left. Like a statue he was suddenly closer, still as death with black eyes glittering on her as if she were naked. She saw sunlight, broken through the trees ahead. She was up and racing toward it.

Suddenly, panting and shaking, she was in the hot light of day at the edge of the woods. Streak was beside her. Whimpering, he stared back into the trees. There was no sign of the man now.

A raven rose from the woods, circled once, and flapped away.

Melanie slapped her sides and caught her breath. She looked back into the woods with an embarrassed giggle. A scan of the manor and its grounds showed her that her mother probably hadn't seen her go where she wasn't supposed to.

"Safe," she told Streak.

Like night fear banished by a risen sun, her scare was over. She laughed at herself for being silly, yet knew she wouldn't go into the woods by herself again.

Sixteen

Dewey Pounds was a man of action. He spent the heat of the morning in the Dodge cruiser on county roads. At every bend or rise in the two-lane blacktop he expected to see Chester Rawlings' corpse propped up, ludicrously suited in funeral clothes, gaping at the road.

But the roads unwound and the hours passed and he saw nothing unusual. He was worried sick. Problems were made to lay big hands on. Criminals existed to be caught, the truth to be wrung from them. Inactivity gnawed his beer belly. It made his lips dry and his hands tense on the wheel. The locality around Bickford, his ground, was getting out of hand. He knew it looked bad. If he couldn't get things under control and get to the bottom of the whole mess, the next election would find him pumping gas or looking for a job in another town.

First it was pets. People complaining about a dog or a cat and once even that goat disappearing. As if animals didn't stray off on their own. Hawks and owls picked them up. Cars knocked them off the road. They got horny and wandered into the woods. But—not so many in so short a time—that was the hitch. Then, the pets were nothing compared to that little girl missing. Probably her old man killed her and hid the body before he stuck his head in the microwave. Suicides did weird things like that. Or she saw her mommy and daddy and ran off and is still lying under a pile of leaves, overlooked by the searchers where she died of exposure. Then Dave's daddy doing himself in. Now the damned grave ripped open and the hard fact of a stolen corpse. But maybe Sam went crazy, too. Maybe he was the one who did it and hid the cadaver and shot at something he thought he saw, some hallucination, and had a stroke and—

Pounds cut speed and turned into the brick drive at Whitewood. No, he thought, none of that shit makes sense. Some weird fucker or fuckers were running around. They had to be found. Satanists, maybe. Hitchhiker from out of town staying down somewhere in the woods. God only knew. Only thing for sure was he had to find out what and not take another year doing it. The specter of a gas pump haunted his daydreams. Folks laughing at the big dumb old boy who used to be sheriff. Man, when he finally got his hands on whoever it was—

Dewey edged the cruiser up the drive. The sight of the mansion, of any mansion, made him tense. He'd grown up in a one-bedroom home with naked bulbs and pull-down shades on the edge of Bickford. Maybe that was why he liked hell out of David. A guy never stuck-up because his folks had something. Damned fine quarterback in high school ball, a boy who could take a hard hit and not get all shook about it. Now he was a doctor and still the same good guy. Hell of a shame somebody messed with his daddy that way. By God, they would pay. Not just in court, neither.

The cruiser halted by the great white house. David stepped off the front porch. Climbing out, Dewey swallowed, wishing he'd found something, anything.

David walked out to the cruiser. He could see from Dewey's uncomfortable expression that nothing more had turned up.

"You look tired," David said.

"I ain't found a thing. I reckon that's good in a way." The big man rubbed the acrylic beige enamel of the cruiser's hood with a thick hairy paw, scraping at a disintegrated grasshopper with his ridged thumbnail. "I wish I could say more right now," he added.

"What about Ruth, Dewey?" said David.

Pounds shrugged. "What about her?"

"Lots of people confide in Ruth, don't they? Think she might know anything?" He had left the fingers in the study desk drawer. Reconsidering, he wasn't sure yet whether he would mention them to Pounds. Ruth and Phelps were tight-mouthed, but Pounds was talkative when he'd had a few down at the Night Spot, Bickford's tonk. There would be enough ugly whispering as it was now.

"I'll sure stop by and talk at her. God knows I'm at the

point where I'd try any damn thing. I feel bad about all this, you know that."

"It's not your fault." David rubbed his face. The sun was bright. He was worn out. "What about this man Sprague? Have you ever seen him?"

Pounds cocked his neckless head thoughtfully. "Well—met him once, called on him during the investigation of the little girl we had missing. One of those tall-dark-and-handsome older types you know the gals go for. Course he's blind. Walks with a gold-tipped cane that's got a funny animal head carved on it. But he was real concerned. Put up a ten-thousand-dollar reward for that girl."

David nodded. "Was he investigated in the course of all that?"

"Being from out of town, you know he was. He's from New York. Rich as hell, way he rebuilt that old DeBois wreck. Never caused one bit of trouble, sure ain't no socializer, stays to himself. Hardly anybody ever seen him except the carpenters and masons, and, man, he paid them good."

David mused. "I met a real weirdo over there. Maybe a servant. Whoever it was wasn't blind."

"I never knowed he had a servant. Course, he'd have to. Big as that place is, and him blind. Surprised he don't have half-a-dozen. Maybe he does, for all I know."

David looked down the end of the drive. Past the arbors, the gravestones were dappled in sunlight through the old trees. The horn of a barge came echoing faintly from across the river beyond. Anger had kept him awake, yet the need for sleep was tearing him down inside.

"You got any reason to suspect that Sprague guy of anything, I want to know it," said Pounds.

David shook his head. He didn't. He just didn't know what to think anymore. It was all so damn crazy. Like some off-center dream full of comically hideous scenes of horror.

"I'll ask around," said Pounds. "Woody Sheehan, Ruth's boy, he delivers groceries out to Sprague's once a week, I hear. Strickly vegetarian stuff. Saw him at the gas station this morning. Said Sprague's been away about a month but might be back now." Pounds stalked around the fender and opened his cruiser door. "I'll be checking by from time to time. You get some rest, you hear?"

"Have to."

David watched the big man back the cruiser out the drive. It was all quite insane. And yet real. Images rushed and wisped of the open crypt, Sam's face bloody, the fingers, the cat attacking his hand, the strange encounter at the restored manor, the raven killing the bluebirds, Sandra's smile and Melanie's smooth white face, all interphases and blearing. His dazed eyes burned. He needed sleep.

Exhausted by the ordeal he went back into the house and collapsed on the leather couch in the den.

Once, he heard Melanie and Streak run through the hall like wild Indians. Then the last thing he saw before sleep was Sandra peeking in the door, her finger at her lips hushing Melanie. Black dreamless waves came mercifully.

Night came and passed uneventfully. Rains came. Black water drummed the heavy walls of Whitewood, lashed oaks and arbors, swept across the vast river.

David had crawled upstairs to bed from the couch in the den.

Cozily, in the den, Melanie was glued to the television. Its snowy images shifted—*Voyage of Sinbad*—it was the same rerun she had seen in Memphis but one of her all-time favorites. Fascinated, she watched the handmaiden turned into a snake-bodied dancing girl. The German animation was superb. She marveled at Sinbad's fight with skeletons the sorcerer had brought from the ground by sowing hydra's fangs. By the end of the movie she was biting her nails as if she'd never seen it. Melanie couldn't take her eyes away. Streak slept beside her on the floor. Her hand wandered aimlessly over his sleek side, over the corrugated bumps of ribs under muscle.

Asleep, Streak whimpered. His legs kicked as if he were running on his side. Melanie rubbed his nightmare away without taking her eyes from the set. Sinbad was creeping up the castle stairs. The tiny princess squirmed in the terrible giant fist.

"Bite him!" hissed Melanie, "make him let you go! Don't be afraid!" Her fists knotted against her mouth.

In the study Sandra sat on the piano bench. She had played Satie's "Gymnopédies" after dinner. The window casements were black with night rain. She watched the water run over the glass like a flashback in an old Bette Davis movie. Thunder shuddered through Whitewood. Sandra ran her fingers over the eighty-eight keys reflectively. The world was so different here. Everything kind of upside down. With David's father's death so much had changed. Life was a door hinged in crazy directions. Teaching would no longer be necessary at all. If she wanted she could find a real teacher of her own, someone who knew piano beyond her wildest dreams. Someone very expensive who could train her, help her find eventually whether she herself could be truly great.

It's so vain to think this way, she told herself. And yet tonight after dinner—softly playing for Melanie, careful not to wake David—she had a vision of an audience of thousands, their faces rapt and attentive with pleasure.

She rose to check on Melanie. So innocent, lovely in the bluish television light, yet never conscious of her own beauty. Sandra hoped adolescence wouldn't ruin the child.

She returned to the drawing room piano. What if a master could be found, someone willing to take her on? Would there be enough time for David and Melanie? To help them in the ways they needed? Give David assurance when he was tired? Guide Melanie through the pitfalls and temptations and quagmires of becoming a woman? And what about this so-called master she wanted, if the person was a real artist, would he bother with her at all? She smiled at herself, caught in her old conundrum—if somebody is willing to take me on, he's not good enough. But that was silly. Rubenstein didn't really get going until he was forty-four. There was her whole lifetime ahead.

In bed with David at midnight, she felt him stir. She woke him with her lips and hands. After love, they slept again like two spoons.

She woke early after dawn. Melanie was up, too. While David still slept, Sandra took Melanie and Streak quietly out of the manor into the early sunlight. It was not only to keep the house quiet because David needed rest, the morbid details of all that had happened were not lost on her. And such events might have a disturbing impact on the child. Outside in the mind-healing sunlight—after the rainy night—she felt emotionally refreshed.

They walked along the edge of the river bluff. The sweep of the river was panoramic. White-capped crests flecked the half-mile stretch of water. Wind rose warmly from the plunge to the flat brown river below. The drop from the bluff to the water was at least six or seven stories.

"Stay away from the edge!" Sandra shouted as Melanie and Streak raced ahead.

The cemetery was shrouded in half-shadows under its copse of oak and elm. Sandra walked past it was consciously averted gaze. Gusts from the river wafted her dark hair. The sun felt terrific and she made a mental note to check out the terrace in the center of Whitewood's roof—perfect for sunbathing.

Melanie slowed as they followed the curve of the bluff toward the western shelterbelt of woods. Sandra paused to gaze in a circle over the surrounding scene. This all belonged to them. It was incredible. A great manor. The old arbors and gardens. The land. The stunning view. She glanced down at the trace of old stone steps leading from a crumbled landing. It was so easy to imagine parties arriving at night by riverboat, laughing couples climbing to the candlelit manor. Violins and piano music. Swishing silk gowns. Crisp cuffs of gentlemen. Dark eyes flashing innuendo. The great house itself aglow with dancing, with a promise of careless gaiety and fruitful life now again a possibility.

She walked on to the first trees of the shelterbelt. Melanie had stopped. Sandra smoothed the child's silken windblown hair with a tender caress.

"Want to explore the woods?"

Melanie stared with bright eyes into the deep shadows of the trees. "Un-uh. Let's just go along the field, okay?"

Streak was statuesque. With one foreleg lifted he stood broodingly watchful, eyes fixed upon the thick woods.

"Watcha looking at, boy?" smiled Sandra. She patted his sleek blue-black shoulders. "We'll just walk along out here in the sun then."

They were a hundred yards from the bluff when the stranger appeared silently beside a huge oak. Sandra halted. Melanie took abrupt backward steps and gripped her mother's hand. It was certainly not the dark man she had seen before, but she instinctively distrusted him and felt fear. Streak stood dead still, a low rumble rising in his throat.

The tall man regarded them from the edge of the shadows. Sandra was instantly struck by his gentlemanly bearing—tall and serene with walking cane and an expensive raincoat slung nonchalantly over strong shoulders, a steely-haired man, middle-aged, or older, with a dazzling smile. She saw at once that he was blind: rather than opaque and repulsive, his eyes were compelling and clear. They did not move but she felt drawn to look at them.

"Ah . . . my neighbors?" His voice was cultured, accentless and virile. His blind eyes seemed to fix upon Melanie. Sandra felt her daughter's small hand grip tighter upon hers.

"You must be," Sandra stammered, "the person who—had that marvelous restoration done?"

The blind eyes shone. "Exactly. Philip Sprague."

Sandra introduced herself and the child.

"You play the piano, yes?" inquired Sprague.

Sandra was abashed. "Well, as a matter of fact I do play a little." She blushed, flattered and puzzled at his sensitivity—How did he know that?

"More than a little, I suspect, and with charm." Sprague smiled, stepping closer. He was tall and moved with dignity and strong grace. His long ebony cane felt the ground in front of his black shoes. Closer, Sandra saw that its head was gold, a crafted animal's eye peered from between his index finger and thumb. His other hand rested in a waist pocket in an antique mannerism.

Sandra fumbled for something to say. "We were just enjoying the sun. Why haven't we seen you before today, Mr. Sprague?"

Melanie squeezed her mother's hand tighter. Sprague stood regarding them blindly within the edge of shade. His eyes covered them without focusing. He smiled broodingly, as if struck by some private irony.

"I have been away but have returned." His blind eyes seemed to pierce Sandra's.

"How did you know I play?" she asked, genuinely curious.

" 'Vibes,' I think is the current expression. One artist's sensitivity to another. I would like you to try my own piano. I'm certain you would enjoy its touch."

Melanie jerked her mother's hand, and Sandra looked down into an impish frowning NO on Melanie's face. Sandra frowned back, making lip movements: *Mind your manners!*

Streak had inched between Sprague and Melanie. He seemed to be staring past the man into the forest shadows.

"I'd love to try it," smiled Sandra. "But I'm not very good, really."

"Do you know Mozart?" solicited Sprague.

Sandra grinned. "Who doesn't? I love Mozart."

"Then you love wit and strength and delicacy. We are already almost friends. I want you to come dine with me, at my home. Bring your husband and daughter, please, of course. It's so seldom these days I meet a person of culture. The life of a retired person has removed me from many contacts I once enjoyed. The locals are provincial, nice but boring."

Sprague advanced in the sunlight toward them.

Stiffening, Streak snarled.

Sprague jerked to a halt. His blind eyes fixed on the

animal almost as if they were lucid yet without focusing. Sandra was mortified. She snatched the Doberman back by the tip of a cropped ear.

Sprague smiled. The pocket hand came out to grip the cane. He reached forward with the other.

Sandra blushed. He's reaching for my hand, for God's sake.

She extended her right hand sheepishly. His hand touched hers and his lips bent coolly to brush her skin. Her hand tingled as she drew it back, as if the spot he kissed were asleep and waking. Sprague groped for Melanie's hand.

Melanie drew back grimacing. Sandra nudged her. Melanie shook her head. Streak snarled and Sandra slapped the dog's head.

Sprague withdrew his hand from Melanie with a cold and knowing smile. Melanie saw the long immaculate nails, as sharp and clear and long as a woman's, but at the end of powerful-looking fingers.

"Please forgive our bad manners," apologized Sandra. "I guess we're not too used to meeting people of culture out here either." Melanie once had an unfortunate experience with a stranger, she began to say, and decided not to.

"Quite all right," smiled Sprague. His teeth were gleamingly strong, white, and even. "The young lady is reserved. I can appreciate that, believe me."

Sandra noticed that the hand that had been in the pocket, the one now gripping the cane, was misshapen. Two fingers were missing. With the other hand Sprague slipped an envelope from a vest pocket. He extended it toward Sandra. She took it quickly, with a curious grin of expectation, wiping a stray lock of hair from her eyes.

"An invitation," he said, "I was bringing it to you. Will tomorrow night at eight be convenient?"

"Sure. . . . I mean we're not exactly booked up for the local social season."

"Until then, adieu."

Sprague wheeled suddenly on one heel. Sandra stood nonplussed. The tall distinguished man strode off into the forest shadows, his cane striking the ground as he went.

"Wow," sighed Sandra, "your daddy won't believe this."

"He's weird." Melanie stared into the woods. Streak was close beside her.

"Huh." Sandra looked down at her daughter. She was watching Sprague disappear through the deep maze of trunks.

"I hate him." Her eyes showed fear

Sandra shook her head. "Child? Is that how Sandy's taught you to act?" She smoothed Melanie's hair.

"I don't care. He's weird."

As they turned to walk away Streak stood staring into the woods. Muscled flanks quivering with rage until Sandra and Melanie were crossing the yellow stubble field toward Whitewood. Melanie called. The Doberman turned and galloped toward her, casting backward glances.

Sandra was starstruck.

Seventeen

David sat up groggily on the bed fighting back thick layers of dreamlessness.

Looking at the clock he realized he had slept a whole day through. Bright slants of sun filled the windows. He could hear Sandra and Melanie playing with Streak on the front lawn. Long sleep always left him deranged, as if he had awakened without personality, frightened until he found himself again. His mind clutched at his family's sounds.

Pulling on shirt and jeans, he staggered through the hall and down to the kitchen. A scalding cup of black coffee brought him halfway back.

Sipping, he leaned against the counter. He thought about developing the film. Putter in his old boyhood darkroom. Good idea. With a twinge of excitement he remembered the shots of Sam, and more— he shots of that raven attacking the bluebirds.

Down the old familiar cellar stairs, he flicked on the darkroom bulb. Orange safelight illumined the small makeshift room. Filled with nostalgia, he entered and shut himself in. The water tap spurted and squalled in the tiny sink. He found and mixed ten-year-old Rodinal, stop bath, fixer, and hypo-clear. In darkness he wound the film from the cassette into the can and developed it with the safelight on again.

While the strip of film was pinned and hanging from a clothesline he squatted and peered through the negatives.

Weird. Something wrong.

The bluebirds were there, desperately fighting, feathers

flying. But the attacking raven was hardly a dark blur, like a mere shadow on the film . . . was the shutter speed too slow? No. The bluebirds were sharp and clear, frozen in mid-action. The camera settings had been right. What then? The old chemicals? But if that were the problem, everything would be off key, not one pictorial element.

He shut the darkroom, left the film to dry, and went back upstairs, puzzled. Cameras didn't lie. They saw what they saw. It was illogical. Did not compute, as Spock would say. Some explanation would come to him.

In the kitchen, Sandra was fixing chicken salad for lunch. David poured another cup of coffee. Melanie sat at the drop-leaf table eating a Twinkie.

"You look dead," smiled Sandra.

David managed a grin. "Yahs . . . I'm a vampire, come unto thee for evil ends." He bared his teeth and crossed his eyes.

Melanie giggled. Sandra pursed her lips scoldingly.

"We've got something nice to do tomorrow night, and I don't want you yawning the whole time." Sandra gave a secret wink at Melanie. Melanie frowned.

"What nice?" asked David, stifling a yawn.

"I don't want to go," Melanie sulked.

Sandra shook her head. "Of course you don't. He's a perfectly nice gentleman. You don't want to know a thing about him, for Christ's sake."

"Huh?" David blinked. "Would you let old dad in on the secret?"

Sandra sat down excitedly and told David about their meeting with Sprague at the shelterbelt.

Listening, David sat more erect, surprised and interested. Obviously the man had made a very favorable impression. He watched the light in Sandra's eyes as she described their newly discovered neighbor.

Melanie stuffed the last bite of sandwich into her mouth.

"He's weird. Looking at me funny."

"Don't talk with your mouth full," chided Sandra. "Because a person is blind you think he's weird. And how could he be *looking* at you if he's blind?"

"Don't know," glowered the child.

"You were the one acting weird."

"I don't care." Melanie slipped Streak a bite of bread.

Sandra handed David the invitation. Penned on parchment bond in a thin florid hand, it invited them to dine tomorrow night at eight.

"The old guy sure is formal," David said.

Sandra was coy. "Quite the gentleman. Kissed my willowy hand."

"Oh yeah?" David frowned with mock jealousy.

Sandra leaned across the table and whispered confidentially, "Don't tell David but I'm running off with him to Paris."

"Mommy!" protested Melanie. She found nothing funny about that man.

"Sure, we'll go." David laughed but serious questions had risen in his mind, hanging just beneath the surface. Nobody ever saw the man, so what was he doing in the woods bringing this invitation? Eccentric? A blind man—how had he found his way? Sun on one side of his face or something? And that gruesome little servant or whatever, would he be there, staring the whole time?

Yes, he thought, we'll go and see what gives with this Sprague person.

"I've been dying to see inside that house," Sandra was saying. "God, which dress? The Von Furstenberg is the only really good one. I've worn it every time we've been anywhere but Mister Sprague certainly has never seen it. . . ."

"He won't see it," injected David.

Sandra smirked at herself. "God, I'm dumb."

Melanie looked at them both. He *can* see, she thought. I *felt* it. . . . Like that nasty old man in the old apartments, the way it felt when he was looking.

Streak licked Melanie's hand for another tidbit. She pinched off bread and slipped it under the table. "Do I *have* to go, huh?"

"You betcha," said Sandra. "I want you to act like a young lady, too."

"If she doesn't want to," David shrugged.

"Who have we got to babysit? Anyway, it won't kill her to find out how the better half lives. It's high time, really." Sandra pinched her daughter's cheek playfully. Melanie grinned and pretended to bite her mother's hand.

"The boogeyman won't get you," Sandra laughed.

No, thought David, he won't. But we will go. And maybe find out a few things about this rich blind man who moved down so recently from New York. So very recently.

After lunch David drove the Triumph into Bickford for groceries, Herbal Essence shampoo for Sandra and Melanie, and Ken'l Ration for Streak.

Sandra saw him off and went back inside to sit at the baby-grand Steinway.

She mused, her lingering fingertips caressing the keys. She realized what an unusually profound impression Sprague had made upon her. Gentleman of the Old School. Cool and casual, yes, but like one of those old declamatory Victorian actors, too, a Kean or Booth. An actor? she asked herself. There was a sense of that in the man. No denying. Like he was meeting you onstage in a subdued role. Subdued enough to make it real and casual. Melanie had embarrassed her half to death. But you couldn't expect a child to encounter physical infirmity without awe. His eyes had no doubt frightened her. And the two missing fingers almost hidden on the far side of the hand that came out of his pocket. Melanie would be okay when she got used to the idea. She had a good heart.

Sandra's fingers plinked the keys aimlessly. She wondered as much as anything about his piano. Was he a master? With all his bearing and charm, it would come as no surprise.

God, she thought anxiously, to have grown up with a father like him instead of no father at all.

She caught herself—boy, you're really one for jumping the gun; what is this, infatuation with an old blind man?

David cut speed on the outskirts of Bickford. His green roadster purred into town.

The gas gauge registered a quarter tank so he wheeled in at the Exxon. Woody Sheehan strolled from the clapboard garage looking like Mickey Rooney with long hair and acne scars.

"Fill 'er up?" He wiped his hands with a rag greasier than they were.

"Extra," said David, standing by the pump.

Woody plugged in the nozzle. "Nice old job. I 'member you tooling round in this here thing when I was a kid."

A lifetime ago, back in the dark ages, thought David. Back in the happy bright dark ages when the future was still seen through a boy's eyes, a boy with his mother and his father. Now, Sandra was the mother and he the father. Growing up was to realize uncertainty.

"Still running good," David smiled at the car. Machines endured but men passed on.

Woody removed the nozzle. David paid him.

"Dewey Pounds tells me you deliver groceries regularly out to the Sprague home," said David.

Woody averted his face. He turned and wiped the face of the new pump with the filthy rag.

"Yeah," he replied without facing David.

"Ever talk to him?"

"Naw."

"You don't see him when you deliver?"

"I set 'em on the back steps."

David sensed evasion. "Who phones in the orders?"

Woody turned, still without meeting David's eyes. "He got a regular order at the store. I mind my own business and do my job."

David saw that Woody's hands were trembling, gripping the rag.

"Then you've never met him, huh?"

"Nope." Woody turned and walked quickly back into the clapboard garage. Passing under the hubcaps over the wide door his dirty face turned with a quick dark glance at David.

He's afraid, realized David. *But of what*?

Woody disappeared into the gloom of tools and jacks and a Ford on a hoist.

David opened the door and eased behind the wheel. The hiss of a lube pump started from the garage. He sat musing. Ruth acting odd. Her boy flinching at the mention of Sprague. Bad things happening the past year.

Suddenly, for a terrifying moment, it struck him—*It's me. It's not them.*

Was he letting this all get away from him? Had his father's death carried an impact greater than he realized? *This is how it starts, you know*. Paranoia. Suspicion of what would not normally seem suspicious. Maybe this was how it had hit Chester. Mother's death. Bad dreams. Things happening as they always did but suddenly seeming odd, everything off-center. But Sam's death—that had been no normal thing. Or had it? Had insanity infected him like some communicable disease? The old man had been very close to Chester. Was this happening to him now, too, in his turn? *Better watch out, old buddy*. But the God damn crypt—it *was* torn open, it *is*.

David gunned the roadster in a U-turn toward the sheriff's office. Down the street he pulled in beside Dewey's beige cruiser and climbed short steps to a glass door in the brick-front office and jail.

Pounds sat behind the desk in a state of sweaty exhaustion. David walked in and saw the big man quickly cap a pint bottle and dodge it into a desk drawer.

Dewey's hoggish face labored into a strained smile: "Hey, old buddy, set yourself down."

David stood by the desk. "Just stopped by for a second. Turned up anything new?" He asked it in a mixture of hope and dread.

"Shit, naw," Pounds grunted uncomfortably.

"We have an invitation for dinner at Sprague's."

Pounds eyebrows raised grooves on his Neanderthal forehead. "Who did?"

"Sandy, Melanie, and me."

Pounds was impressed. "That's something new. Hardly a soul in Bickford sees him, now you get an invitation. But y'awl are neighbors, anyway. Course, I think he had Holly and her family out once for dinner, when they was making arrangements to pay labor and such for the restoring."

David stiffened. "He did?"

"I think so. Probably why he put up that big reward for the little girl. She was a sweet thing. It sure galls me."

"Yeah," David said. "I can see why."

Pounds seemed to shrink slightly. Rocking back in his swivel chair, he sat up abruptly, reddening. "David, I'm doing everything a man could do to dig up something about your daddy. Don't get on me. I'm trying, you know I am."

David looked at the big boy grown into a big man, suddenly realizing the position Pounds was in. His job was no doubt on the line. Small-town Mississippi people had little patience with a fumbling lawman. Without results, the next election could easily wipe him out.

"I know you are, Dewey. Keep in touch."

Pounds stood. "You know it, Dave. Lemme know how the feast turns out."

David left the office. He backed the Triumph into the street and drove to Davis' store. He realized with a dark fatalism that Dewey would turn up nothing. It was up to him. He was alone with this thing. He should have known it all along.

He parked in front of the store and went inside past two old whittler-chawers who nodded their greetings somewhat askance. He nodded back, irritated. The whole damned town knew about the crypt.

Inside, old man Davis met David with grave condolences. "I don't know what the world's coming to. Kids. You know it's got to be some of these no-good kids we got nowadays. A man as fine as Chester, too. And pore old Sam. I don't know what to think no more."

David gathered the things he needed. Davis brought the

Herbal Essence from the shelf behind the register. In the back of the store old men idled and argued around the air-conditioner.

While Davis totaled David's purchases three times, he overheard the idlers.

"My old woman, she saw a UFO. I tell you it's just a matter of time before. . . ."

"Pore old Samson Johnson, for a nigger he was as good as any white man. . . ."

"Shet up, cain't you see who's up front?"

"Grave tore open like that, makes my spine get the sillies, to think. . . ."

"I say that Sister Ruth is a God damn witch. Setting out there conjuring and spelling. I say. . . ."

Davis glanced up anxiously as David paid the bill. The old man strode to the back of the store.

"Cain't y'awl shet up a minute? Y'awl ain't got the sense of a outhouse rat."

Minutes later, David was driving home. The speed felt clean, white, free. He accelerated on the curves, letting it out. The car felt solid and good.

For the moment he was escaping. The four claw-marks on the back of his hand were mere pink spots in the sun. The town was behind and Whitewood still ahead. He was one with the car and they were alone with speed. The road fled past.

Sprague's manor came into view. He accelerated, gunning it, feeling a high pitch of vibrating speed through the wheel like a tuning fork in harmony with the road. He roared past the restored mansion.

A half-mile past Sprague's, a half mile from Whitewood, it happened.

The left rear went first. It blew like a gunshot. The old car veered sharply toward the ditch on the right.

David jerked the wheel with a cry.

The right front bumped against the weeds. Then it blew.

David ground his teeth, jerking the wheel against the high-speed skid, flat tires slowing the car, helping him but steadily dragging the car toward the ditch. His feet jammed the brake. The grind of steel and pavement shuddered the car like an earthquake trying to shake it apart.

The old Triumph came to rest inches from the fifteen-foot ditch drop-off. David sat there zombielike, shaking. He breathed deeply with an effort to gather his wits.

"You just about bought it," he whispered aloud. His voice croaked through the din that echoed in his ears.

With a deep sigh he climbed out and surveyed the damage. No way to change the front with it hanging on the edge of the ditch. He pulled out the spare and jack and changed the right rear.

The woods along the roadside were strangely quiet. He worked with the unsettling sensation of being watched. No birds sang. The click of the jack and the ring of his hammer on the spinner were startlingly loud.

Throwing the shredded flat tire into the trunk he noticed, with a ripple of nerves, that the rubber was cracked with rot. Yesterday he had checked every tire. Each one solid and smooth.

He circled the car, examining each tire—deeply cracked, as if they had been buried for years in a grave.

He stared off into the eerily quiet woods. The feeling of being watched increased even as he stood there.

He climbed in and cranked the engine. With a lurch he guided the Triumph slowly back on the road, eyeing the dark groove of the ditch one last time before nursing the hobbling roadster back toward Whitewood. The steering dragged leftward against the right-front flat, the wire wheel grinding the pavement and setting his teeth on edge.

On the leather couch in Whitewood's study, David fell asleep reading a *Time* magazine.

The dreams that assaulted him came quickly, irresistibly. He was at his father's deathbed. Half the forehead blown away. Gray custardy brains on the pillow. He bent down to kiss the blood-flecked lips. There was a rasping whisper. The whisper told a string of numbers. Hands clutched in savage fear at his face and throat.

He sat up without screaming. Blinking, he gazed around the room. Unnerved, he rose with trembling hands and went into the kitchen for coffee.

A string of numbers chased through his mind like an annoying but unforgettable television jingle. He thought it was some number printed in *Time*. Or some long-ago phone number remembered suddenly in a mechanical malfunction.

Then he knew what it was. A safe combination. He was sipping scalding black coffee and put the cup down with a clatter, sending brown liquid across the drop-leaf kitchen table.

He hurried through the hall to the library. He opened the padlocked closet and knelt with fingers on the dial of the floor safe.

The handle turned and clicked. He stared in amazement—How did I know those numbers? *How did my mind get that data?*

The thick door eased open. He peered into the safe, frowning at what he saw.

Catching his immediate attention was an odd device. He lifted it out carefully into the light. A clear glass bell jar was glued like a dome onto a heavy wooden base, within which was a strangely altered clockwork. The wheels and gears and levers shone through the glass. The apparatus seemed to center around a thin brass or gold disc atop the altered works. This disc was suspended upon a central spear of bright metal, like a needle. The outer rim of the disc was etched with vague archaic symbols. David realized that something was supposed to cause the disc to spin, but he could not determine what force could act upon it to cause its motion. The needlelike spear in its center certainly could not. Nothing else was connected.

"Rube Goldberg was here," he said aloud to himself, an attempt at humor.

Rising, he set the odd device upon the desk glass, and returned to the safe. There was something else inside.

It was a hand-worn diary. Carefully, he thumbed it open. His brows knitted in confusion.

It seemed to be written in some ancient language or in code. He couldn't make it out. Yet, somehow it was strangely familiar. He stared at the pages. They seemed written in his father's meticulous hand, but absolutely unreadable. He shut the safe and closet and put the diary on the desk.

Leaving the library he paused—how had he known those numbers?

It was almost as if his father had spoken to him in a dream, wanting him to know the contents of the safe. That was absurd, he knew. Had he learned them long ago as a child and forgotten till now?

Must have, he decided without conviction.

Eighteen

It rained at dawn.

David awoke to the caress of hands and lips. Beads of rain glistened on the panes of the high windows. The branch of the oak outside lilted, heavy with clinging water. Sandra's hands moved lower and lower down his back in delicious tantalizing pirouettes that sent urgent tingles racing through his body. He rolled over, taking her in his arms.

She whispered, smiling, eyes closed, lashes long and darkly heavy, "Did I wake you up?"

She giggled girlishly and he kissed her. His own hands began their hungry ritual motions. The muscles under her smooth skin tensed as she responded.

After love, he lay on his back watching the slow deep rise and fall of her breasts, glad they hadn't sagged after Melanie's birth. Gently kneading her thigh, he let his eyes drift over the white sensousness of her long slim body. Sleep and sex were revitalizing. He felt washed clean, ready for whatever he would face today.

Sandra sighed, stretching like a long lazy cat.

David watched rain trickle down the high narrow glass of the casements. Rectangles of bluish-pink dawn. Clouds breaking. First tentative notes of a bird. In spite of everything, he loved this place.

For an hour the light grew brighter, pinkish then golden as the clouds outside continued to break. He forgot the growing tangle of tragedies twisted like dark vines around his mind and heart, eroding security and perhaps even his sanity during the long passing week. Life seemed suspended. Nothing could reach him in this hour with Sandy.

"Melanie needs real stimuli, honey, instead of TV and the rest of that junk kids today feed on, you know?" Sandra whispered, touching him.

"Ummmm." Her touch was delicious.

"Good schools aren't out of reach anymore. Think of the education she can have now. It's just fantastic."

David thought how lovely and bright Melanie was becoming and he knew he could never bear to send her away.

"God knows, we need a real vacation, too," mused Sandra.

"Wouldn't hurt."

"Wonder if I'm good enough . . . I mean, to find a real piano master. Sure, it would mean years of hard work day after day at a good piano, but Rubenstein didn't get going until he was forty-four. You think I'm silly?"

He grinned, kissed her.

"We can have somebody in to take care of things," she said, "find a really neat woman like a nanny sort-of, couldn't we? Then I'd have time."

David grinned sarcastically. "Somebody about eighteen, young and cute."

She pinched his thigh. He squirmed around and grabbed her. His fingers dug into her ribs, tickling. She gasped, giggling uncontrollably, legs kicking.

He stopped and looked down into her eyes and kissed her. Her hands moved slowly again over his back, drawing him down. The sensuous ritual began again. This time more slowly.

Twenty minutes later their bodies unlocked. David lay back breathing heavily.

"Love ya," whispered Sandra. She rubbed his back.

Streak's pads thumped in the hall. Melanie shouted at the door.

"I'm starving!"

"The master's voice," winked Sandra.

As David ate breakfast the unnatural but blessed calm of rest peeled away. Anger rekindled as he ate slowly, hardly tasting Sandra's flawlessly poached eggs and slowly crisped bacon.

"What a fabulous kitchen," she was saying at the range. "You believe I could actually enjoy cooking?" She stroked the big dishwasher.

David glanced at the bird feeder. Desolate, its small oval

mouth gaped darkly like the violated mouth of the crypt. Like the grave Sam would be lowered into.

A redbird landed on the birdhouse platform. The bird leaped backward into the air as if recoiling from the touch of his feet on the wood, flapping and wheeling suddenly away.

"They don't like it anymore," Melanie pouted.

Sandra smiled. "Don't be silly."

David knew it was true. Other birds had landed there and flown away just as quickly. He thought of the raven with anger that he knew was unreasonable. The black bird seemed almost supernatural and evil. He remembered the dark blur on the film where an image of solid living form should have registered. Sam firing without effect. The raven staring down immobile as the servant from the eaves at the DeBois place. When Ruth was here, the birds screeching and bursting from the tree when the raven landed.

Again, David caught himself—*Watch it, boy*. Want to wind up in a rubber room?

Strain manifested itself in fantasy. Fantasy could be an enemy as real as poisoned food on a plate. What was it the doctor told Dylan? It's only in your head, boy. David smiled grimly. No worst place.

"You've hardly touched a thing," implored Sandra.

He looked at her. At Melanie. Streak's head peeking greedily over the edge of the table. Warmth surged, welling in his chest. They loved him. They were real. They counted. He was damned lucky. God, they were beautiful.

With a sudden squawk of chair legs he was up, startling them. He bent over and kissed Sandra. Then around the table to Melanie. She grabbed his waist and hugged.

Sandra and Melanie traded uneasy glances.

When David left the dining room Melanie touched her mother's hand. "Is Daddy okay? I mean. . . ."

"Honey, he's been through lots of strain. First granddaddy, now Sam. Sure he's okay. But he needs us now. We have to act special. See?"

Melanie picked up two plates loaded with flatware. "I wish sometimes we never left Memphis, mommy."

"Everything will be just terrific in a couple of days. You'll see. Tonight will be super, I bet."

Melanie remembered tonight. Dinner with that man in his house. "Do I *have* to go?"

"You betcha."

Sandra urged Melanie out of the kitchen with a slap on her rear. Going to do something special was the best medicine for them all. Distraction was exactly what David needed. And, God, she couldn't wait.

The rain returned after breakfast and continued through morning.

David phoned Pounds. Still no news. Pounds' husky voice gushed apologies, embarrassing and angering David.

After lunch Sandra played Chopin "Etudes." David realized she was warming up for tonight. If nothing else it would be a break in the dark monotony of all that had happened. He clutched at one consoling thought—once his father's remains were found and reinterred, nothing worse could happen. And yet life had taught him never to believe that it couldn't. He was tortured by grisly images of the pathetic corpse somewhere in the rain.

He idled through early afternoon cleaning Chester's fine shotguns. Their hard lean feel brought floods of memories. Bird dogs stalking sage in coppery twilight. A boy moving beside a tall man in understood stealth. A fine mist sifting through a duck blind. Frozen ground crunching under boots in deer woods.

His father's passing was the passing of a generation. Of a lifestyle. He would probably never hunt again. All taste for it lost during the years in Memphis. He would never farm the land. A man's life ended so much more than the man. All tenderness, all wisdom blasted in a split second of madness.

But David had no more tears. Sorrow was diluted in reflection. He knew that the man lived in him, that wherever he went or whatever he did he would carry within him all that was good to remember. That was true continuity—not the house nor the land but the warmth, that sheer faith of having been loved.

He finished the shotguns and replaced them neatly in the walnut cabinets along the den walls.

Melanie was trying to watch television. Rain drummed outside. *Sesame Street* was on but waves of snow kept blotting out Cookie Monster. David read to her from a leather-bound copy of the *Odyssey*. She stiffened at Scylla and Charybdis. Odysseus was as brave as Sinbad, fighting monsters.

As David read of monstrous beings, the fingers crossed his mind. The two fingers stolen from an unknown cadaver. He had put them—it seemed incredible now to him—in the desk drawer. Why hadn't he given them to Pounds? Scandal? Then why not destroy them? Prints.

Of course! He would take prints of the fingers and have Pounds send them to Jackson for an FBI check. Whoever they had belonged to had certainly not been dead more than a month. *Prints*! Find out whose they had been. That would erase one bit of the puzzle, perhaps point to the vandals.

He walked through the hall toward the library. No need to tell Pounds everything. Pounds owed him discretion. If the prints turned up anything interesting, there was still time enough to let Pounds in on where the prints had actually come from. Sam would be buried by then, anyway. Let ugly rumors fly after his funeral. Until then, Pounds didn't have to know everything.

He entered the library and went to the desk. His mouth fell open in surprise. The drawer was half open. The envelope was there, its flap open. The fingers were gone.

He stood looking at the envelope and the drawer in wild disbelief.

Quickly, he strode to the door. The rain was halting outside. Melanie gaped up at his pale angry face.

"Have you been playing in the library?"

"No, Daddy."

"Are you lying to me?"

"I haven't even been in there," protested Melanie. Streak gazed up beside her.

"What's wrong?" demanded Sandra. She had heard the harsh words and came from the piano. She stood behind David in the hall.

David turned and shook his head. He knew he must be crazy. Melanie obviously knew nothing. Streak? Streak couldn't open a drawer no matter how smart he was. There was just no one else. Sandra? No way—she would have come running to him at once, with damned good reason. Thank God she hadn't. No one except himself.

"You storm in here like a mad man," snapped Sandra. "God knows things are under enough strain without—" She caught her sudden impatience.

"I'm sorry." David blew out a long breath. He knelt to kiss Melanie's forehead. Streak stared up from deep eyes.

"It's okay, daddy." She kissed his face tenderly.

"Come on with me to the piano," Sandra told Melanie.

David walked back into the library. His hands trembled. He heard Sandra playing a Chopsticks duet with Melanie. For Christ's sake, he thought, they're on your side.

Steeling himself, he opened each desk drawer. Nothing. On hands and knees he searched under the desk. He felt like a damn fool, but had to look.

He gave up.

Bewildered, standing at the windows, he watched the blue sky appearing through the high boughs of water-laden oaks. Something caught his eye.

Looking down he saw them. He flinched back.

They lay together, hidden by the heavy drapes, their long nails pried into the crack of the window jamb.

Nineteen

David stared at the fingers on the sill.

He knew he must be going mad.

I must have put them there myself, for Christ's sake.

With a pencil he flicked them back into the envelope, recoiling as they slithered red against the paper with a scuffing friction. Lightning flashed outside. The thunderclap made him jump, almost dropping the weighted envelope.

A key protruded from the center desk drawer lock. He put the envelope there this time, locked the drawer and put the key in his pocket.

Nobody but me, he thought. What the hell am I *doing* with them, anyway?

Fingerprints, he remembered. But he didn't want to touch them again or see them. Later. In the morning.

Lightning flashed again. Thunder rattled in the windowpanes. Fresh rain buffeted the glass as the sky suddenly darkened.

David slumped in the desk chair, rapt in thought, staring at the cartooned cover of a *New Yorker* lying among agriculture reports. He should have turned the damn rotten fingers over to Pounds right away. Hell with rumors. Nothing could hurt Sam anymore.

But suddenly he knew why he had not.

Face it, he thought. What you really believe is that Sam was crazy, obsessed, mad enough to open the crypt himself for God knows what wild reason—you know the fingers must belong to Chester.

He winced, knowing it was true. But where . . . where was the body? Sam knew Whitewood better than anybody. It might be hidden anywhere, the secret locked forever in Sam's dead brain. Pounds had found nothing because nobody would ever be able to. And now instability, borne on a crushing carrier wave of events, was infecting him in turn. Without remembering, he had to have moved the fingers—now they were locked in a drawer. And if prints were taken? He knew whose name would come back—Chester Harlan Rawlings.

He stared at the clockwork device. With a shudder he stood up. He no longer trusted the labyrinthine passages of his mind.

He unlocked the padlocked closet and gazed down at the safe. How stupid, not to have realized it that morning when he had somehow *known* the combination. He had found the numbers on a slip of paper in a box or in the desk, found the combination and not remembered. He was suffering from an obsession grown out of guilt. Guilt that he had not been with his father in time of great need. Instability could lead to insanity. He was on dangerous ground.

He returned to the desk. That crazy clockwork device glued inside its bell jar. He fingered the hand-worn diary. Its cryptic pages made no sense at all. Yet it was somehow familiar, like a word so tantalizingly close to recognition, just on the tip of his tongue. . . .

He closed the safe and the closet door and left the library with an uneasy mixture of relief and dread. Relief that at last he was now aware of a dangerous obsession with his father's death. Dread that it was necessary now more than ever to stay here, to face whatever was happening, to master it before he could leave.

At 7:35, fifteen minutes before they had to leave, Sandra made last minute adjustments to the three-year-old bamboo-motif Furstenburg, admiring her willowy figure in the full-length Victorian mirror on the master bedroom wall. Not so bad if she did say so herself. Good hair. Face could be a little less cutesie-pie, but what the heck. Good calves, makeup okay.

She knew the man wouldn't see her in any event but it felt terrific to have an excuse to really dress up for a special occasion. And David would see her.

Glancing at the mirror she realized—We're wealthy enough, I could be wearing a Halston if I'd been to New York this week.

With a girlish pirouette of delight she giggled. Melanie came stomping into the room, her bottom lip pouting fully.

"Button me up, mommy." The child stopped beside her mother and turned around.

Sandra almost laughed aloud. Her daughter wore her Lady Deb evening gown, simple white satin that emphasized budding breasts and long legs. But those atrocious cowboy boots, too.

"I feel like a ballerina or something," pouted Melanie, hips cocked, boot heels awry, smooth arms crossed.

Sandra bit her lip to keep from laughing. She buttoned the back of the Lady Deb. "Take off those boots, honey."

"I can't stand those white Mary Janes, mommy."

"Then wear the white ballet slippers."

"Just like a dumb ballerina." Melanie clumped back to her room.

"And keep away from Streak!" called Sandy. All those tiny black hairs.

David came out of the bathroom with a dab of toilet tissue on his chin. Sandra kissed him and, when it was time, tied his tie. She brushed the nap of his old Harris Tweed jacket—sure had seen its better days. Hints of darkness still lurked in his blue eyes. She hoped tonight would help. Any good distraction would—and good company was definitely good time.

Melanie ran into the room, halting with a quick spin.

"Okay?" she asked.

Sandra and David stopped simultaneously to stare. David had never seen the girl more hauntingly beautiful, supple and dark-eyed and long-legged in white satin.

"I look funny or something?" Melanie frowned. She ran to her daddy. David swooped her into his arms, hugging.

The night was warm. Whitewood's lawns shimmered under a cloud-veiled new moon.

Minutes later they were on the front steps.

David shut the front door, making Streak step backward into the foyer. "Keep an eye on things, Big Boy."

They drove over to Sprague's in the Scout. It began to drizzle as they slowed, the massive DeBois manor rising dully luminous among its evergreens and oaks, its lower windows tall cold rectangles of draped light shrouded in unblossoming magnolias.

Talking among themselves they did not see a dark face watching through the leaded glass panel beside the great carved oak doors.

Its black eyes glittered. It was immobile, staring as the

Scout halted on the looping drive under the magnolias. A slanting breeze drove beads of mist against the thick panes. As they parked and stepped from the Scout, the dark eyes pressed closer to the glass as if held back from what it wished, checked in loathing and fear at the collecting rivulets of rain-water on glass. Behind it in the foyer Sprague appeared. His blind eyes flared in opaque rage. His cane lifted, pointing at the thing at the window, making it glide back from its perch.

Outside, David held his jacket over Sandra and Melanie. They ran through the blowing mist toward the high front steps. Wind hissed through the magnolias. The wraithlike limbs of random ancient oaks scratched at the clouds, creaking as their topmost branches resisted the gusts of mist. A huge iron lantern hung from a thick brass chain over the carven doors. Its yellow light cast a sullen pall across the heavy columns and down the high steps.

At the door David lifted a huge knocker—an ugly leering timeworn face of bronze. A bull mastiff? Lion rampant? No—it was a demon, he saw, not remembering it from childhood visits. He let it fall. The boom reverberating.

Sandra felt chill, hugged herself. Melanie was tight against her side. The boom resounded again as David dropped the knocker a second time. Cold mist blew across the porch and the doors abruptly swept open.

David gazed into a marble-paved foyer that led to the marble stairway he remembered, carved more than a century ago in Italy. Mirrors glittered. Antiques stood darkly. A huge chandelier hung unlit above the Carrara marble.

"Hello?" called David.

He motioned Melanie and Sandra inside. Melanie hung back. Sandra led her through the doors and David followed, shutting the door.

"Well, I feel like a damn fool standing here," said David. "Let's go back home."

"Yeah," agreed Melanie quickly.

Sandra saw a drawing room on her left. "Come on, we'll wait in here."

"For Christ's sake." David followed her into the room. Melanie grabbed his hand.

Marble steps led down. The sunken floor was paved in French verde antique, deep green marble polished to high luster. Indirect overhead lighting cast somber shadows over rich furnishings. Sandra was awed by medieval wall hangings. A six-fold Japanese screen. *Makimono.* A Korean bowl in a niche. And an eight-foot Buddha in one alcove.

Melanie flopped on a severe white couch. David watched as Sandra continued around the walls, gaping at dark paintings —a real Goya, his black period—a Hopper of a solitary man in an empty room contemplating an empty sea—a Picasso, Cubist period. Seeing the Picasso, David thought of the African mask locked in his father's closet. Same madness of dissociated eyes, misshapen mouth, twisted reality focused into something obscenely powerful. David found all the paintings as grotesque as Sandra did impressive and charming. He saw artists in dark chambers haunted by years of madness.

Sandra was on one knee fingering a thick Oriental carpet, trying to decide whether it was Bokharan or a nomadic copy, when she looked up and saw Sprague leaning on his cane at the top of the steps. He was smiling.

His blind eyes were not on her but slanted toward the couch where Melanie sat twiddling her thumbs. Sandra jumped up anyway with an awkward embarrassed smile.

"Forgive me, my friends," he said, "my man told me just now that you had arrived."

Sprague said "man" with the slightest oddness, perhaps irony, David wasn't sure.

"Everything's so. . . . It's just beautiful," gushed Sandra. She caught herself—too effusive.

Sprague's brow lifted. "You approve of the restoration, then?"

"Good work," David nodded.

It was actually marvelous, far better than good. He could hardly believe the attention to detail. Exquisitely carved moldings. Flawless plaster. The marble like new. It was as it might have been a century ago, undisturbed. The impression of newness was unnerving. He had played in shambling ruins here as a child.

"I had help from craftsmen of Bickford," Sprague smiled fiercely. "But when they were through, my man and I added final touches."

Again, that hint of irony at the mention of the servant. David realized he was very impressed. The man had dignity, grace, and, most of all, an imposing bearing. He was at least six feet one or two. He must have been seventy but the years had not made him bend. His hair was white, brushed back in the style of *Luftwaffe* pilots. His face was lean, wrinkled perhaps, but as stark and strong as if cleft from stone. He stood straight-backed in a posture of austere self-assurance that did not quite border on arrogance. And his blind eyes almost shone with depth. There seemed to be life there, uneasing

David. They didn't follow motions in the room. Yet they seemed to seek out things with a will of their own. It was as if Sprague saw with his mind rather than through his eyes.

Adaptation, David surmised. Acute sensory readjustments, auditory and otherwise. Not uncommon. But to this degree?

"Would you care for cocktails?" suggested Sprague with a backward wave of his cane. "The bar is this way."

The bar was in a small reception room adjoining one end of the mammoth central ballroom David remembered from secret explorations as a boy. Dark paneling and rich leather.

David antagonistically requested Bushmill's, expecting Sprague to have none. Sandra offered to make a vodka-and-tonic for herself. Sprague lifted an arched hand in polite disdain. He moved unerringly to each bottle on the carved wooden racks behind the walnut slab bar counter.

Melanie sipped ginger ale from a Baccarat goblet while David sipped his Bushmill's double in grudged admiration. There was something unlikeable about Sprague. Yet he could not fail to be impressed.

"I understand you and my father became acquainted," suggested David, peering over the rim of his glass. He was fishing. For what, he did not quite know.

Sprague was disappointingly nonchalant. No jerky movement or undertone of guardedness.

"Your father was a cultured man. Such a terrible tragedy. We visited from time to time, I enjoyed his company."

"Really? You knew one another well?"

"Well enough, for neighbors."

A touch of mirth? wondered David.

Sandra winced and changed the subject. "You must be a very successful collector of antiques. My God, a Picasso, a Goya!"

"Your God?" grinned Sprague. "Yes, Goya was quite mad when he painted that scene of a black sabbath. Witches and hobgoblins and such. One would have to be mad to believe in such trash." Sprague sneered theatrically, mockingly.

David thought curiously of the things he had found in his father's library.

"But he painted with such passion," added Sandra.

Sprague nodded. His blind eyes flitted over Melanie.

"Yes . . . to bring to birth a desire, to feed, develop, foster, excite, and satisfy it—is one long poem. According to Balzac, at any rate. I have other paintings a person of your obvious taste would no doubt enjoy."

David saw how floored Sandy was. He gave a stab at intellectual comment. "You seem to collect the iconography of cults."

Sprague smiled an affirmative. Sandra glanced at David in wonder. He looked again at Sprague—the man seemed to have been staring at Melanie and then suddenly looking away.

"Are we ready to dine?" Sprague inquired.

"Famished," answered Sandra.

Sprague led them down a hall, tapping his cane. It was lifted before him but not in all directions, rather swaying like a cobra's head or a radar antenna. They followed through the long marble hall, their steps echoing crisply.

Sprague's dining room was larger than Whitewood's and more elegant. Its chandelier was twice as massive. Myriad glitters sparkled over the long table and high walls. Dinner waited on a gold service. David expected the dark servant to be here, was vastly relieved to find him absent.

Sprague waved a hand. "Too many formalities spoil a good meal. And I prefer to help myself, rather than half-a-dozen servants stumbling everywhere. Please seat yourselves as you wish."

Dinner was an odd combination of family help-yourself and exotic cuisine. Sprague sat at one end of the table apparently identifying dishes by their scents.

"*Grey Sole Bonne Femme*, or *Homard à l'Américaine* if you prefer, lobster with wine—Côtes du Rhône this time—and tomatoes and herbs and garlic. My servant is proficient in preparing various things. His talents are quite varied indeed."

Again, David sensed the detectable irony.

"Some authorities call the recipe *à l'armoricaine*," continued Sprague, "after the ancient province of Brittany where lobsters thrive. Others proclaim *armoricaine* nonsense, since the tomato is quite untypical of Brittany—they say the recipe is rather more likely that of some Parisian chef with Provençal inclinations."

Sprague went on that way through dinner. Sandra listened in rapt appreciation.

David endured the near-pedantry with irritation, but the food was excellent, and the wine. At one point Melanie announced that she hated fish, but Sandra smoothed the slightly jarred mood with compliments.

Dessert was *Gâteau de Crêpes à la Normande*, delicious mounds of *crêpes* with apples *flambé*.

Melanie dug in, smacking her lips. Sprague seemed to gaze on her with an interest more than cold, and she noticed. His blind attentions made her squirm. She kept thinking—He can see me. And she felt as naked as if he stared down upon her in a bath.

Sprague raised a glass to his. Startled, David noticed a maimed hand—the index and forefinger were missing. His mind clicked hard—*odd, you know, old boy, but I've extras locked in a desk drawer at home—they're in kind of rotten shape, though. . . .*

He dismissed the wildly absurd and ugly thought. His eyes wandered to the head of Sprague's cane. It rested against the table. The golden beast seemed to peer over the Belgian lace, marvelously detailed but hideous in the twists of its jowls, its suggestion of horns, and the flat slits of bestial eyes inset with tiny rubies.

This guy is really cornball, thought David.

Sprague pointed to a silver tray of liqueurs: "Cognac and cordials."

David declined, surfeited. Sandra sipped her brandy appreciatively.

"Won't you have some?" Sprague admonished David.

He politely demurred. Sprague was having none, either. Sandra finished hers.

Sprague rose. "Now the piano, my dear?"

Sandra winked at David as they stood and followed their host.

"My dear," David whispered comically as they passed close together, following Sprague into the hallway with Melanie tagging close behind.

Sandra elbowed him impishly, a finger to her lips.

An immense black nine-foot Baldwin stood like a Viking warrior in the high-ceilinged study. Its cover was raised and propped like a giant black wing. Sandra took in the vision with a quick gasp. This was like college again; she was in the home of some idolized professor, a piano master; she was in the presence of something great and powerful—a machine that could be induced to move the hearts of men.

Sprague smiled.

"I believe the popular song says, 'make the mountains sing, or the angels cry'?"

Sandra was stunned. Sprague seemed to read her mind.

"I would like very much for you to play," he said. "Music was made for after-dinner, you know."

Sandra blushed. "I just couldn't—"

"She's good," protested Melanie.

"Oh, I'm *not*—"

Sandra found herself sitting on the piano bench staring

down at eighty-eight keys. Melanie sat in a Louis XIV sedan chair. David stood by the nose of the Baldwin. Sprague stood at Sandra's shoulder, resting on his cane.

They were waiting and she knew how horrible she really was. It struck her now in sheer waves of dread that accumulated as queasy humiliation in the pit of her stomach. The eighty-eight keys were powerful and profound. She was no good.

"Play," whispered Sprague.

She did. And it was like losing herself in a dream.

It was not her fingers that attacked the keys. Yet her fingers dove, flew, tapped, trilled, slid, and punctuated, and the great piano rang and thrummed the Chopin "Revolutionary Etude" as wondrously as if she had studied the piece for years. She felt the music come through her fingers from her heart. Her *desire* was doing it. Quickly she followed with the Shubert A Major Sonata. It was intoxicating. The immense instrument seemed to have taken over; she could do no wrong.

Then she was leaning back from the keyboard, panting lightly, trembling, and perspiring faintly. Handclaps. Grins of appreciation. A wonderful look of surprise on David's face.

Melanie was not clapping. She squirmed in the chair. Sprague's blind eyes passed over her again; she felt unnerving urges beyond her years. She felt naked and frightened and alone, and something—something like wanting to peepee, a funny sensation that made her hands want to rub there. She slipped off the chair and stood beside her daddy.

"When can we go?" she whispered, tugging his hand.

David shrugged. The night was not going badly at all. At least Sandra was having an okay time. Wild difference a good piano could make in her playing.

Sprague opened an inlaid cabinet. He returned to the piano with a violin and bow. "An Amati," he said delicately.

David watched them confer. New music began. He stood with Melanie through a Brahms duet. Sprague fingered with his good hand, bowed with the maimed one. They played superbly together. The melody wound on, dark and brooding. Watching, David thought of the perfume-ad kiss—"White Shoulders"?—and then they were finished, Sandra gazing up at her accompanist with regret that it was over.

"That was really wonderful," she beamed, hardly able to retain modesty.

Sprague touched her shoulder unerringly.

"You should have a master. One worthy of teaching you all you are capable of knowing." His blind eyes shone.

Sandra tittered, out of character, irritating both David and Melanie.

Sprague leaned somewhat toward Melanie, "I will teach you, too, if you would like to learn."

Melanie shrank slightly against her daddy. Sandra flashed her daughter a scolding look, warning against bad manners. Sprague grinned cheerlessly.

"Why don't we climb to the cupola," Sprague suggested. "My servant tells me the view of the river is superb. You may enjoy it."

Sprague led through the marble hall again. Dull yellow light fell in pale rectangles from each passing room. David glanced into each, some were richly furnished, others empty. In the dead center of the house rose the ornate wrought-iron stairwell David remembered. Moonlight filtered down from above on clear nights but tonight its upper reaches were hidden in shadow.

Sprague flicked on a light. "For your benefit."

They climbed up behind him, Melanie staying close at her daddy's legs, looking back down as they approached the top. The marble floor was four stories down.

The interior of the cupola was round and glassed in. Mist trickled on high narrow panes. Lightning glowered in the distance, showing the half-mile-distant roof and oaks of Whitewood. On the west was the river far below, wide and black, golden in occasional flashes of lightning. Its sweep was breathtaking from this height, added to that of the hundred-foot bluff itself. The vista was so wide the water seemed to David not to move at all.

Sandra stared in awe. Even Melanie was affected.

"Neat up here. Wow, look at the little boat!"

David had to strain to see the tiny red lights of a distant barge just rounding the far river bend. Probably just behind Whitewood right now. The river bluff was higher here and the manor closer to the river.

"The view is just fabulous," Sandra said in awe.

Sprague nodded. She felt instantly guilty—it must be awful for the man not to be able to see all this and she was making it worse.

Melanie glanced down the iron stairwell. She almost screamed. At the bottom of the deep spiral the dark face was staring up. By the top step she was aware of his eyes looking up her legs, of his staring straight at her with that perfect photographic immobility, like a doll's head fixed on her with black glass beads for eyes.

Looking at her daddy, gripping his hand, she looked back down a second later and there was nobody at the bottom of the stairwell. She blinked. It was like nothing had been there at all.

"I understand my servant was rude to you when you came to call once here," commented Sprague urbanely.

"He was very silent," David said, not without humor.

"You may have taken reserve for rudeness. He is not my servant, actually. More friend and companion, you see. His lineage is most ancient and quite noble. In ancient times his forebears were great rulers."

David stood beside Sandra staring through the glass at the sweep of the river beyond and below. The barge was slightly larger now, still a toy pushing upriver. It seemed out of place, as if something from the twentieth century did not belong near this house nor this man Sprague; as if the house itself were a fantasy, atavistic and unabridged.

"How do you spend your time out here with so little company?" asked Sandra.

Sprague smiled coldly. "I have guests from time to time. I observe the stars, listening to the firmament so to speak. I seek into matters of reality. So often one's life is dissipated in illusion and fantasy such as politics and television."

Sandra couldn't agree more—if she could only learn to play the piano that way forever and ever.

"What do you watch the stars with?" asked David. He had not meant to be cruel. The question was not rhetorical. He had forgotten Sprague's blindness, so adept was the man in his movements.

Sandra recoiled at the seeming brutality of David's question. She elbowed David hard. But Sprague only smiled.

Then he said: "I will tell you two things. In the year 1989 Great Britain will become a satellite of this country. And within thirty-three hours there will be felt a substantial tremor along the New Madrid fault zone, which lies roughly along the Mississippi River . . . in other words, under our feet here and at Whitewood."

Sandra frowned and traded uncertain glances with David. Then she steadied herself on a rail, feeling suddenly wobbly.

"Kind of sticking your neck out on that last one, aren't you?" asked David. Something about Sprague made him hostile, he had to keep repressing it—that urbane *kultur* bit, or maybe it was just the whole place was so overwhelming that he was intimidated. To be fair, that could very well be, he admitted to himself. And yet he sensed something else about the man. A distance, a chilling remoteness. Like the sensation of being watched in a crowd or when no one could be seen. These feelings he resisted just as he had resisted the backwash paranoia following his father's death and Sam's and the violation of the crypt. Just the same, he didn't want to stay here any longer. Rain clouds were clearing. Something about the clear night sky made him want to be home.

"I tell these small things to amuse you," Sprague was telling Sandra. "Because you are my friends now. My advice? To the vulgar speak only of vulgar things. Keep for your friends every secret of a higher order."

Sandra had to steady herself again. A tiny pinpoint in her mind was spinning.

"Time to get Melanie back home to bed," said David.

Sandra protested but Melanie yawned. She was ready, very ready—enough to fake a second and a third yawn until her daddy noticed.

"For her beauty sleep," smiled Sprague, passing his shining blind eyes over the girl.

They went back down the spiral stairs, through the marble halls, into the foyer to the huge front doors. Sprague walked out onto the veranda with them. The lawns were fog-layered. Magnolias rose out of the grayness against the appearing moon.

Sprague found Sandra's hand and brushed it to his lips. Again, she felt something raw-nerved in her fingers and the back of her hand where he had kissed.

"Will you play with me again?" he asked. His smile held strange irony, obvious now to David.

"I'd love to," answered Sandra.

"Then we will play again."

David watched that dry smile, that taste of veiled mockery. It uneased him. Probably his own damn paranoia, he told himself.

Perhaps.

As they walked to the Scout he realized he knew hardly more about Sprague than when he had rapped on the door. In spite of all the urbane chatter, the pedantry, the charm, Sprague was still an unknown. But they had told about themselves. It was as if Sprague had casually manipulated the evening. But why? For what reason?

David found himself feeling like a fool again.

He climbed behind the wheel of the Scout. His mind was

taking offbeat tangents. More and more he had to run to catch up with it and bring it back to what was real. "Leave stray suspicions alone" was fast becoming a new rule. Stick to fact, avoid fantasy.

As they drove the short distance back to Whitewood, Sandra was obviously uncomfortable. She sighed deeply and rubbed her face and shoulders.

"You okay?" asked David.

"You two nearly embarrassed me to tears tonight, for God's sake," she snapped. "Like two hicks who never heard of manners or tact."

David frowned and shrugged defensively.

"It was like he was playing with us," said Melanie in the back seat.

Sandra looked back viciously. "Sure he was, Melanie. We're so special he should toy with us." She glanced at David. "He's genius level at least. Maybe you were a little jealous, David, just a tad?"

"Don't get bitchy." He turned the Scout into the brick drive. Whitewood loomed pale in broken moonlight through the oaks.

A half-hour later in the master bedroom, David lay apart from Sandra for the first night in months. It had been her choice.

He listened to the night birds, the night insects crying tragic songs. He wanted to touch her but he knew what it meant when she slept with her back to him, her shoulders like the impregnable walls of an alien city.

David woke, sitting up, never remembering falling asleep. He wondered what time it was. Moonlight washed the floor through the high narrow windows.

The grandfather clock downstairs chimed. The thin metallic tones rose stringily through the house as he counted them. It was four A.M.

He yawned and rolled over to put an arm around Sandy.

She was not there.

He was alone in the bedroom. Alarmed, he rose from the bed. She was not in the room.

His peripheral vision caught motion. The balcony door was open.

Sandra stood nude on the bedroom balcony like a blind white goddess in frozen moonlight.

Twenty

David stared in waking blinking disbelief. It might have been a dream. Through the balcony door and windows, Sandra looked like a nude marble goddess, lustrous with moonlight. For a moment he dared not move, as if the fabric of some delicate and sinister spell might be torn.

Then he was edging to the open balcony door. He paused only a few feet behind her.

She seemed to be gazing out into the bluish patches of moonlight weaved through the great oak shadows of the front lawn.

With a start David realized—somnambulism. Sandra was sleepwalking.

"Sandy?" he whispered, reaching guardedly for her.

She did not move. A breeze stirred her long dark hair against her white shoulders and arms. The rest of her body was as immobile as a photograph. He bent to peer around her face. Her eyes were open but glazed. They were almost like Sprague's, gazing blankly at the milky grounds below.

She stood in the open end of a long narrow marble hall. Her shadow ran before her as long as the hall itself, a dark streak all the way to the other end. Sprague waited at the end. In his hand was the head of her shadow. He drew it close against him. He was chanting. Misshapen forms moved in the darkness behind him. Her shadow stretched like thick rubber and she felt his elastic pull upon her body. She felt urged to glide through the long hall until she was with him. The floor tilted, the hall filling with piano music. *Wonderful.* Yet now there was something behind her. *Hideous.* Something too dreadful to turn and face. Claw-tipped hands touched her bare shoulders. Her body was accessible, vulnerable, she realized she was nude. The hand lay heatedly on her cool naked shoulder. But she wanted to go to Sprague. He was pulling her shadow and hissing in sudden rage. She wanted to take Melanie and go to him but the hand was—

Hands on her shoulders, David tried to turn Sandra without waking her. He thought he might lead her back asleep to the bed. Her hands gripped his shoulder with amazing strength. Her body convulsed at once. Her eyes opening in fear and dismay. Shuddering with stifled cries, she allowed him to guide her from the balcony. In the bedroom she wept and giggled and then wept again, terrifying David.

As they left the balcony, slowly returning to bed, neither saw the thing in the massed shadows of the great oaks below. It was motionless. Even if David had stared straight at it he would have seen only a fragment of the weave of shadow and moonlight. It was gone, and then there were only the clotting shadows.

Sandra slept peacefully until morning. Troubled, David lay awake beside her most of the night. The last time she had walked in her sleep—the only other time he knew of—had followed the incident with the middle-aged plumber in the old apartments, the attempted rape of Melanie. Three nights in a row Sandra had risen and walked to Melanie's bed. Each night David had followed, watchful but not interfering. Somnambulists were potentially dangerous to themselves and to others, acting out repressions, attempting bizarre acts unthinkable during consciousness. For the world of dreams to cross with the world of reality was dangerous—prognosis uncertain and possibilities equally uncertain, ranging from the sufferer fetching a glass of milk to committing somnambulistic homicide, from *Alice in Wonderland* to *The Cabinet of Doctor Caligari.*

He hoped it was not beginning again. Psychiatric aid had been considered before, but the problem had cured itself. And he wondered—what was triggering it this time? Perhaps nothing new. As in LSD experiences, bits of scar tissue might float to the psyche surface from old wounds. He resolved to keep a sharp eye on her for the next few nights.

Another pound or two of pressure on the already heavy

load, he realized. He remembered Sam's funeral—tomorrow afternoon.

He was still awake as the pinks of dawn trailed across the gray-blue window panes. He almost wished he was a boy again. Nothing bad could have happened yet. But that morbid wishfulness was erased by the first sounds of Melanie and Streak in the hall. He grinned. Melanie's cheerful whisperings. The joyousness of her. Her grace, her silliness, her loveliness.

Red-eyed from sleeplessness, he sat up on the bed. Morning brightened the windows as he went to the shower.

It was half past ten as he drove the Scout toward Pordrey alone. Pordrey was halfway between Bickford and Jackson.

Sam's funeral was at the white clapboard Methodist A.M.E. church on the black side of town. Among old men and women, his face the only white one in the crowd. He sat through bugle and organ dirges, through the beautiful soulful sailing of flower-hatted meaty sopranos. An hour later Sam was lowered into a red clay rectangle under an elm in the black cemetery behind the church. David threw a handful of gritty dirt upon the casket. On the way back to the Scout he was too stunned for more tears. He felt dry and squeezed inside.

He sat in the Scout and found a dry cigarette butt in the bottom of the glove box. He lit and smoked it down. Heart hammering, he reflected upon tragedy. If man was the only animal who knew he must die, then man was the only truly tragic animal. He thought of Holly. Jackson was only an hour away. He wondered if anyone ever went to see her there, if anyone dared see her in the state she might be in.

Decisively, he started the Scout. Accelerating, he drove toward Jackson.

In the fast-food and new-car-crowded outskirts of the city, he stopped at an Exxon for directions to Whitworth. A buck-toothed attendant eyed him suspiciously and handed him a city map.

A half-hour later David sat at a metal desk in a Spartan office, explaining his old friendship with Holly McDaniels, now Holly Butler, widow of the deceased Hamilton Butler, Bickford banker. The aged female psychiatrist-administrator listened tolerantly with sad baggy eyes. At first she was reluctant to allow the visit. David found it necessary to use medical credentials to win her trust. Minutes later she led him down a long motellike corridor into several adjoining wings. Attendants in clinical uniforms of different colors—

red, yellow, blue, green—nodded or paused to confer with his guide.

Like a human doll, Holly sat in the dimmest corner of her sterile room, staring at the opposite corner. Her blank eyes held catatonic darkness. David felt chills of anxiety and sadness, peering through the plexiglass prism in the door. Someone sobbed hysterically down the hall. Holly's heart-shaped face did not register. David remembered her slender supple form warm with vibrant life, her splendid vitality. Now she was a mere husk of the girl he had known. The patient psychiatrist accompanied him into the room. Holly did not see them.

David conferred with the aged woman as they returned through heel-clicking corridors.

Driving back toward Bickford, leaving Jackson, David remembered what the psychiatrist had told him—Holly's only words, sometimes repeated for days: "Sleep no more. Sleep no more."

It was early afternoon. Wrung out, arid, David turned the Scout onto the brick drive of Whitewood.

Sandra met him on the lawn.

"Was it very very awful?" She consoled him with a cool hand inside his unbuttoned and wilted oxford-cloth shirt.

"Brassy," David smiled. He kissed her and they walked slowly to the house.

He had decided not to mention her sleepwalking. Last time such mention had only succeeded in throwing her into spiraling anxiety, a kind of reacting alarm whenever she almost dropped off to sleep that perhaps had even extended the somnambulism as a backlash.

"I've been trying to play that awful thing in there," she mused. "It's so out of tune, it sounds so bad compared to that big baby last night."

She had sat dreamily at the piano bench, craving the excitement of playing as if she were a Rubenstein or a Richter.

"Guess you're spoiled," David grinned.

"I wish."

He kissed her. "I'm going to really spoil you in a few weeks. How about a couple of months in Europe?"

Her eyes flashed wishfully. "Don't tease."

"I mean it. We both could use a real rest. We'll board Streak and bring Melanie. Have a real sabbatical and then get back on our careers with both barrels."

She jumped up and down like a little girl, then hugged him until he begged for mercy. For a moment in the shade of an oak they necked like they used to in what seemed to David now another world, another age.

After a hot lunch of tomato soup and grilled-cheese sandwiches—welcome to both David and Melanie after the complicated dishes of last night—David wandered into the library.

Irritating and obscene, lodged in the back of his mind, the fingers were undealt with. He looked down at the locked drawer in disgust. This was incredible, filthy and inexcusable. He had to do something else with them.

Abruptly, he peered closer. Was the drawer pushed out slightly, as if straining to open against its lock? Better just open the damned drawer and throw them out, bury them. God, yes, get rid of them.

David frowned in confusion. It was as if another voice were interfering in his thoughts. No, he didn't want to see them now or deal with them. The fact of their existence was itself insanity. When Chester's body was found—if it ever was—they could be added to the remains which would no doubt be missing two digits. He thought of Sprague's two missing fingers. One more weird coincidence that if pursued by an overactive imagination could only worsen his mental composure, could only weaken it.

Wrap them in tinfoil, hide them in the back of the freezer. Yes, I'll do that a little later. That makes sense. Doesn't it?

He rubbed his face. Tentative chords echoed through the house. Sandra was at the baby-grand Steinway picking out a melody that David did not recognize. Something in a minor key, brooding and romantic in a sinister way . . . Liszt? Berlioz? No, more like Bartók or Prokofiev, or some obscure Shostakovich piece that he didn't know.

He stared down at the weird clockwork device in the bell jar. Crazy. And that cryptic little diary in some kind of a code. Turning toward the windows, he lifted the diary toward the light and opened it near the glass.

It *was* certainly like his father's handwriting, somehow, but—

His eyes widened. He saw the reflection of the writing in the window pane. Perfectly legible.

The diary was mirror-written.

With a hiss of excitement David read the first few lines, squinting his eyes at the windowpane.

In an age when men were burned for dreaming, Leonardo wrote in this way, and so will I. The I is Chester Harlan Rawlings, who sets these ugly things down with the useless twenty-twenty clarity of hindsight. I do this to keep track of occurrences which, if I cannot remember them all, I will at least attempt to recall and make some sense of while brief moments of lucidity remain to me from time to time, such as now.

Pulse quickening David sat quickly at the desk. A small hand mirror was wedged between two *New Yorkers.* Placed beside the open journal it worked perfectly, as it must have for Chester. He swallowed. His fingers trembled on the wrinkled pages as he read.

This was my first meeting with Sprague. I was on the field beside the western shelterbelt. I was hunting birds. My bird dog Linda worked on ahead. No coveys there so we worked on farther through open patches of the woods toward the old DeBois place that I knew had been purchased and was in the process of restoration by the purchaser whom I had not met. My curiosity was whetted by his ambitious project of rebuilding a fine old house actually much greater than Whitewood in its day.

It began to drizzle. Still no coveys in the woods where Linda and I had always found some. We have noticed a raven, rather a large one, in this area . . . perhaps that is why the game birds are scarce. Linda seems shy at the sight of this big bird. But no sign of raven or others with the rain. We turn to return to the house. Linda suddenly stops. She races off through the trees. I run after, shouting for her to come back. There in the bottom of a low ditch a white-haired man has fallen. Water rises about his unconscious face. I slide down on my heels and help him upwards. He mumbles. I am surprised—It's Latin. His clothes, muddy, are expensive, of a New York cut. I am carrying him out of the trees across the field through the rain, almost to Whitewood, when he comes to in my arms. Unbelievable strength in the man though he must be seventy. Blind eyes, I realize, but, too, as if he can somehow see. At Whitewood he insists on having no medical attention. I give him hot coffee. He wants me to take him back to that place where he fell, instead of returning him directly home. His name is Philip Sprague. My new neighbor! He seems very grateful. We take the jeep through the rain and I find what he seemed to want desperately—a cane he had dropped. Hadn't noticed it before. He grips it tightly as we drive onto the road and to his place, the DeBois manor. The head of the cane is gold, carved with the head of some apparently mythological beast. As I drop him off, half expect-

ing him to invite me inside, which he doesn't, he assures me he never forgets a debt.

Quivering with anticipation, David paused. A note had been scribbled apparently later in red ink—*"If I had known then. . . . I wish to God I'd kicked dirt down over him instead of helping him out of that ditch."*

He stared at those words. What had his father learned of Sprague to warrant such condemnation? His face was flushed with emotion. Cheeks burning, he read on.

Leah—tonight she returned to me in a dream. Almost touchable. I awoke and remembered all the nights with her. And how horribly she was taken away. Almost not like a dream at all, so real, yet so much more the torture when I wake."

Looking up, David winced. He knew he had found the source of insanity, a haunting dream-image of his mother, tantalizing Chester, opening half-healed wounds torn by her premature death from cancer a mere three years before. Had his father grieved too much to share it? But you were not here for that, he thought. Were you?

With difficulty, he read on through sporadic entries that dealt with a similar theme, that of Leah returning in dreams.

I write this after waking to the most real sensation of her. Even her perfume, "Joy," the attar of roses clinging to me like soft hands. No sleep. When I sleep she comes. I want her to come but the price must each time be paid in grief, I hate the pain but want it. Sprague has invited me to dine. Anything for distraction. . . .

David closed the journal. He was unable to read more. Slipping the thin volume under a sheaf of papers, he left the library. He had opened a wound of his own. A fissure released black welling guilt. It rose like long-held vomit in his chest and throat.

He needed sunlight and Melanie and Sandy. He went outside to find them. Bad things had happened and he knew that to dwell on the unchangeable was a strong seed of insanity.

They were eating at the drop-leaf table in the kitchen when the tremor rattled the house. David's and Sandra's faces jerked up in alarm. Utensils clattered on the wall. A hanging plant swung in pendulum motion against the windows. Glasses and dishes shuffling inches across the table.

Instead of screeching in fear, Melanie jumped up from the table with a clap of her hands.

"Wow! A real earthquake, man!"

She had never experienced a noticeable tremor though she knew from Earth Science that feeble ones happened along faults all the time, too small to feel normally. Sandra and David were on their feet. Streak threw his head back and howled.

The tremor was suddenly over. Melanie ran to Streak by the door and knelt to comfort the dog, grinning that the big baby should be afraid. She and the dog slipped outside. He had made a urine puddle.

"You think we should go down in the basement?" Sandra asked David, eyes wide, clutching his arm.

But the tremor did not return. They felt nothing more. And it hit them at the same time—they looked at each other, staring, realizing—

"His prediction," said Sandra in awe.

"Yeah," nodded David.

"How could he *know*?"

David shook his head, didn't know what to say. Seismograph in his basement? "His time was way off," he commented lamely.

"Huh?" frowned Sandra.

"He said thirty-three hours. Its been maybe . . . eighteen."

Sandra sat back down. "Oh, David, that's reaching. I mean, he made a pretty accurate prediction."

David shook his head. She was right. A miss by fifteen hours was better than maybe anybody on earth could have prognosticated.

"Probably has a background in geophysics or something," he said.

Sandra was not convinced. "What about his other prediction? About England?"

David smiled—that was easier. "He won't be around to be proved right or wrong, so that one we can skip."

The back door slammed open. They both jumped in their chairs. Sandra's glass of iced tea, unspilled during the tremor, flooded the table, dripping through the hinge cracks onto her lap.

Melanie came running inside with Streak. David and Sandra looked at each other. Their exasperated faces broke into laughter.

Sandra found herself playing masterfully again. She sat on the bench of a black Baldwin as long as a football field. Each fingering brought vast melodic tonality. Beside her stood Sprague, playing a lewd and sinister violin counterpoint, his breath warm and damp on the back of her neck, making her play faster, faster, faster. Then his violin ceased. His strong arm was around her waist, lifting irresistibly. Her face turned. His incredibly penetrating eyes saw into her, through her pupils. His face swept over hers like a shadow. It was dark and he mouthed a strange chant near her lips. Inhuman life swarmed in the dark. She glimpsed shapes blacker than shadows about the piano, things that tittered and scraped and dragged slithering tentacles. Sprague drew the tip of his cane along her belly, between her breasts, down toward her belly. . . .

Melanie awoke. Her mother's hands were sliding under her, trying to lift her from the bed. Blinking, moaning, she saw her mother beside the bed in the shadows. Moonlight streamed through the windows and her mother's eyes glinted with it, open but staring like cat-eye marbles.

"Mommy—?"

Melanie's first thought was that there might be a fire, her mommy trying to lift her, get her out. But there was no scent of smoke. She saw her mother's face closely and knew mommy was sleepwalking again, like two years ago.

"Mommy—?"

But her mommy's hands had much more strength than they did that night two years ago. They were lifting her easily from the bed, as if she were a pillow made of down.

At the foot of Melanie's bed Streak snarled. He sniffed toward Sandra as if she were unknown, an intruder. Melanie jerked her mother's hair. Sandra's arms went limp. Melanie turned back onto the mattress.

Sandra woke sitting on Melanie's bed. She felt a half-formed urge, something unremembered and darkly important. It was terrifying. She shuddered, helpless, at the point of tears. Melanie was stroking her back.

"What was I doing here?"

"I don't know. Mommy, you scared me."

Sandra hugged her daughter. The last time she had done this was after that obscene old man had—she didn't want to remember. But this was horrifying: to go to bed and then suddenly be somewhere else, doing God knew what or why.

"What was I doing, honey?"

"You weren't doing anything bad, mommy."

They kissed. Sandra felt Melanie quivering. She was glad David hadn't awakened.

"Let's keep this to ourselves, okay? Daddy's under enough strain right now. Agreed?"

Sandra gently tucked Melanie in, then patted the mattress. Streak jumped back onto the four-poster with a nervous whine. He watched with distrust as Sandra left the room.

She returned to the master bedroom. Long window-molding shadows fell across the floor from the moonlit casements. David slept in tangled covers. He snored lightly as he did whenever he was totally exhausted.

She sat beside him on the bed, wondering what she had dreamed. It was like a flavor just behind the tip of her tongue, disturbing because somehow she did not want to remember.

As she lay back she could not sleep. She felt a waning urge. For some reason she had wanted to take Melanie down into the moonlight.

Naked, Woody Sheehan sat cross-legged like an ape in the middle of his mother's trailer floor. It was night. The full moon flooded the dense shadows of the unlit room. Ruth's hands passed over the smooth surface of her son's back. From a gourd in her hand a dark liquid spilled on his bent head and wide shoulders. She anointed him. Woody seemed to struggle in place at the touch of the unguents but did not rise or move. Ruth's voice came in a low ululating chant—

"These doors open, these doors close; palms upward I anoint this son, to free him from the spell of one, a hidden spring of hell."

There was a space of frozen moments in the moon-flooded trailer.

"I feel better, momma," Woody said.

The air beat and moaned though no wind stirred the curtains.

"He can't make me do for him no more," Woody said, half-rising. "You saved me, momma!"

Ruth hissed for him to be still. Then she flinched. She fell back against the trailer wall, shivering and twitching, gasping for breath. Something unseen struck Woody. He rolled on the moonlit trailer floor. He began to shriek, his face gross with agony. Then he was still. Ruth gazed down at him. He stared back up at her, leering, his eyes reflecting a hideous cynicism and mockery.

Twenty-one

After breakfast David went out to the garage and put the old Triumph on jack stands. He hammered off the spinners, worked the wire wheels off the axle splines, and rolled the tires to the tailgate of the Scout.

Loading them in the hatch he frowned at shards of dry-rotted rubber coming off in his hands. The tires were all flat. Completely deteriorated. Practically in pieces though just a week ago they had seemed all right.

He drove the Scout toward Bickford. Passing Sprague's manor he saw no one, yet there was that feeling of presence, that dogged sensation of being watched that made him feel more and more like a fool—*dumb Mister Paranoid.* But he hadn't forgotten the note scribbled in red ink in his father's journal: *"I would have kicked dirt over him if I had known—"* Known what?

Yes, he told himself, try to figure it out. He was crazy, so you try to figure out something crazy and when you understand it that means you've managed to attain craziness too. Congratulations.

The Scout passed Sister Ruth's, then the outskirts of Bickford. The abandoned cotton gin. Brick houses. The clapboards built at the turn of the century and then the main drag of stores.

David pulled off at the Exxon.

As usual Woody came strolling out of the garage wiping his hands. He did not look at David. David got out and dropped the rear hatch.

"Got some pretty bad flats, Woody. You-all carry radials?"
Woody glowered. His eyes glinted darkly. "Special order."
"Well, let's order some."
Woody turned and walked inside. David followed. The office was walled with used parts, its floor thick with greasy lint and studded with bottle caps ground into old linoleum. David filled out an order form himself when Woody did not offer assistance.
Back outside, David closed the hatch. "Been back out to Sprague's lately?" he asked.
Woody reacted with a long deep tremulous exhalation. His averted face blinked spasmodically. David saw the grimy hands twitching.
"You done asked me about him once," Woody said.
David frowned, watching the nervous hands twist a filthy rag.
"All I do is deliver groceries out there," Woody said.
"Didn't say you did anything else."
Woody turned and walked back into the garage. David stared. Woody was far more than defensive. Defensive of what? Maybe he just doesn't like me, David thought.
He climbed into the Scout and U-turned across the warming blacktop, back toward the sheriff's office.
Dewey stood heavily beside his metal desk, scalding his mouth with a fourth cup of black coffee. He flinched as the door opened and David strode in.
David slapped Dewey's shoulder good-naturedly. They shook hands, David's face expectant.
Pounds slumped gloomily in his swivel chair and David sat in a folding chair by a big manual Underwood.
"Dave, I ain't turned one single thing. Just like it hadn't ever happened."
David hadn't stopped by to harangue Pounds, nor did he want to discuss his suspicions about Sam and the manner in which the crypt was probably violated. The thought of that night brought a green taste filming the back of his throat. He was even relieved that Pounds had found nothing.
"I just stopped by the filling station," he said. "What's with Woody? Does he always act weird?"
"In what way, Dave?"
"Like flinching at the mention of Sprague."
Pounds shrugged. "You know that kid. Always been a little off ever since he was a baby. Eating bugs in the school yard, remember? And chasing chickens and killing them when he was older."

"Doesn't he worry you? I mean, with all that's been happening?"

"I keep a strong eye on him, Dave. You know he's the one I'd take first look at." Pounds rubbed his red-veined neckless face with hairy hands. A wet frayed toothpick popped into the corner of his mouth, having been on his tongue.

David sat forward in the folding chair. "What about that thing that happened, Dewey? What did happen to Holly?"

Pounds exhaled between closed lips, making them flap together like an exhausted horse. He shook his head. "Pore girl, just sitting in the middle of her living room floor. Buck naked. Fairly covered with her own blood, we checked it for type. Like she'd bit and torn at herself pretty bad, staring right at me but never making a sound. She was hurt kind of bad down you-know-where, too. Doc said she must of done it to herself with a bronze statue they had of a lion, heavy thing about three feet long. It was laying on the floor in front of her, blood all over it, too. We found her husband in the kitchen. Head in the microwave with a finger holding the button. That house smelled bad. I puked three times off by myself. Of course, you know the worst thing, we never found a trace of their little girl. Eleven years old. Still makes me sick. FBI, they came in but couldn't turn nothing, either. Just like she disappeared. Searches in the woods and everything else."

Pounds let out a long disgusted breath.

"FBI turn up anything interesting on Sprague?" fished David.

Pounds shook his head. "Clean. Look, since you keep asking about him, if you want I'll check through New York myself."

David nodded.

"You want?" asked Pounds rhetorically.

"Yeah," David affirmed.

"Just for an old buddy, I'll do it. But don't say nothing to nobody. Sprague spread round lots of cash during that restoring. And put up that big reward for Holly's little girl." Pounds leaned closer toward David. "Why you want to know so damn much about him, anyway? You don't figure he had anything to do with yore daddy's trouble; do you?"

"Maybe I'd just like to know, okay?"

Pounds leaned back. The toothpick disappeared inside the heavy red lips. "Okay, I'll put in and let you know when it comes back. Just keep it between us."

David stood and slapped Pounds' damp warm khaki shoulder.

He walked out and stood on the sidewalk looking up and down the sun-blinded asphalt center of his boyhood town. He looked at the Scout with widening eyes.

Was he losing his mind?

The Scout was dark green. The license number was right. But it wasn't yellow.

It was dark green. *Dark. Green.*

He put his hands on his eyes and turned sideways, taking long shuddering breaths. Some elaborate practical joke?

He stalked back into Dewey's office. Dewey was tippling from a pint which he quickly stored in a drawer.

"Come look at this!" said David.

Pounds was instantly up. They went outside. David gaped again at the Scout. It was yellow.

"It was dark green a second ago!" he said aloud, in disbelief.

Pounds glared at David. "Green?"

David realized he looked like a complete madman. Saying more would only make it worse.

The Scout had changed color or he was mad—the choice was that simple.

"Forget it," he told Pounds.

Pounds stood scratching his head on the sidewalk. He watched David climb in the yellow Scout, back out, and drive away.

"Pressure's getting that boy," Dewey told himself with a shake of his neckless head. "Better keep an eye on him instead of Woody."

Melanie followed Streak along the weedy edge of the field beyond the tennis court. He nosed in low thickets, sniffing, lifting his foreleg, glancing left and right as insects fluttered over the tops of the lilting damp grass. Tassels dislodged pollen.

Melanie laughed as the great dog sneezed big hearty explosive snorts. She did not have to bend very low to hug his silky black neck. "I love you, you bad big boy!"

Suddenly the Doberman's ears pricked erect. A brown cottontail burst from a snarl of ground-vines, bounding in short rapid leaps toward the shelterbelt a hundred yards away.

"Wait!" shouted Melanie, but Streak was already fifty feet away even as she called. She shouted again but Streak was almost catching the rabbit, a brown blur dodging left and right just ahead of him.

She began to run through the weeds. The huge trees loomed closer as she ran. Ahead of her, Streak slipped, trying to cut left of the smaller, quicker animal. Down tumbling, he was up again. The cottontail had gained ground. It was almost to the trees. Streak put on speed. Dog and rabbit disappeared through the dense wall of growth.

Melanie ran to the dark edge of the shelterbelt woods. She panted, peering fearfully into the shadows. She could hear the crackling brush of the chase but couldn't see them. She stamped a cowboy boot in frustration.

"Streak! Come back here, Streak!"

Nonplussed she stood indecisively for a moment. Then she pushed through the brush into the heavy shade of ancient oaks and cypress.

The woods were still. No birds, no animals moved. It was so quiet she could hear her own breathing. She stepped forward gingerly. Brush and leaves crackled underfoot, startlingly loud, like a TV—she was the picture with the sound turned up, and millions of eyes were watching from the deep gloom on every side where huge trunks rose against farther darkness.

She paused in a thin leaf-shattered patch of sunlight to listen. "Streak?" she cried, panicky.

Her small voice seemed absorbed by the woods, quickly gone without echo. She did not call out again. It had made her more afraid. She glanced left and right, the back of her left hand against her front teeth.

The slithering rustle came without warning.

With a choked cry, Melanie strained her vision into the dense thickets. She began stepping backward. Something rustled again. She whirled with a scream.

The blackish triangular metallic head of the moccasin lifted from the leaves ten feet from her. It rose, swaying. The glassy eyes were fixed upon hers.

Melanie could not move. Tears started in her eyes. She could not step backward. The snake was so beautiful and so ugly, so perfectly made in glittering interlocking scales, it's movement somehow soothing, its eyes holding a dark serenity that she could feel stronger and stronger. She wanted to turn and run with all her heart and mind but her legs and feet felt dead, felt sunk in the cold ground. The top half of her body twisted.

Streak had quit the chase. He heard Melanie's cry. Padding silently through the shadows, his hackles stood up as he saw

Melanie, as he saw the head of the thing rearing mere feet from her. He knew that it was no more a form of animal life than was the thing he had faced once before in these woods, the thing that outwardly resembled a man. He snarled, advancing.

Melanie heard the dog. Her head jerked around. She cried in a fit of relief at the sight of Streak stalking into the glade beside her.

She turned to run but was fixed by what she now saw. There was no snake. A tall man stared at her. He stood where the snake had been. His black eyes were piercing like the snake's eyes. He was Sprague's servant and he was a foot taller than before and he was naked. His arms hung by his side. His legs were parted beside his maleness. He was as frozen as a movie poster but his reptilian eyes were vibrant with evil.

Streak snarled in rage. The black eyes turned on him, angering him more.

Melanie watched in horror as suddenly Streak gathered himself and attacked. She saw nightmarish slow motion of dog rising with black jaws open and fangs wide. In the collision there was no reaction, no sudden whirl of fighting. She blinked and could not be sure of what she saw—Streak lay on the ground on the *other side* of the dark figure as if he might have passed *through* it.

The Doberman did not shriek or thrash. He was dead.

Melanie fled. She ran with open mouth in silent screams. Her boots skidded. The naked man stood between her and the trees, black eyes piercing hers. Warm wetness poured down her thighs.

His eyes stared into hers. He was shorter now.

She was up and running again at a tangent toward flecks of sunlight she knew marked the edge of the shelterbelt. She felt his darkness reaching inside where her insides began, where she could not bear to feel it.

He stood in front of her near the edge of the trees. She didn't fall this time, cutting sideways with soccer agility, darting for the light.

"Melanie?" came her mother's shout from far away.

She saw the opening, the field, the big white house beyond, her feet lifting and falling as if she were on an escalator going backward without getting anywhere.

Then she was in the sunlight.

At the edge of the field she stopped, twenty feet from the wall of shadows. Her face was ashen. She heard her mother call again from the house. With backward faltering steps she stared in terror at the trees.

"Streak?" she stammered through building tears.

And she felt the being staring at her again, finding her from those thick shadows. It was like being touched all over, a thousand times worse than that old man with his bony cold hands trying to—

Streak stood at the edge of the trees.

"Oh, Streak!" She knelt, wild with joy, clapping her hands. "Come on, boy!"

He stared at her with black eyes. She felt ugliness crawling over her body. His eyes were not Streak's eyes.

Wild-eyed, Melanie broke into a frantic run across the weedy field. Throwing herself over broken ground, she was beginning to bawl. Twice she fell in the field without looking back. Past the old stable and the tennis court, she raced toward Whitewood. She took the veranda steps two at a time.

Sobbing on the top step she stared across the lawns. Nothing was after her. Nothing moved in the field or near the tennis court or garage.

Sandra was mixing brownie batter in a bowl on the kitchen counter. Melanie burst into the kitchen. Sandra turned so abruptly, startled, that the bowl wobbled off the counter. Glass and brown spatters shot across the floor, over her feet and Melanie's, as the girl came to a halt, gasping for breath, eyes red with frantic tears.

Melanie hugged her mother desperately, heaving ragged sobs.

"What on earth?" asked Sandra.

Melanie could not begin to frame her words. It was all so confused—she didn't even know what had happened exactly. Her head rocked from side to side. Her hands found the countertop. She looked down at broken daggers of glass bowl rearing angrily from dark foothills of brownie batter.

"Honey?" Sandra knelt, taking her daughter by the shoulders, bending her face to look up into the dazed young eyes where dark lashes trembled under heavy uncontrollable tears.

Twenty-two

When David returned to Whitewood he found Sandra comforting Melanie on the leather couch in the study. The child's face was red and puffy. Sandra held her close, rocking her, talking low. Sandra looked up at David in the hallway door.

"I think a snake bit Streak. Melanie says it was in the woods. Apparently Philip's servant was there, too, and Streak tried to bite him, for Christ sake.

"Wish he'd *killed* him!" stammered Melanie through tears.

Philip? thought David. He entered the room, sat, and put his arms around Melanie. She snuggled into his chest.

"Please, daddy . . . *please* find Streaky. . . ."

"I'll find him, don't you worry." He stroked her dark hair. Damp and warm with stray tears, it clung to his palm. Her bleary blue eyes rose hopefully to his.

"Promise? Promise you'll find him?"

He kissed her tenderly. "Would I lie to my prettiest girl friend, huh?"

She grinned hopefully through her tears. He made her stand and go with him to the hall.

"She needs a nap, David," Sandra said. She took Melanie's hand.

"I want to go with daddy to look," protested Melanie, snuffling.

"Go on," insisted David. "Mommy's right."

Melanie stared a moment at her daddy. She thought of the dark man's nakedness, thought of her daddy naked under his clothes, wanted to tell him that the man had made her feel ugly. But could not. She let her mother's hand pull her into the hall.

Sandra hustled Melanie to the foot of the stairs and ran back down the hallway to catch David in the kitchen.

"For God's sake take a gun if you're going outside to look for that dog. He's a *Doberman,* we forget that with him licking and being so close to us all the time, but he still is."

David shook his head. "That dog would never hurt one of us. Whatever he was doing out there, it was to protect Melanie."

"From what?" frowned Sandra. "Thank God it wasn't Philip himself that the beast attacked."

David looked at her. "It's Philip now, huh?"

Sandra shook her head in exasperation. Without turning back to find a gun, David went outside through the kitchen veranda door.

At a kitchen window Sandra watched him descend the veranda steps and walk past the tennis courts, calling the dog's name. She bit her lip, tore off a handful of paper towels, and knelt over the dark mess of glass and batter. The instant her free hand touched the floor she lifted it and stared at a thin bright three-inch needle of glass that hung suspended from her index finger, slow drops of her blood beginning to find their way down its broken edge. A breeze brought the odor of the ivy through the window. She had not noticed before today how vile it smelled. She would have to pull it down tomorrow.

For an hour outside, David searched for the dog. At first he expected Streak to come bounding across the lawns at his first shout. But there was no response. He worked his way completely around the house, through the arbors, past tennis court and garage and stables and back through the oaks and arbors again until he was along the river bluff past the cemetery. Finally, he stood at the end of the brick drive, back where he started.

Hands on his hips, he shook his head. "Where are you, boy?"

He gazed across the field at the western shelterbelt of trees. He knew he should go check there but the shadows were growing long. The sun was getting low. In a half-hour those dense woods would be too dark to see in. Yet a vision of Streak dying alone, snake-bitten, in solitary agony, was too much for him to bear.

He crossed the coarse field quickly and peered through the

wall of brush, calling the dog's name. Nothing. The murmur of a breeze in high creaking branches.

He pushed through the thickets into deeper shadows, staring at huge trees where he once played Indians—was that twenty years ago? Really? Here he had hunted with his father.

Tearing himself from reverie, David turned to push back through the wall of brush into the field.

He saw it. Gasping, he blinked, a captive of his own stunning disbelief.

His father's body was propped up against the coiled roots and trunk of an oak. The pasty eyelids were closed. No funeral suit. The body was naked. Not a grey hair out of place. White hands folded neatly over the ashen face. Like a manikin with legs outstretched, the white soles of the feet slick and unmarred, facing outward. Half the forehead was gone and the abdomen was stitched in a mortician's puckered V.

The eyes snapped open. Black gleams stared at him. His mind rattled in horror. Medical texts. Cadaveric spasm. Inspect the corpse. Take a look, Doc. Isn't that the thing you've been looking for?

With one step backward David shuddered, his hands quivering and useless at his sides.

The mouth of the corpse fell open. The jaw moved with a grating of bone. David heard a voice in his mind, words that did not pass through air to reach him—*Timor mortis conturbat me.*

The fear of death unsettles me. . . . Latin . . . his father's voice.

With an animal whine he turned and ran three steps. The urge to flight was involuntary. He caught himself and halted. He forced himself to turn again.

It was insanity. Looking now he saw nothing but a tree. His father wasn't there. Whatever he'd thought he'd seen was gone. And now he knew it had never been there. And the Scout hadn't changed colors. Nor had the fingers moved.

It was insanity.

David staggered back through the brush into the field. The low sun pierced river bluff trees with yellow slanting rays that threw uneven grasses into sharp relief at his feet. Once he glanced back from the middle of the field. Of course there was nothing there.

We leave in the morning, he thought, we don't stay here another day. Sam had been right—when a place is going bad you get away, you quit asking questions. But—*Sam stayed.* And he died.

We leave in the morning, David reiterated. No matter what, we leave.

As he crossed the drive and mounted the veranda stairs, he did not cast haggard eyes toward the bluff, toward the face-broken crypt. Perhaps he would not have seen it even if he had.

Dark in itself, it crouched in the deep shadows of the broken tomb. It watched David with baleful eyes that glimmered above curving fangs. Within Whitewood, the clockwork device sat on the library desk, its central wheel turning slowly, catching glints of sunset light on archaic symbols.

Twenty-three

At dusk Woody Sheehan's battered once-red Dodge pickup came to a chugging halt at the juncture of the two-lane blacktop and the driveway of the restored DeBois manor.

Woody's face stared pastily out the pickup window toward the great house. His eyes were overbright. His hands trembled. They could barely light a cigarette, the lighter burning a finger, his eyes not registering pain, gazing upon the house.

"Don't," he said, flinching.

Sweat popped from the coarse pores of his face. He whined. He hugged himself as if he were a cold little boy, rotating his shoulders, moving his head slowly from shoulder to shoulder. "Please don't. . . . Not no more."

He convulsed. His hands dropped onto the scarred steering wheel. The truck clutched into gear and edged up the drive, the black-windowed mansion looming in swarming purplish dusk.

The truck halted at the end of the drive. Woody's cigarette burned down to his sweat-beaded lips. It blistered them, leaving a blackened half-moon before hissing out against perspiration.

Two boxes of groceries rested against the tailgate in the dented pickup bed. Woody climbed down and pulled them out. One of them he hefted under each arm. He carried them through the portico and set them on the bottom brick step under the ornate black grillwork. Ashes between his rigid lips fell as he stooped.

He returned to the truck and seemed to hesitate beside it.

He flinched and reached into the bed and unlocked a long high toolbox bolted in behind the cab. He lifted out a two-by-two-foot wire cage.

Within the wire a calico cat hissed and clawed at Woody's fingers. Gnawing at the wire, hissing, howling in panic, it shrieked as he carried the cage around the darkening house. Woody placed it beside the groceries. For a moment he stood bemused, seeming to contemplate the trapped animal. It paced the cage. Now and again it whined up at him. Woody frowned once as if remembering something. His body inclined to bend and pick up the cage again. Then he stiffened. His face jerked aside as if something had slapped it.

The caged animal listened as the click of Woody's heels went away. The pickup's engine wheezed and started. The chugging tailpipe and howling differential faded and were gone. The silence of the house poured back in.

The cat stood in the center of the cage without touching the wire on any side. It turned to peer up at the house.

The back door was opening, slowly, soundlessly.

Every hair on the trapped animal's body stood straight out. It pressed back against the wire. Its body arched. It shrieked in stiffening horror at what it saw. The door was open and the animal screams went deep into the shelterbelt of woods.

It was night. A quarter-moon rising over Whitewood. Thin languorous breezes from the river stole through the great oaks. While nocturnal insects made discreet sourceless songs, moonlight clung feebly against the house like ocean phosphorescence in the wake of passing monsters.

Upstairs, Melanie was asleep. Sandra read in bed, waiting for David to come up.

He was outside on the veranda. Gazing on the moonstruck lawns where he and Sam had watched together, he sipped whiskey from a shot glass.

Now that he was certain that in the morning they would return to Memphis, he savored a bittersweet nostalgia. It seemed that a kind of nightmare already receded backward into terrible days that could hardly have ever happened. He would never have thought, given any such problem a few weeks earlier, that he would leave with such things in question—the theft of his father's remains, the unapprehended vandals who may have contributed to Sam's death, the disappearance of Streak. But those things were not as maddening even as the fingers in the window that he must have moved *himself,* without realizing it. Or the shadow of the raven on the film, shadow instead of substance. The threat of his own crumbling sanity. His paranoia regarding Sprague, a blind old eccentric and nothing more. The Scout seeming to change colors for Christ's sake. Worst of all, the image of his father sitting under the tree. Abominations of the mind. Seeds of insanity. There were no vandals—Sam had moved the body—it would never turn up. Streak would show up in the morning with a sheepish wagtail grin. Dogs that lived long enough in the country began running off sooner or later, all of them.

He was suffering from a dangerous mental deterioration. The crush of events had been too cruel and too quick to absorb. What he must have now is rest. Ironically, that meant returning to the hospital. The sooner the better. A week or two back in Memphis would make clear the guilt-ridden associations which had combined with tragedy to bend his mind out of shape. Hindsight was always twenty-twenty, his father had said.

David sighed miserably. His poor father. And yet he had his own family to consider, the living. He had to have been guilt-crazy in the first place to try and stay here—even to think to do it—seven weeks to watch a crypt. The idea must have worked on Sam to such an extent that Sam had done the thing he started out to keep from happening. Such was the mental labyrinth. Return to Memphis would be a return to sanity.

With comforting mood of having settled a difficult problem, David rose from the chair and walked down the veranda steps into the moonlit pallor of the lawn. He was not yet aware of the thing that moved now from the crypt shadows. That had watched him at dusk, waiting, and now for the past hour. He could not hear it coming. It made no sound.

Within Whitewood's library, the clockwork whirled on the desk casting a lurid red glow over nearby papers.

David strolled hands in pockets toward the garage, past the tennis court, wondering whether to rent a tow-bar and haul the old Triumph back to Memphis. If the tires were in he could. If it didn't mean waiting too long.

Out of peripheral vision he caught movement.

He turned. He spun, stumbling, almost falling backward. The double gleam of eyes, the frontal black shape ran through the arbors straight toward him. It was something that looked like Streak. He saw and knew in an instant it was not Streak.

He bolted for the garage doors only yards away. He heard nothing but felt the creature closing in behind with incredible speed. His own rasping breath and the slap of his shoes in the grass were the only sounds.

Stumbling between the garage doors his hand closed on an iron-tined rake. He whirled, thrusting the rake blindly backward. The thing was leaping at him. He cried chokingly, both hands feeling its weight hit the rake. The wooden shaft snapped and he staggered back into the garage blackness.

He had heard the thing laugh in the darkness with him. Backing, his hip cracked against the car. His hands grabbed wildly along the garage wall, stuck by unseen nails, by hanging garden tools. He heard a snarl. His hands clutched something from the wall and he turned in the blackness with a desolate cry of fear. He saw a shadow rise between him and the rectangle of moonlight in the doors. A weight struck him. Gasping in horror he felt himself borne to the dirt floor of the garage, expecting fangs to tear into the soft flesh of his throat and face. But the thing on him shuddered, relaxing.

He felt warm sticky liquid oozing over his hands and chest. He felt the mass flutter and become rigid. Sharp hairs were prickling his cheek. His groping hands felt lifeless paws with long nails.

Hardly daring to breathe, David crawled out from under the thing. He tried to stand in the darkness but his legs were stalks of water. He pulled himself up with both hands on the back bumper of the Triumph. His hand swayed overhead until it crossed the string of the light switch. He found and snatched at it.

Light flooded the garage, blinding for a moment.

Streak lay beside the roadster. Like a giant scissors, one cutter blade of an old pair of hedge shears was buried in his chest. A triangular steel tip came out again between the shoulder blades. Blood pooled under the sleek black body of the animal he had loved, that his daughter had worshipped.

But he knew that had not been Streak.

It had laughed.

Had it? Or had he thought so? He stooped to examine the body. His hands shook as his fingers lifted the head, touched the fur. It could not have laughed. He was so scared he thought it had laughed. Not *it,* Streak. Had the dog even attacked him? Had it been glad to see him? Had he murdered it senselessly? Was *he* the dangerous one, not the dog?

No, he told himself, *that wasn't Streak.*

What, then? Hydrophobia? A good possibility—Something logical had caused erratic behavior, the attack.

He examined the dead animal. No froth on the jowls. Still,

the head would have to be sent to Memphis. Brain analysis for hydrophobia was atavistic but standard procedure.

Grimly, with deep revulsion, he stood.

The head would have to be taken off tonight. He could take no chance that Melanie would see or ever learn of this. Streak's head would be sent in a crate, his body secretly buried tonight. Better that the child think he ran away than even a hint reach her of what must now be done.

He was a doctor, yet the act sent disgust and sadness in ugly waves through his chest. He thought he would vomit as his hand gripped the hacksaw over the workbench.

He knelt and lifted the head with a firm grip on the muzzle. He ground his teeth. The saw grated.

It was over quickly. All that remained was the vibration of sinew and bone through the indifferent steel tool. He blinked constantly. Tears dripped off his nose and collected at the corners of his mouth. Breath caught in small jerks in his throat.

"I'm sorry, old boy," he whispered. He tugged the decapitated carcass outside by one leg, taking a shovel as he passed the rack of lawn tools behind one door.

For a half hour he shoveled out a deep rectangle in the edge of the field. Then the work was done. Walking back to the garage, shaking his head, he steeled himself for one last thing. Wrap the head for shipment. Take it into town early, before Melanie wakes up. Boxed securely so that no post office clerk would have questions. In the garage he found a tractor battery packing crate. That would do.

Biting his lip and fighting an enervating sorrow that bleared his vision and melted control, he cradled the head tenderly in both hands to lift it.

The death-lidded eyes jerked open and glared blackly up at him. The mandible locked open and crashed shut like a trap trying to catch his fingers.

David croaked in horror, staggering back, flinging the thing toward the garage doors. It tumbled through the air. Jaws clacked, fangs caught the light, a last glitter of an eye watching him as it struck the edge of one door and went through the open space into the night outside.

Twenty-four

Unaware of time, hardly remembering where he was or what he was doing, David stood shakily by the car. His feet were frozen in place, eyes riveted on the garage doors. At any instant he expected some unspeakable horror to appear in the vertical opening between them, hoping he could convince himself that it was mental malfunction and nothing real.

Yet nothing appeared.

Sweat itched in stringy rivulets between his shoulder blades, under his armpits, and in the orbits of his eyes. Obscenity returned like a needle jerking perpetually on a broken record—the repeated feel and image of Streak's snapping jaws, eyes open in the bodiless head, eyes that were not animal, that had never belonged to the puppy Melanie had loved and raised.

His mind raged. Get a hold on yourself before you lose touch. You hacksawed the head off. You freaked, imagining it moved. You threw it and it hit the doors and tumbled outside. It's lying out there on the grass. *For God's sake go find it.* What if Melanie came rushing out of the house in the morning and there it was?

His shaking hand found a battered two-cell Eveready between two nails over the work bench. Its brass switch slid crustily. A weak yellow glow grew slowly into a beam.

He edged past the car toward the doors. Swallowing, holding the light ahead, he came to the doors, passing the beam over the grass outside, seeing no trace of the head that had to be there.

The garage doors clattered and David screamed.

It was only Sandra. Holding her nightgown together at the throat, she frowned. "David? What on earth?"

David let out a long breath and shook his head. He kissed her. She wanted him to return to the house.

"What're you doing out here, anyway?" she asked.

Not knowing what to say, he lied. "Working on the Triumph." He promised to be in shortly.

She kissed him and went inside, leaving him a quivering mass of nerves. The head was not on the grass outside the garage doors. *It had to be.*

But it wasn't. Not even flecks of blood. His flashlight beam whipped back and forth over the grass, showing nothing. He circled the garage. Wandering with the flashlight he felt a kind of collapsing inertia of logic. The part of his mind that told him what to believe and what not to believe was failing. Like a weird game with bases being switched on him.

He wondered about sanity. There was no way he could have seen any of the things that scared him—was that how it came? Little horrors at first? then worse and worse? until it verged on madness? Then full-blown?

How much worse could it get? He knew the answer—his father had known the answer. Sam had. It could get bad enough to blow your brains out. Or have a stroke.

He felt chilly.

The open air was unnerving. Looking across the tennis court and the wide jumping course beyond, its posts milky in moonlight, he felt the chill associate with a terrific sensation of being watched.

He wanted to go into the house. There was nothing to be done about the head. He had searched. Maybe he hadn't even sawed it off. Was he sure? Maybe Streak hadn't even attacked him. That was becoming a definite possibility.

He closed the garage and went to the house.

In the kitchen he paused at the sink to wash his hands. He wanted to wash them because—

Blood on his fingers. *Dried blood.* It had all happened out there. Yes it had.

Had he buried the head with the body? Maybe. The only thing to do would be to wait seven days, then take a blood sample for analysis. Take the damned shots if the test returned positive. He toweled his hands dry and sat at the table.

Not sleepy.

He made a pot of coffee. While it perked he took a shot of whiskey from the kitchen cupboard bottle. With the first cup of coffee he took another shot. His father had loved good whiskey. Distilling was an ancient art. He thought of furry Celts in Scottish hills scarfing down their potent beverage. Fragrant peat fires sending smoke into the Highland skies. Skill and experience passed on from father to son. Father to son.

With a ragged sigh he rose from the chair and walked through the hall. He found himself standing at the library door.

The disciplined walls of books echoed back at him his own sense of broken continuity. He wanted somehow to reach out to his father. To make any kind of contact. And he thought of the journal.

He went to the desk, snapped on the desk lamp, and took the chair. The odd clockwork device glinted in the light, its wheels still. He opened the thin volume to the mark where he had quit reading days before. The realization that he sat at a desk with two human fingers locked in its drawer made a ripple in his thoughts. He almost laughed at this grisly absurdity. How important and weird it had seemed only days ago, when his behavior in handling them should have been the first warning signal.

He adjusted the desk lamp, situated the small hand mirror, and began to read:

Last evening I dined at Sprague's. Estate-bottled wines. French cuisine outdoing anything I've had this side of Paris. Better than what I had there. During after-dinner innuendo in the high cupola, I began to think that somehow he knew already of the appearances to me of Leah in dreams. How could he know this? I asked, in my own blunt way. Sprague stared at me. He talked of my sensitivity, of saving his life. We had liqueurs. I left late, with the funny feeling that I had left something behind. . . .

Wincing, David found passages seeming to confirm his suspicions as to his father's progressing insanity. He read on compulsively.

Leah . . . she comes again and again in dreams. Tomorrow night I dine again with Sprague. Perhaps he knows something to help me. The doctor in Jackson—pill-peddler—gave me little pink pills that don't help sleep at all. But why should I think he knows anything of use, this Sprague person? And why am I, admit it, intimidated by this man? His attitude almost seems to indicate that he resents me for having saved his life—or if not for that, for having handled him, having carried him in my hands and my arms. He avoids the least contact. Dinner over, he invites me to view a collection of memorabilia, as he calls it. We climb down the old stone steps below where I have always believed the foundations of the DeBois manor to be. The temperature drops ten degrees on those steps. A candle is lit in one corner. Of course he would need none, being blind, so I know he's expected all along to bring me there. The basement smells faintly foul. In the uncertain light I see that it's like the chamber of some antique magician or sorcerer—a weird old crank, I say to myself. I thought so then. I still took him lightly at that time, still was unaware of his powers. There is a table heaped with archaic instruments of doubtful origin or utility. Cryptic charts on the walls are something like Ruth's trailer but very different, certainly not commercially printed. A censer—which looks to be stolen from a Catholic church—stands in one corner. I look up at the skeleton of a large snake suspended like a mobile above us. Within a niche cut into the stone wall above the table are carefully placed old volumes bound in moldy stinking leather, with greenish and rusted hinges. I have some Latin and Greek and can make out some of the less badly rubbed titles. Demonology? the black arts? Bullshit of lesser antique minds, I say to myself. Yet Aristotle and Plato both delved into such matters. On the stone floor are faded evidences of chalk diagrams drawn and wiped away. The feel of the room is unnerving, an atmosphere of obscene and vulgar superstition. My opinion of Sprague as a man drops even lower. He turns at me with his blind smile, as if waiting for compliments but mocking me as well. I should grin at this hodgepodge of repulsive and corny objects. But the feel of the lonely deep cellar room, and something about being there alone with this strange dismally mocking old gentleman character, makes it hard for me not to want to strike him. I realize I'm a little afraid. It's as if I have stumbled through some idiotic panel into a class-B melodrama that is all real. I ask if he collects objects of occult origin. He dissembles on a long study he has made of sorcery. I watch his blind eyes seem to search mine for hints of ridicule. I ask myself what in hell am I wasting time here for? I am disgusted, unamused. He goes on talking, mentioning ancient texts and so forth. I am hardly paying attention to their names or sources, but I begin to be aware of an odor. Maybe it's the source of black sensations in the room. Like decay. I smell it coming stronger.

Breathing deeply, David paused. He remembered the stench of the book from the safe. The woodcut of a sorcerer, a raven on his shoulder, arms high in invocation, the sacrificial maiden, the vague horned specter rising savagely over her.

He poured another shot of whiskey and read on with a compulsive curiosity and dread:

I am an ancient man of ancient tradition, Sprague said, and I pay my debts, I must—for the saving of my life I bring you another. He told me that, and I didn't understand. His mocking tone was sharper. I said I was tired. He told me that a few more minutes would be worth my wait. His cane described a shape upon the floor. He stepped into it. Bending down, he reached under the heavily piled table. What he pulled out was hard to see at first. Then I saw it was a dead cat. My God, I thought, the damned man is utterly crazy. He touched the furry body with the cane. It was suddenly writhing, screeching, and he began to chant. I started to move forward and knock him aside to put a stop to the obscenity. And then she was there—at first a kind of whitish shadow, then solidifying like a developing photograph—Leah was standing in the circle with Sprague, she was looking straight at me. So real I thought I could reach out and touch her.

And the next thing I knew I was waking in my own bed at Whitewood. Tantalized, I sat up bawling, wondering whether it was all another bad dream. . . .

David shuddered. The things he was reading seemed to slur the already shaken memory of his father. He wanted to throw the small book aside but could only read on. His eyes skipped frightening passages describing nightmares as Leah haunted nights and sleep. From an aged book scout in New Orleans, Chester had obtained ancient texts at outrageous sums— *Malleus Maleficarum, Formicarus, Discours des sorciers,* titles David remembered seeing in the padlocked closet. The journal told of Chester digesting these medieval tracts, of learning to devise a clockwork to warn against the approach of demons. Yet Leah kept returning in dreams, maddeningly real, until he returned again and again to Sprague for help, wanting her, to have her again. The strain of Asian ivy was cultivated around the walls, a protection against demons. Still she continued to come, pushing him deeply into neuroses and black spells of madness. And Sprague promised help, mockingly it seemed, and yet the haunting grew worse.

David read in the morbid fascination he had felt in dissecting his first corpse. Yet it had to be sheer fantasy. Chester had been a rock-hard rationalist. It was as hard to imagine Chester degenerating into superstitious backwardness as it was to—what? believe that he himself might have seen, or thought he saw, the things in the past days that had shaken his own sanity to the core? He stared at the clockwork, shook his head, read on.

Now I am considering the murder of Sprague. Or the end myself. No night of rest. . . .

I spoke with Ruth. She is more afraid than I am, if that is possible, and she knows nothing we can do. What can we say about the little girl? What would the authorities believe? That we are mad? That we've lost our minds?

David paused, eyes wide and heartbeat quickening—*little girl?* Holly's daughter? He flipped back through earlier pages but found no account to explain the new passage.

I am convinced. Sprague is a black master who must be somehow destroyed. Yet that familiar is always nearby.

Familiar? wondered David.

A changeling able to alter its shape. I have seen it myself. He is a raven, or a snake, or that dark personality that appears human. I can only guess his powers. It will have to be a night of rain, when I can do it and escape. The familiar cannot follow through rain. He cannot cross free-running water, the grimoires *say. I will have to act soon before I am destroyed. He is obligated to make periodic sacrifice to retain his powers. What child is next?*

David stared at the maddening pages, but now the journal tapered into scripture scribbled in a shaky hand—

> The beast thou sawest was, and is not;
> and shall ascend out of the Bottomless Pit . . .
> they that dwell on the earth shall wonder. . . .
>
> And all that dwell upon the earth shall worship him
> whose names are not written in the Book of Life
> of the Lamb Slain from the foundation of the world.
>
> And when the thousand years are expired Satan shall
> be loosed out of his prison.

Then David read a passage that momentarily stopped his breath. His eyes widened in awful surprise.

No one would believe what I have witnessed tonight—How can I even bring myself to tell what I saw on Sprague's cellar stairs, too late to save the girl? But now Sprague is dead, his thing pursues me. It wants his body but I have it buried, hidden. I sit here now watching my device on the desk before me, knowing I am quite mad. There is still my revolver in its drawer. Better that than the thing outside.

The last pages of the journal were blank. David stared at them in hollow-eyed dread. He saw a train of events. Pets disappearing. Chester dead. Holly's little girl. Sam. Broken crypt. Sandy's sleepwalking. Streak. Hallucination of his father in the woods.

He was flirting with madness. But the journal was written with conviction and a wild logic all its own.

No—in the morning he would return to Memphis. In the city nights men stalked, but they were only men, not figments of nightmare. He would fling himself back into his work. He would not think about any of this for a long long time.

It had become a matter of self-preservation, of keeping himself from flying apart from abuse. Sandra and Melanie came first.

For a long while he stared at the last empty pages of the journal. Its madness taunted and swirled in bits and pieces, disjointed and surreal. He began to nod, whiskey glowing. Finally, he slumped in the desk chair.

Upstairs, Sandra slept. The light was still on. A fat paperback lay across her breasts.

She sat up and opened her eyes. They stared, unseeing. The book fell from her lap, unnoticed as she got out of bed. She stood by the moonlit balcony casement and a breeze moved the sheer nightgown fabric against her body in dreamlike slow motion.

Twenty-five

The supplicant knelt humbly on the uneven stone floor. His back was bowed. His thin chant rose singsong, nasal, enticing more than demanding. His chin touched the stones, his back rising from the gloom.

There was a dim light in the room. But a pentagram described in chalk about the supplicant wavered, glowing brighter on the floor. Its dull greenish glow grew stronger as the chant went on, rising, beseeching. In the sullen radiance the calico-furred sprawl of a cat was visible. One of its fore-paws twitched as it might in a nightmare. The chant continued.

It was Sprague's voice, trembling with eagerness.

"Arator—Lapidator—Monitor—Omator—*woman* bring the child, *woman* bring thy child virgin child to consecration with God of kings, God of my fathers—King of men, I ask in the name of Cernunnos the Horned One—*woman* bring the virgin child to consecration—"

A wind hissed across the stones. The light wavered. Now there were outlines of a second form and a sound like the beating of heavy wings.

Sprague's hand extended, gripping his cane. The tip of the cane swung toward the cat. It touched the furry ribcage. The cat shrieked, twisted as if impaled, every fiber of limbs and back and tail and head tensing but trapped, vibrating under the constant tip of the cane.

The chant continued in the voice of him who used the name Philip Sprague, who had used countless other names and countless other lifetimes. It was voice whose knowledge of merciless ingredients was profound in hateful mirth.

"*Woman*—I command you to bring the child—in the name of Cernunnos!"

Sandra stood in a plain tilled over the course of centuries by simple folk in simple cottages. Pure mountain water flowed in rock-lined streams. Pure mountain air passed over her face. She waited. Something loomed darkly behind her. She turned, her naked feet swishing against cool smooth grass. It was her lover. He had come at last. He had no name but his blind eyes were no longer blind. She panted as he drew her close, bending her body, touching her until her head fell back and her lips parted with desire. His head was a cold shadow upon her face. Her lips were open to him. Her breasts urged hotly against his cold chest. . . .

There was no sensation of rising from the bed or of walking.

She was unaware of leaving the bedroom, of passing through the dark hall to Melanie's room. Her eyes were open, unseeing, yet no part of her body touched a wall or bureau or doorframe as she entered Melanie's room.

The child lay among twisted covers, whimpering in an uneasy sleep. She was dreaming of Streak chasing his red rubber ball under the King Kong poster in her bedroom in Memphis. She hardly felt the pressure of her mother's arms under her buttocks and her back, nor the lifting followed by the soft press of her mother's bosom.

With open glazed eyes Sandra turned with her daughter in her arms. She carried Melanie from the doorway into the hall.

David awoke in the library. He heard footsteps on the stairs. Rising, stumbling into the hall, sleep-dazed, he looked up the curving century-old staircase. His burning eyes widened.

Sandra stood in the middle of the stairs. She gazed into space. A whitish form slept in her arms—Melanie. He was stunned. She could not be carrying the eighty-pound child without a strain. But she *was*. She came slowly down toward him, not seeing him. Her right foot lowered unerringly onto the last stairstep.

Reaching, he pulled Melanie from her arms. They were pliable, unresisting. She stood still, her blank expression becoming a frown of doubt. Her eyes blinked, closed, then popped open, pupils still unfocused.

"I'm coming . . . coming. . . ."

David felt Melanie waking in his arms. He had to get her back to bed before she knew what had happened. Frightened, he nudged Sandra with his foot, hoping she would follow him back up the stairs. It was too late.

Melanie's body squirmed. She moaned. Her dark lashes fluttered open.

"Daddy? Huh? What's wrong?" She was afraid, hugging him tightly.

"Nothing, honey, shhhhh."

Sandra was waking now, muttering incoherently. She turned and held onto David's arm, following as David gently carried Melanie up the stairs to her bedroom.

He laid her back on her bed.

"What're we doing?" she whimpered.

"David?" Sandra said in the hall. "What . . . am I . . . ?"

"Everything's okay, go back to sleep, doll."

He hurried to Sandra and led her back to their room. Her naked feet hissed beside him on the polished hardwood. Her breath came in short anxious pants sliced with sharp jerking breaths as if she had been crying uncontrollably and wanted to stop now.

At the door, Melanie's plaintive whisper stopped him. He looked back. She was standing in her doorway. Diffuse moonlight from her room illuminated her cotton nightgown, showing the shadow of her young female body.

"Daddy—did Streaky come back?" she asked.

He lied. "Yes, honey, go to sleep now."

"Can't he come in?"

"Hush now. In the morning." He had to get Sandra back to bed.

Moonlight lay across the bedroom floor. Leading Sandra through it, he saw that she was asleep again, her eyes open but glazed. He whispered her name. She did not answer. He led and she came docilely into the bedroom and allowed him to place her across the bed. He knew that was incorrect. She should not be pliable. Not in textbook somnambulism anyway, not as he had studied it.

Trembling, nearly in tears, he sat beside her on the crumpled sheets. Moonlight fell across his toes from the windows. They looked like ghostly worms.

Staring, he felt something alien, something close. He knew it might be his own madness. Some part of him seemed no longer disciplined, no longer controlled at the helm. And yet the presence seemed not risen from him. It was outer. Darker than he had power to be. Alien, not very close now but lingering in traces. As if he remembered a prehistoric hunter crouched in night thickets, having escaped the near pass of a night visitor, monstrous and hungering, something felt without hands and smelled without nostrils and feared without ever hearing the deadly stealth of its tread.

But he knew he had seen the fascination of its eye. Those had not been Streak's eyes. *No way*. No way on earth.

David rubbed his face. His feelings, his thoughts and fears were all muddied. There was no focus anymore, only baffling confusion and fear. Work would erase horror in time. If the sleepwalking continued he would find appropriate psychiatric help for Sandra. Maybe buy a puppy for Melanie—nothing eased the pain of death more quickly than new life. His own shaken foundations would need time to fuse together into the solid base that had been and would be again.

Yet, he was unconvinced. Beside Sandra on the bed, watching her and the movement of tree shadows against moonlit panes, sleep was not even a remote possibility. He kept seeing Streak's head wrenching alive in his bloody hands. Those alien eyes, reptilian, evil.

Exhausted, he was nodding when he heard her whisper. ". . . . Cernunnos?" he thought he heard.

He was instantly awake, bending his head over her lips. She said the word again. It sounded like *Sir-noose-nose.*

Sir Noose-nose? He straightened and imagined Sir Noose-nose, a comic Don Quixote on a swayback nag with a big nose with nostrils wide as nooses. A monster that grabbed things with its nostrils. He grinned until he saw Sandy begin to sit up. She threw her legs off the opposite side of the bed and stood before he realized it was happening.

"Cernunnos," she whispered, not a questioning now but pure affirmation.

David reached quickly across the bed for her arm.

Sandra stood at one end of the long ballroom lifting her face toward him who waited at the other end. The guests were misshapen forms in shadow. The light about him was tranquil yet shifting, a movement of illusive shadows, and only his eyes were revealed as she felt herself moved with smooth motions toward him. She felt her weight lightly urged forward as a wave moves a swimmer. Halfway across the grand ballroom she glimpsed his ancient face, his golden-horned skull, the cloudy green serpentlike eyes with splinters of red their pupils. . . .

David gripped Sandra's arm. She jerked against his weight, her strength startling him.

"Sandy!" He tugged harder, afraid of harming her but afraid too of what was happening.

She tumbled backward across the sheets. Her mouth clapped open and shut like a mannequin's, eyes were wide open. Her own long thin hands lay palm upward in dim bluish moolight.

Loosing control, David shook her desperately. He rasped her name in hard steady whispers as much for himself as for her, the sound of his own voice unconvincing and weak. He felt her body beginning to relax. She sighed and her eyes opened.

He looked down into them, Sandy's eyes, warm and lovely and well known.

"Was I having a nightmare?" she yawned.

He let out a long troubled breath. Trying to smile, he nodded and lay down beside her. As he held her, fear was running all through him like an animal. His courage was at a low ebb. His father's insane journal kept returning wildly in his thoughts.

Is madness my legacy?

Fear was there around him in the room as palpable as the humid air. He lay staring at the ceiling through the hours. Predawn darkness gave way to pleasant faint colors of dawn, delicate insinuations on the fringe of the bedroom curtains.

He woke. Daylight filled the room. Downstairs, the grandfather clock chimed ten times. Sandra was sound asleep. He sat up sharply, left the bed to begin packing.

Standing by the armoire, he heard something. His fingers tightened on a shirt, knuckles turning white. But he didn't hear it again—that clatter of a large dog's nails on hardwood flooring.

Sandra sat up on the bed. "David? What're you doing?"

He turned. Her face was puffy with sleep, a slender hand rubbing her eyes.

The phone rang.

David flinched. The shirt slipped from his hand.

"Honey? You all right?" asked Sandra. She rolled over to the night table and lifted the receiver.

The second grandfather chimed ten times.

"Ummmm? Uh-huh, he's right here."

Sandra stuck the receiver out at him. Swallowing, he went to take it, remembering another phone call that now seemed years ago, in Memphis when Barksdale's voice had come huskily on the line. He felt that same dread now.

"Dave?" came the thick crackle of Dewey Pounds' voice.

"Yeah." His voice broke. He cleared his throat and coughed.

"I arrested Woody Sheehan last night. Caught him stealing old man Davis' pet cat last night. Funny. Like Woody didn't know who he was, or at least he was acting that way. I'm gonna make him talk. Thought you'd like to know. Maybe the dumb bastard knows something about your trouble, huh?"

David's pulse quickened. "I don't know, I mean—yeah, wait for me, Dewey. I'm coming right down."

"Come in the back way, through the alley, Dave. There's a few pissed-off folks starting to gather outside here."

David hung up. A voice told him to go away, leave this place now. Take his wife and daughter and get away and don't come back. Another voice cried louder of anger and suspicion, of love for his father and Sam and Streak, of revenge and retribution.

He snatched his jeans off a chair and jerked them on, grinning now with anticipation. Woody. It was that damned Woody. Poor Ruth.

Sandra swung off the bed, stifling a yawn.

"What was that all about?"

Pulling on shirt and weejuns, David related Pounds' message. Sandra listened with deepening concern.

"Why torture yourself, honey? Let the sheriff handle it. You're just tearing at your own wounds."

"I'll be back early this afternoon, should be. We'll pack and go back to Memphis." He was at the door, buttoning the shirt.

Sandra wiped hair from her eyes.

"Back to Memphis?" she asked, incredulous, taken utterly by surprise. He walked out and she sat there shaking her head as if she hadn't heard right.

"Just starting to enjoy the damn place, and BAM—he wants to leave."

She screwed her nose at the scent coming in the windows. Funny it never bothered her before. "First thing goes are those vines."

Morning light flooded the foyer. At the base of the stairwell David halted. The dull fear of past days was clearing, replaced by logic. So that bastard Woody was the answer. Something flesh and blood and real. Not imagined. No prowler of the mind, after all.

He almost laughed with delight. Then felt guilt. Poor Ruth. Her son had a hell of a lot to answer for. But what if he refused to talk? What if nothing were solved?

David stood rigidly concentrating. The stubborn rational discipline that had gotten him through tough years of med school and half-starvation washed away the frightening uncertainties of the past days. The threat of madness and decline was burned away. Now that he had a material handle—someone to blame—he stood on solid ground. But what proof besides Pounds' feeble charge of pet-snatching? Could he bluff Woody into a confession of other things? Was he grasping at straws?

But—maybe there *was* evidence. Or at least something to confront Woody with.

David went quickly into the library and unlocked the desk drawer. The envelope was open. The fingers seemed to have slid to the front of the drawer. A pallid stench reached him.

Revulsed, with a Bic pen he slapped them back into the envelope and shoved it in his pocket. He thought he felt them twitch against his thigh but knew it was a nerve in his leg. His imagination had been escaping him these past days. He had to keep it in check now. The answers were soon at hand. He hurried outside to the Scout.

Twenty-six

Sheriff Dewey Pounds peered through a crack in the yellowed pull-down shade that covered both front windows of his office and triple-cell jail. Squinting past a quarter-inch rusted iron bar and bleary glass, he studied the street. Ever since he had brought Woody in, they had begun clustering in shadows, the town men and working women who watched the jail with arms crossed and mouths twisted in gossip. Some waited in hushed curiosity, mildly watching the jail, but others seethed. He knew any of them could be dangerous to him in one of two ways. If they got drunk and stormed the jail, he might hurt them or be hurt. If he let that happen, or if he couldn't get Woody to confess and clear up Bickford's unexplained crimes, the gas pump was always waiting.

Dewey licked sweaty lips. If Woody had been only a car thief or bank robber or if he'd only killed a man in a fight, people would let the law take its course. But a pet-snatcher was something else again. And the little girl missing. The town had been waiting to focus on something, on somebody. And word moved faster in Bickford than over Ma Bell. The fact that his deputy hadn't shown up proved that.

The big man let the shade go. He rubbed his face and belched, tasting a vague eggy foodness on a chemical wave of whiskey. He peeked out the window again. The faces of the women scared him most—how was he fixing to stop a woman if she wanted to get in and tear that Sheehan punk's eyes out?

Beside the desk drawer he took another drink. Something

hit the door. Sounded like a rock. He capped the whiskey pint and slid the drawer shut, thinking that maybe David would know the best thing to do. Sure he would—always did, that quarterback. And he hoped David wouldn't get too mad when he figured out why he really called him—because he was scared to be alone.

"Bring him out!" shouted somebody outside.

Pounds took a deep breath. Should he open the door and try to poker-face them? With a grunt he turned and strode heavily back into the dank heat of the dim cell corridor.

Woodrow Arlis Sheehan sat miserably on the rumpled edge of a fold-down iron cot. One lean hand gripped a rusty supporting chain. He stared at the two-tone green wall, concentrating on a crack in the peeling paint and trying to remember why he was doing what Pounds caught him doing. It was as if he wouldn't have remembered any of it if something hadn't gone wrong, like he'd done it a dozen times before without ever remembering. A backyard. A fence to climb. A fishing net to unfold and toss. Cat struggling in the net. Twist it tight around him so he can't scratch and bite. Put him in the cage. Take him—take him where? Take him somewhere? Who would hurt me if I didn't?

The window set high above him in the cell wall was teethed with three iron bars. Its panes were broken and missing, only pieces of rotted molding hanging at the edges. Sweat poured down Woody's face. He could hear them outside, distant murmurs punctuated by an occasional growling shout. He looked up and Pounds was standing at the cell door looking at him.

"Pissed off, ain't they?" Woody grinned bleakly. He felt the eyes of the huge man in khaki boring in on his. He knew Pounds could bust him up like tearing rotten string.

"I ought to kick you out there like a piece of meat," said Dewey. He jerked on his Sam Browne belt with two thick thumbs. He rarely wore it—the stiff strap chafed his left shoulder—but he felt that today it lent added authority to his image, made him feel stronger and wiser.

"You think I wouldn't?" demanded Dewey.

Woody hung his head in confusion and self-pity.

"You better tell what-all you been up to," tried Dewey as he had tried before.

Woody shook his head fatalistically.

"I done said I don't know," he whined.

Dewey shifted tense muscles. "Listen to me, you make me a full confession. I'll get you out of Bickford the back way, get you a Highway Patrol ride to Jackson. You had something to do with that little girl, didn't you?"

"Little girl?" Woody eyes widened.

"You know what girl. And Holly. Messed her up, too. Killed her old man and made it look like suicide. Robbed pets. Broke into a tomb. Is that weird momma of yours in on this? Talk! Maybe you need me to shake up your memory?" Pounds laid a thick sweaty hand on the humid cell door lockbox, distraught at it all. He had known Ruth all his life. Now this.

"Got it all bundled up together, doncha?" Woody covered his face with both hands. "I don't know, man, I just don't know. . . ."

Pounds cursed through gritted yellow teeth. His hamlike fist hit the bars in frustration. He tugged at the key-keeper on his belt and rattled the key into its orifice. The lock clanked. The door creaked open. Neckless, sweating, Pounds stood in the open door, big hands opening and closing, looking down into Woody's widening expression of awe.

"Guess I ain't got much choice," Pounds said, lifting a white-knuckled fist studded with hair-swarmed fingers.

David slowed as the country blacktop smoothed and straightened into Bickford. Ahead he saw twenty or thirty people milling slowly in the street as if waiting for a show or sale. Closer, passing the filling station, he saw the hard lines of their postures and the anger in their faces, jaws working in heated agreement. He parked a block away, in front of Davis Variety and Grocery.

Old man Davis stood on his high storefront porch alone. Watching the crowd, he adjusted his thick glasses. He squinted, trying to see clearly.

"They ain't got the guts to get that witch's spawn, give 'em about half a day they might work up to it," the white-haired man snapped as if David had asked him a question.

Without retorting, David strode on the street toward Pounds' office.

Davis called after him. "I'll join in if the rest of them got the guts!"

Witch? thought David. He felt sudden fear for Ruth. The people probably thought Woody had been stealing the pets for her. Both the feed store and Barksdale's office were shut and deserted. At an alleyway a few doors from Pounds' office, he saw that the windowshades were drawn. A few stones lay on the sidewalk near the closed door. Some of the people in the street were ones he had known, mostly decent quiet types, not drunks or misfits. They grumbled, mouthing Woody's name bitterly.

"Bring that bastard out here," one shouted.

The nerves in his legs twitched violently. The skin shivered under his pocket where the fingers lay together in the envelope. The fingers he'd brought to confront Woody. The twitch rose from his leg into his stomach and he fought an impulse in his epiglottis, suddenly wanting to vomit. The nervous flick faded, leaving him momentarily giddy, swallowing to scratch his throat.

He ducked into the alley to avoid the crowd. He realized that if they found a champion, trouble would begin.

He went quickly through the alley, turning at the corner toward the back of the jail. The back alleyway was deserted. Pounds' cruiser waited by the back door. The steel-faced jail door was locked, as he expected. A buzzer was fixed to the molding. He leaned on the button. He kept leaning on it, knowing how it infuriated anyone inside, remembering the ring-and-run game of boyhood.

Dewey's fist had dropped like a bone-studded club into Woody's ribs. Woody rolled off the cot with a grunt. Lifting knees frantically, he took the kick of a size thirteen boot in his right calf instead of his right kidney. He tried curling in a fetal ball but the huge grunting man had a handful of his shirt collar, tearing and lifting.

Dewey worked the midsection. He knew he couldn't leave facial marks. He tried to crack a rib. A cracked rib hurt bad, he remembered from football and a tractor accident. It wasn't too serious but it might make him open up.

Woody writhed on the dank floor trying to cover himself with arms and lifted legs like an armadillo.

Dewey threw a boot into the cage of ribs, making arms and legs fly.

"Wait!" screamed Woody. "I'll say whatever you want, goddammit!"

Dewey paused. But suddenly Woody was staring up at him with mocking confidence. He kicked at the grinning face. His boot swooped, but Woody's hands caught it easily. Woody's hands twisted. Dewey found himself flopping in terrified surprise against a wall.

Woody was up, lurching for the cell door. Dewey tackled the splindly legs. Woody whirled with wild animal strength. Dewey felt his hands fly loose. He clutched desperately at his prisoner in disbelief at Woody's sudden strength. It was impossible that the bony frame he felt within his grip could force his arms apart, and he couldn't bear to look into Woody's green cloudy eyes. Dimly, he heard the backdoor buzzer begin ringing.

Dewey hit the floor, dazed. Through bursts of winking light he saw Woody leaving the cell.

Dewey scrambled heavily to his feet. The mindless insistence of a dazed lineman helped him plunge into the hallway, reaching for Woody's back. Woody jerked him toward the back door. The buzzer kept ringing. Dewey strove to haul his man down. He threw all his weight sideways. They floundered against the back door and Woody's hand was snapping back the draw-bolt.

Outside, David heard the bolt. His finger slid off the bell button. The door slammed open. Woody's eyes glared wildly into his. Woody hissed staring at David's pocket. His arched fingers raked David's jeans.

"Help me!" bellowed Pounds, thick arms locking around Woody's chest.

Woody shook sideways, frantic, eyes riveted to David's jeans pocket.

"God damn!" cried Pounds, struggling to work a man backward who was half his size.

David dove his arms around Woody's legs. They hauled Woody toward the open cell door, snatched left and right by violent convulsions, his tongue now gagging from his mouth, red eyes bulging. They staggered into the open cell and suddenly, Woody was limp.

David felt the tensed legs relax, soften. It was more than cessation of activity. Woody's muscle tone itself seemed to deteriorate instantly. The swell of the calf muscles sank to flaccidity. Woody's eyes fluttered and closed. Panting, David and Dewey stared at one another in amazement.

"Let's put him on the cot," suggested David shakily. Dewey nodded.

They stretched him out and stood back as if Woody might regain his nearly superhuman strength and agility. But Woody seemed merely asleep.

Dewey panted. "I never knew somebody who could sleep after a fight, after hard licks to the ribcage."

Nodding, David remembered Woody's hand raking his leg, digging at the pocket that held the fingers. Was there some connection? There could be little doubt that Woody was somehow at the source of everything.

"I don't know what the hell to do," muttered Dewey.

David heard the shouts of people outside. Dewey slapped his arm.

"Come on, let's go in the office a minute."

They moved into the hall and Dewey locked Woody's cell. In his office Dewey opened the drawer, had a shot, offered the bottle to David. David shook his head. Dewey took another shot and tossed it back into the drawer. He slumped in his creaking swivel chair. Something hit one of the front windows, making the big neckless man flinch.

"You ever seen anything like that power in a skinny man?" Dewey asked.

David hissed through clenched teeth. "Hysteria, maybe. I don't know. There are cases on record of supernormal physical capacity during stress. Large muscles aren't necessarily the strongest at any time." He heard himself speak without conviction. His words relieved Pounds somewhat, but David sensed far more than sheer physical reaction. He had seen something hideous in Woody's complusive staring eyes, felt it in the frantic grab for his jeans pocket.

"I reckon so," allowed Pounds. "David? What the fuck am I gonna do with them damn people out there?"

"Get Woody out of here, if only for his mother's sake. Have you told her?"

Dewey shook his head. "She's probably the one making him do it all, David."

"You know that isn't so, dammit."

He picked up the phone, asked the operator to ring Ruth Sheehan. Pounds took another drink. He was eyeing David oddly now, recalling how David thought his car had changed color. Nobody made sense no more, Dewey thought.

In his cell, Woody's eyes snapped open in sudden glaring dread. Staring up at the cell window, Woody began to shiver as if against intense cold. Footfalls clicked in the dim corridor. Eyes straining, Woody shrank against the cracked cell wall.

When he saw it was David his stiffened frame relaxed. His hands wandered upon each other in relief.

David had the key and opened the cell. He stepped inside glaring at Woody.

Woody was still relaxed, rubbing his face.

"What do you know about—" David could hardly articulate the words, the thought that keyed the obscene image, "—the opening of my father's crypt, Woody?" Something vulnerable callow, and yet mockingly sinsiter in Woody's face made

David want to crush it in like a doll's face of thin plastic. Woody was mute.

"You want the blame shifted onto your mother?" David demanded, anger rising.

Woody whined and shook his head. "Dunno, man."

Surprising even himself, David's sudden backhand smacked, echoing through the dim cell and corridor. Woody's head snapped back against the concrete-block wall. Blood oozed from his left nostril. His eyes were bright with involuntary tears that sickened David. He had no stomach for cold-blooded torture yet he felt an overwhelming urge to damage Woody, smash him, destroy him. His fist lashed out again. "You were strong before, Woody. Come on."

"Don't hit me no more," Woody whined.

David's other hand cut air, stunned itself against Woody's face, making the tight cell ring like a paddle slapping water.

Woody snuffled, sobbing. David's hand was raised again. He caught himself, shaking a red cloud of hate from his mind. Panting, he stared down at Woody—appalled at his own violence.

"I'm sorry," David said. "Pounds is getting a car to get you out of here."

"Don't let me be alone," begged Woody. He grasped David's leg.

David jerked away in revulsion. Woody sank to the floor with a desperate cry. Nonplussed, David watched Woody hunched double in racking sobs. The sight made him half-sad, half-furious. Tears would never change what he felt against the man.

Still, he believed that Woody held the key. He knelt to play the sympathetic role.

"Tell me all about it, okay? I want to help you, you know how long your mother and I have been friends, don't you? Hey, come on—" Insincerity revolted him but he wanted desperately to learn whatever was locked in Woody's tormented mind.

Woody stared up at David. Suddenly, he clutched David's hand as if in mortal fear of something very close, shifting his eyes into dim corners. "I got to tell somebody, but I don't remember. I swear I don't, not all. . . ."

"Not all . . . what?" urged David, thinking at first it was an act, then seeing the wild desperation in Woody's sunken eyes.

"Oh, Lord God. I don't know, don't know. I was out

there just delivering my groceries one day, long time ago, last year. I didn't mean no real harm. . . ."

"At Sprague's?" David's pulse quickened.

"Yeah," nodded Woody, excited now, with halting sobs. "I broke in and he caught me stealing silverware and such. I know he could see me, pointing that cane thataway. With them blind eyes of his. But next thing I know I was waking up the next morning in bed at home. It was like I had this weird dream. And after that, like ever since, I have these devil kind of dreams. I don't know what I do anymore. I see myself leaving cats out there with the groceries, but a dream—a dream, it ain't real, is it?"

"You tell me," said David tersely. An image of Sprague was forming, forming, an image he wanted to tear to shreds.

"I swear I never had nothing to do with your daddy's body or nothing else bad. Like, one time I dreamed I was out at Sprague's, I thought it was night, and I heard this funny-sounding talk, like something called out over and over. . . ."

"A chant?" asked David.

"It kept going on and on and I thought I heard a little girl crying but it was nothing but dreams, you know? And like, well, I don't know, I just don't know. . . . Momma tried to help me but didn't do any good, just scared her, too."

David removed the mortician's envelope from his jeans and opened it.

"When you were trying to get away you grabbed at these. Recognize them?"

Woody's eyes glazed in abrupt terror. Trembling, he groped backward against the rusty cot frame.

A sudden thought struck David: "Sprague is missing two fingers—did you know that?" The thought was insane. He knew that it was and yet spoke as if on the edge of discovery.

Woody stuttered. "I—I ain't see-seen him since that time I broke in, two or four or, I don't know, some mo-months back, but he didn't have no missing fingers." He shut his eyes tightly and ground dirty knuckles into the sockets, sobbing again.

David stood in anguish and disgust and pity. Shoving the envelope back into his pocket, he heard a distant door slam. The voice that came from the office was wailing and pleading, crying Dewey's name. It was Ruth. David winced, moved by deep pity.

"I'll be back in a minute," he said huskily.

Woody sobbed in a pathetic quivering heap.

David left the cell, tugging the door shut. Its massive iron frame reverberated in his hand.

For a moment, David stood in the hallway door between the cells and the office. He could hear Ruth pleading with Dewey in the office. Outside, people shouted "Witch!"

Surprised Dewey had let her in, David smiled bleakly, glad that Dewey had pity for those weaker than himself. In one long blanketing moment the whole thing seemed suddenly incredible; he was convinced of an evil emanting from Sprague as surely as his father had written of it. No, he was not mad, nor had Chester been.

He put a hand on the wall, trying to concentrate. The old slogan of civil rights activists came back—when you feel paranoid, its because there's a reason. It was crazy but the fingers somehow belonged to Sprague. Woody was directed by Sprague in some way. The cats were brought to Sprague for whatever insipid black ritual Sprague indulged in; there had been a cat in the journal, a sacrifice when Sprague had supposedly shown Chester the image of Leah. The supernatural part had of course been Chester's own mental aberration, just as Streak's head coming to life had been his, or Chester under the tree. All twisted and obscene, yes, but materialist. A mystery with its source in Sprague, who held the ends of obscene strings.

Undoubtedly Sprague knew about the crypt, the pets, even had something to do with what had happened to Holly, her husband and little girl. There was no black magic, only the resources of an ugly and demented rich man whose basement held absurd superstitions and torments. He was a freak who had led Chester into delusions and madness and suicide. Hypnotism? Possibly. Drug-induced fantasy? Holography? Whatever, it wasn't important now to know what it was exactly, only to stop it at the source, and the source had to be Sprague. David reeled at the wild chain of reasoning. Was he the madman, lurking in a cell corridor with rotten fingers in his pocket?

In his office, Dewey slumped in the swivel chair with an expression of sadness masked as indifference. Ruth's ample hip spread toward him on the desk. At first she had pleaded to no avail, then she had said something that unnerved Dewey.

"Look, you can let him out the back, honey."

She edged closer, unbuttoning the front of her polyester tent dress so that two big red print flowers fell open from heavy pale breasts tipped by thick dark nipples. She fluffed orange curly hair, voice was shaky, thick orange lips quivering with desperation.

"I always thought you were real nice, you know."

Dewey squirmed. It was pitiful, saddening. The way she leaned over at him made her breasts hang like water bags. He could see down her dress how much smoother and whiter she was underneath than he would have ever guessed. Her breath smelled like his, but Scotch instead of bourbon.

"Are you that damn desperate?" he asked bluntly to make her quit it.

She giggled falsely. "Desperate?"

"Witch!" they shouted outside. Something hit the office window. Dewey's eyes flicked toward it. Dewey felt her hand reaching down his leg. His chair scooted back. He was suddenly frightened, thinking her a real witch, then catching himself.

"Ruth, goddammit, this ain't like you!" he glared, embarrassed for her now.

She regarded him with tiny eyes of panic which suddenly dropped large rolling tears. The plywood door to the cells slapped open and hissed shut.

Ruth slid off the desk as David entered. She waddled weeping toward him with fat open arms from which meat hung jiggling as she advanced.

He patted her back while they hugged and she bawled. He looked over her shoulder at Dewey. The sheriff jumped angrily from his chair as something huge hit the office-door window with a crash of broken glass. Ruth shrieked.

"God damn, that does it!" growled Dewey.

The big man angrily snatched a nightstick from a drawer. It was black and chipped and scarred but not from use against men. One night at a country road site, he had whipped a concrete block, believing rightly that the violently scarred wood was just as threatening as a blow itself. Now, stick in hand, he unlocked and jerked the office door open, grunting with rage. Bits of broken glass glittered across the floor. A clutter of paling faces retreated from the door in awe and surprise.

Dewey slapped the club in his palm, standing, David thought, like John Wayne: "Who gets it first, boys?"

In the eight-by-eight-foot cell, alone, Woody shivered and sobbed. Crying made him feel shitty.

"I got to tell somebody," he moaned. "But tell what?"

His wiry buttocks ached on the hard damp concrete floor.

He tried to get up and sit on the cot, tried to pull himself together, to remember what all had happened. What had he done to get here? What-all was happening here? He gazed down into the water bucket in the corner of the cell.

He flinched with a choking cry. Black eyes leered up at him from the water's surface. A wild kick sent the bucket flying. The cell dimmed. He looked up at the ceiling bulb in its wire cage. It flickered and went out. He was cold.

"Help . . ." he tried to say, voice dry and feeble.

He looked up and saw the raven in the cell window. It did not preen or flutter, frozen and staring down at him with expressionless obsidian eyes. With a cry of horror he covered his face. He looked up again. It was gone. He panted and tried to shout. One of the three window bars quivered. It fell with mortar dust to the floor, ringing as it struck concrete.

The bar rolled to a halt in the water-spilled corner. And it began to change.

Woody's eyes widened in panic. His hands turned white, tightening on his thighs. The bar elongated, becoming pliable like grey swelling plastic, stretching and swaying, one thinner end whipping and twisting, the closer end thickening and growing blunt and assuming a shape that he began to recognize. He cringed against the wall in silent shock as it formed twin eyes in its blunt end, as the eyes saw him. The blunt end was a head flicking a black forked tongue.

It came for him.

Woody could not move. The thing bumped his face tentatively. Its throat curled around his throat with chilling sensuality. He quivered to a slither of coils. Scales caressed his skin in what seemed an incessant looping.

Twenty-seven

Dewey knew the men in the street and the scattered women among them. The men were hardened, most of them, used to lifetimes of struggling with broken machinery and stubborn land. He'd grown up with half of them. He did not expect to disperse them with the stick. Embarrassment was what he counted on. When they saw him there, symbol of the law whom they had elected, they would look at one another in shame. They were voters but he was past worrying about the gas pump; that was a foregone conclusion now.

"Who the hell busted that window?" he growled, legs spread, stick slapping his open palm.

"Get that witch and her devil, you coward!" a woman screamed.

Half-a-dozen men rushed Dewey. His stick was knocked away.

In the office, David and Ruth were thrown back by the human wave that carried Dewey shouting helplessly.

David heard Ruth's shrieking, the onrushers cheering one another on. Faces and elbows and bodies swarmed through the office. The plywood door to the cells was torn off its hinges.

The mob's momentum halted at Woody's cell. Men slammed into men in front. Shouting ceased sporadically. Men's mouths hung open working in speechless amazement.

"Jesus," whispered someone.

Woody sat in one corner of his cell on the floor. A rusty

cell window bar lay beside him. His eyes bulged at them in eternal agony and surprise, red bulging orbs center-punched by black dilated pupils. His purplish tongue protruded like a sausage filling thin lips. His own bony hands were locked around his throat. Blood oozed over the hands, from tear ducts, nostrils, from rigid corners of his mouth and the tip of the swollen tongue.

Coughs and gasps came from the crowding men. Those behind pressed closer to get a better view through the bars. Some in front were trying to get away.

Ruth fought her way through them. Elbowing, butting with her shoulders, her asthmatic breath came wheezing in anger and panic. Then she was at the bars. Her own doglike dumbfounded stare joined others. She couldn't tear her staring eyes away. Her fat fists locked on the iron bars. Like a wild giant zoo ape she howled, snatching at the bars, making the iron frame clank and rattle.

The men around Ruth—a superstitious mob bent on murder minutes before—now closed about the woman, trying to lay soothing hands on her, to urge her back from the gape of her son whose red eyes accused them all with swollen bloody stare.

The sight had stopped David like a fist between his eyes. Not its ugliness. Not even his pity for Ruth. What stopped him was the medical impossibility of what he saw. A reality that reduced itself to an absurdity. No man could possibly strangle himself to death—Of course someone could try—but as their hands squeezed, closed the carotids and jugulars by external pressure, unconsciousness would quickly ensue. Signals from brain to hands would cease. Oxygen-rich corpuscles would move again and life would resume. David knew that Woody's suicide was impossible and yet there it was. Like the other impossible things he had been seeing. Streak's attack, his coming to life. Chester under a tree mouthing Latin. The raven. The color of the Scout. Sprague's servant. Fingers somehow on the window ledge. Woody's inhuman strength and impossible death.

David tried to face it all. He knew now that it was all real. The insanity of his father's journal became a terrifying logic. He could no longer discredit anything. Could no longer assume that empiricism was without holes. Woody was proof of that.

Ruth's howling gradually penetrated David's confusion. Dewey had her, tugging her heavily from the cell door through the knot of men who spread aside, some in sorrow, some in disappointment. Most turned to look at Woody again like something unbelieved in a Memphis Cotton Carnival sideshow. David joined Dewey. They brought the heaving woman to the rear alley door. Ruth stumbled outside and threw herself across the cruiser's hood, sobbing wildly. She sank to her knees in the dust.

"Let's go out there and look around, at least," David said, nudging Dewey.

Dewey frowned, looking down at Ruth. "Where? Look around for what?"

"Sprague's. His cellar. His house."

Dewey glared at David. "I got no reason to mess around out there, do you?"

"What would it hurt?" insisted David.

"Look here, you losing a daddy and a good friend so fast and all, I understand you're a little off. But that don't mean I'd go dig a search warrant out of the judge in Grange."

David knelt to console Ruth.

What more could he say? That he'd read a wild story in a mirror-written journal? That Woody had suggested having stolen something from Sprague's and had dreamed of stealing cats after that? He gripped Ruth's heaving shoulders.

"Ruth—won't you tell what you know about all this?"

Ruth shuddered, shook her head.

"Leave her be," directed Pounds, towering over them.

David realized there was no use with Pounds. No way he could tell Dewey any of those things without sounding utterly insane. Either he had gone over the edge into total self-convinced madness, or Sprague had some kind of singular sinister power that had to be stopped. He had to talk to Ruth alone. She knew more than anybody else about what went on in and around Bickford, and she knew more now than she would tell. She was obviously terrified—those weren't only sobs of grief.

David stood, putting out a hand to her. "Come on, I'll drive you home."

Ruth looked up at him with a wide flat red face, blinking tiny puffed eyes, her sparse short lashes stuck together with tears. She looked at Dewey Pounds. He hitched his belt with both thumbs and sighed.

"Want me to drive?" Dewey asked. "You ought not be here no more today, Ruth."

Ruth coughed, striving to regain composure.

"Da-David," she stuttered.

"Come on, let me take you home, Ruth."

David helped her up. She heaved mountainously, swaying from side to side like a tethered elephant.

He guided her through the alley. She waddled shakily against him. On the sidewalk the sun was slanting low. David hadn't realized how much time had passed. It was at least four. The street was practically empty. From random storefront windows faces disappeared as they came haltingly toward the yellow Scout.

Minutes later, they were driving out of Bickford.

Ruth sat mute now in what David sensed as interior rage. She bounced and quivered as they rode.

"Ruth—we're not with Dewey Pounds now. I know you might have felt you couldn't talk too much around him."

She did not answer. They passed the abandoned cotton gin, the shacks at the edge of the country farmland, and patches of timber. David spoke again.

"When you said I should leave a couple of weeks ago . . . I didn't know what I know now, Ruth."

Mute, Ruth stared fiercely ahead, eyes glittering, lips pursed.

"It's Sprague, isn't it?" David probed. Ruth shivered beside him as if she were fighting off a sudden chill.

Her trailer appeared through the trees ahead. David slowed and nosed the Scout down through weeds toward the trailer.

Ruth opened her own door. David got out and she was already through the weeds, climbing on the concrete block steps. He caught up as she was opening the weathered screen door. She did not invite him in or try to stop his following.

The screen door flapped shut behind them. The trailer was dank with the sweet stench of cooked greens. Ruth slumped into her tattered plastic recliner. David stood in the dimness looking down at her face, the savagely painted small eyes and thick orange lips, the spotty rouge where no cheekbones had ever come through the layers of fat, the cold shivering huge body that seethed stoically with repressed emotion. Whether fear or rage, he couldn't tell.

"What do *you* know?" Ruth demanded abruptly. Her painted mouth opened and snapped shut like a trap.

David stood nonplussed in her glare.

"You said you didn't know then what you know now," she demanded. "What do you *know* now?"

Bewildered, he sat on a straightback chair with loose legs. What *did* he know? What, really? He tried to articulate the weird fragments into a workable context.

"I found a kind of journal at Whitewood. Chester wrote it."

"And what did he say?" she eyed him with tense darting impatience, as if she too were attempting some kind of understanding through the shock that had numbed her.

David told her most of it in short simple sentences. She listened with increasing attentiveness. Her small eyes softened, she began to shake her head as he finished telling of the last entry, of killing Sprague, of the pursuing familiar, of Sprague the sorcerer wanting his body back and wanting Chester's body for purposes of rebirth. Even as he told it he felt his own feeble conviction faltering. It sounded completely crazy. His leg twitched once and he remembered the fingers in his pocket—a doctor with fragments of a human corpse in his pocket. He stood outside himself for an instant of stern and unforgiving observation, seeing himself, a young, promising medical man, degenerating with tragicomic horror into a Woody Allen character—*fingers in my pocket,* for Christ's sake, and talking seriously about a dead man coming back to life.

But Ruth wasn't laughing.

Her eyes flitted redly from window to window and she seemed to be listening to him and to something outside.

"And today," David finished, "Woody told me a dream he had, about stealing pets for Sprague. And I saw—how he did that to himself—physically impossible, asphyxiation would have released his grip long before . . . before the end."

Ruth wept silently and bitterly, biting her lower lip without the impulsive grief of before. "Killed my boy," she hissed through clenched yellow teeth. "Killed my Woody, God help him. . . ."

David watched her face lose its heat, freeze to a pallid hating fear. She stared into his eyes as she spoke the next words that made his world reel.

"Sprague is a sorcerer, a warlock, or a wizard, whatever you want to call it."

David stared back. It was all true. The conviction in her words left no lingering doubt. She licked orange lips nervously, glancing up at the windows, staring back at his eyes.

"Your daddy came to confide things to me over the years, since your momma passed away. He couldn't bring himself to make up to you, maybe because he loved you too much. Men are stupid in their pride sometimes. He just needed a shoulder now and again, nothing more. But then Sprague moved in. All that work for the man, all that money. And your daddy found him and saved his life, like you read. The dreams started. He came and I tried to talk it out. But after he saw Leah at Sprague's, or what he thought was her, he was doomed."

David shook his head. "But . . . he didn't kill Sprague, Sprague is *alive*, I've seen him."

Ruth's tiny eyes bored in. "There is another thing you don't know. What else your daddy saw there one night. A little girl dying in a black rite, a sight that nearly blasted his soul and the last of what was left of his mind. Sprague knew Chester's mind, he controlled him, like a kind of game. He told Chester he'd done the sacrifice many times before. It was necessary to keep a pact he had made. He was arrogant in his power, all right, he knew Chester would never try to convince anybody of what he'd seen—who would have believed? No evidence, nothing but crazy talk. He hated Chester, I think, just because Chester put hands on him that day he saved him."

The little girl, David thought. "Holly's little girl?"

Ruth nodded tensely. "But Chester waited for a rainy night. He knew Sprague's familiar couldn't follow through rain. He shot Sprague at the front door, carried the body through the rain with that demon howling because it couldn't come after them. That thing *is* a demon, all right, summoned from Hell. A changeling that can take any form."

David rubbed his face gravely. Chaotic pieces of a puzzle were tumbling eerily into place. "The raven is one of its forms?"

"Yes it is."

"It could take the form of a dog, a corpse, a snake?" he asked, remembering.

"Anything it chose to be. And if its master is completely destroyed, it has to return to Hell from where it was summoned. Chester made one bad mistake. He hid Sprague's body in the old cemetery instead of burning it. Instead of using fire like I told him to. Only fire will completely destroy Sprague. Madness overtook Chester, he shot himself that same night. But it rained and Sam discovered him the next morning and took him to town. The familiar wanted his body but couldn't act right away. I wanted you to leave, son, I would have watched the crypt. Even in death a powerful sorcerer can act. But he needed Chester's remains to reincarnate, only the body of his slayer could restore him. Sam stood in the way and they brushed him aside. They used my Woody for a tool. I tried to break the spell Sprague put on him but it was too strong. He told me what he was being made to do. Told me all about Chester and what happened, but he was helpless sometimes, and sometimes his memory would quit for days. I'm not evil like that-there man. People come here for titillation. I tell them what they want to hear."

David took strong deep breaths. He felt swamped and mind-blown, like a medieval man confronted with proof that the earth was not flat but round. He remembered what Sprague himself had said—"Keep for your friends those secrets of the highest order"—and he sensed the terrible irony of those words, *friends*—had Holly, her husband, her daughter, had they too been his *friends?* What grisly secrets had they suffered? What dark savagery?

Pieces kept tumbling into place—Sandy carrying Melanie downstairs, sleepwalking, perhaps summoned somehow by Sprague—the fingers even now in his pocket, found clutched in Sam's grip, snatched from the hand that now bore two nubs, Sprague's and—Streak trying to defend Melanie from a snake that was not a snake, the familiar moving in on her, later taking Streak's shape, that snapping decapitated head—the fierce claw-marks on the rock-hard marble slab of the crypt—the shadow on the film where the raven had been, shadow instead of substance—the familiar outside even while he slept, killing Sam. David remembered the inhuman mobility of the demon familiar, the staring photographic stillness like something watching in a dream, those same eyes of the raven, of his father under the trees in the woods, of Streak in the dark, attacking—

He rocked dizzily in the chair, almost choking on the brutal succession of indigestible truths.

Ruth leaned close at him from the recliner, eyes tight and earnest as she whispered urgently. "Holly's little girl was the bride of something far beyond our knowledge, it had her, David. Sprague gave her to it as part of his pact and surely has done that before. Go and take your child away now. Go now, this minute. Drive back to Memphis. I'll fend for myself."

He stood, breathing deeply. Chester had tried to stop it, Sam died trying to stop it, Woody had told too much. Fear blazed up in his chest—it wasn't Sandra that Sprague wanted, it was *Melanie.*

"Go now," urged Ruth, "take them away!"

"Oh my God." They were alone at the house, he had left them alone there all day, nothing could have suited Sprague better.

He turned, knocking the chair aside. He jerked the door open and leapt down the blocks into the grass.

David stopped, teetering, eyes fixed in horror.

The thing crouched on the hood of the Scout leered at him with glittering dead black eyes.

Twenty-eight

It was Streak but not Streak. David stood transfixed. The thing hissed, catlike. From between bared fangs flicked something David knew he could not be seeing—a black forked tongue. Its hissing filled his mind. As if in dreams he realized he was on his knees in terror.

There was a scream from the trailer.

David tore his eyes from the thing and saw Ruth on the top concrete block, her thick face twisting with fear overwhelmed by hatred. Her right fist clutched a thick rolled newspaper, its end aflame. Lurching down the steps past David she brandished the flame, screaming bestially.

David saw it happen with maddening clarity—Ruth attacking the thing with fire, it rearing on hind legs apelike from the flames, hissing, forked tongue piercing bared fangs, attacking Ruth, her arms hugging it as it bore her to the ground, the flames spreading over them both like wildfire.

David was on his feet. He screamed as Ruth rolled in the grass aflame, shrieking. She tensed rigidly and lay still. The thing blazed beside her in the grass. David slapped at patches of flame in her clothing, feeling her flaccid body underneath. Her sightless head turned aside. White tendons curled in a black-red hole. Her throat was torn open to the bone, her larynx gaping. Blood pooled under his hands.

He turned his face, sickened, and flinched back. The thing burning in the grass beside her was Streak's head. Its open eyes stared, its fangs champing slowly in the flames like some faltering appliance.

Grinding his teeth, David pulled Ruth's body away. He stared in horror as flames reduced the dog's head with unnatural speed to a skull. The jaw snapped in one last weak impulse and crumbled to a fine white ash dispersed through flame-withered weeds by a rising twilight breeze.

He stood staring down as the last ashes withered and were gone. It was as if he had fallen through some flaw in the ages of mankind. He had seen through a kind of wall. The monstrous seen as real.

He bent and lifted Ruth by the armpits and dragged her, panting up the concrete blocks into her trailer.

Then he was quickly outside again, climbing into the Scout, his mind reeling back through ages of barbarism—*thou shalt suffer a witch to be burned.*

He raced the Scout backward out of the drive. Gunning forward on the road, new fear struck him with sickening force—*Sandy and Melanie are alone.*

Twenty-nine

At three o'clock, when David still had not returned, Sandra decided to check the roof terrace for sunbathing. It was a beautiful sunny afternoon and she deserved a break after cutting the roots of the foul-smelling ivy that covered Whitewood's walls. She had watched the ivy wither and curl in less than an hour. Its smell had died with it. She showered. Then she and Melanie, both in swimsuits, climbed the steep hall stairs to the terrace.

The door was stiff. She shoved and it gave mustily. Melanie followed her out onto a wide brown tiled terrace. They halted breathlessly. The view was magnificent, the sun-gleaming river expanse visible beyond arbors and the bluff on one side, the tops of the great oaks going away and away on the other.

They brushed oak leaves industriously into a corner and sat on wrought-iron loungers, rubbing each other with a baby-oil and iodine mixture, Sandra's own. Melanie dropped the shoulder straps of her navy tank suit. She still felt a little funny about bras and she hated the little bralike white marks straps left in a tan.

Sandra sprawled on her lounger with her bikini top undone. Lying on her stomach she fell deliciously asleep while reading a paperback historical romance in the hot slanting sun. Then they were both asleep.

The sun shifted westerly. It fell below the roof level and the eaves. Hours passed. A breeze rattled the pile of dead oak leaves. One leaf drifted over the wall, down past the library windows where a faint redness shone in the dimness.

It was the glass-encased clockwork on the desk. Its wheels spun, blurring with increasing speed, casting a lurid red glare that spilled from the desk.

On the terrace, Sandra's book dropped to the tiles. It was dusk. She sat up on the creaking lounger. Her untied bikini top slipped away softly but her hand did not rise to cover her nakedness. Eyes open yet unseeing, she rose and bent over the curled slumbering form of her daughter, lifting the child against her breasts.

Melanie awoke.

She was in her mother's arms. Her mother stood at the terrace rampart. Frightened, not moving lest she fall, Melanie clutched her mother's arms. She saw distance in her mother's eyes and looked down onto the dusk-shadowed lawns.

The dark face gazed back up at her. The one from the woods. The one who hurt Streak. The one at Sprague's. His black eyes gleamed, staring at her and her alone. Melanie screamed and jerked her mother's hair.

Sandra heard Melanie shrieking in the dark. It was a nightmare. She heard her daughter's cries of terror, trying to reach her, trying to kick free of the darkness covering her like a smothering damp blanket. She too was screaming now.

Mother and daughter shrieked once together at the terrace rampart. Then Sandra was awake, appalled, kneeling with Melanie still in her arms, weeping now and covering the terrified child with kisses.

Melanie's eyes were riveted upon the dusk-gathering lawns. Nothing stared darkly up at her now. Nothing was down there. Her gaze raced from tree to tree, from shrub to gargoyle to stone walkway, from shadow to clotting shadow, in desperation.

"Momma! He was down there!"

On her knees, Sandra hugged the child, wild with fear of herself. She realized her breasts were naked, that she might have dropped Melanie off the roof to a deadly plunge of three stories. Her daughter's cries made no sense.

"Who?" she wept. "Who was, honey?"

Sandra and Melanie stared down at the lawn, Sandra's hands covering her breasts.

"Mommy!" shrieked Melanie, clutching her mother's arm.

Below them the weathered gray stone gargoyle seemed to quiver. The first movement was hardly perceptible. It had crouched there a hundred years facing the distant road through the long corridor of oaks, guardian of the great house. Now, as Sandra and Melanie clutched one another, gaping down in helpless fascination and horror, the stone head turned on stone shoulders. There was a grinding friction as the bestial face grinned up at them. The eyes within stone lids were dissolving, suddenly black and glittering with an obscene mockery that Melanie felt as an unbelievable caress. She shrieked in fear and shame, muscles frozen, her mother's body stiffened in horror against hers.

The eyes of the thing did not release their eyes. The stone grated and groaned as the gargoyle tore itself from the lawn, turning with a leap onto the side of the house that shook the terrace under their feet. Sandra gurgled in terror.

"Mommy!" screamed Melanie.

Jerking at Sandra's arm, she urged her mother to the terrace doors. Then they were running down the stairs.

Stone claws locked in the wall, the thing climbed. It shattered a window below and entered, its stone tail slithering through the casement.

Silence came from within Whitewood.

Sudden panting screams pierced that silence; unanswered sobbing pleas broke into wild shrieks of agony and hysteria that weakened and faded as night quickly overcame dusk.

David cut the Scout's wheel hard, broadsiding into the long brick drive. Through the oaks he saw the withered ivy. Slamming on the brakes at the house he saw the torn lawn, the gargoyle missing. One wall of the house was damaged as if something heavy had been slammed and dragged against it. An upper window was smashed. The house gaped at him darkly.

With a cry, David ran from the Scout through dense shadows. The front doors stood wide open, a mouth of blackness in the face of the violated house.

He stared, trying to see inside. He called out for Sandy. For Melanie. The house gave back a frightening silence.

Trembling, he crept inside and paused—a fetid bestial odor lingered in the foyer shadows. He listened. Nothing. Floorboards creaked underfoot as he came toward the library. He halted at the door, gasping.

Shredded books and pages covered the dim floor. The desk was upside down, the clockwork device smashed, the closet door hanging on one hinge, the steel safe door torn open. Hair pricked on the nape of his neck, chilled at the shattered evidence of inhuman forces.

In the hall again he stopped and picked something from the floor—Sandra's bikini top. Fear for her blazed up, his eyes searched the hall. Rage replaced fear as he moved quickly, unthinkingly, toward the study.

David stood in the study door, blinking in sickly numbing shock at what he saw. Had he not seen the things he had seen in the past days, he could not have believed it. "God, oh God," he gasped.

Naked, Sandra sat like a wide-eyed doll in the middle of the study floor, pale arms at her sides, palms upward on the floor, legs apart, her white skin covered with blood and huge darkening bruises. Her blank eyes were fixed upon the stone gargoyle. It lay on one side covering half the floor, moss and earth on its base as if hauled there from the yard. Blood was smeared on the stone. Tensed in disbelieving horror David remembered the broken casement and torn lawn and wall.

Quickly, he was kneeling beside her. His hands manipulated nerveless limbs. He laid her on the couch, wincing though she did not, repeating her name though she did not answer. Her dull eyes gazed past him at the ceiling.

His hands caressed her bruised face and terms rolled meaninglessly through his reeling mind—catatonia, trauma, psychotic paralysis, shock. Helplessness brought tears blindingly across his vision. Sandra's pathetic face wavered in his quivering hands, a whitish blur. And all at once he realized something even worse that brought him wildly to his feet.

"Melanie!" he screamed, hands becoming fists, eyes wide. "Melanie!"

A quick frantic search through the house—made with no regard for danger to himself—brought no sign of his child. He found himself praying, *please God let her be okay.*

David halted at the darkening base of the stairs.

Sprague, his mind seethed—*Sprague.*

He ran from the house across the dark lawns. Skidding to a halt by the Scout, he racked his brain. . . . Fire. He must have a weapon.

Flares.

He ran to the garage and pulled the doors open with breath hissing between clenched teeth, half-ready to encounter some new madness. Quickly, he found the taped bundle of road flares under the workbench. They were old and covered with oily lint. He struck one. It sputtered, then flared. He jammed it into the garage floor to put it out.

The garage doors slammed shut. David whirled with a choked cry.

Fire burst from the walls, from the old Triumph, from the ground under his feet, smoke crowding the flames.

Arms over his face, staggering blindly against the garage wall, his elbow smashed a window pane. He felt the rush of cool air. Turning, he drove the flares through the glass, coughing and hoisting himself through the opening.

He fell to the grass outside, clothes smoking as he rolled in the grass. He sat up and stood shakily, falling once before gaining his feet. He coughed. Acrid tears streamed down his sooty cheeks and jaw. His body reeked of burnt hair. Staggering, he reached the garage doors. One arm thrown across his face, he snatched the doors open, leaping back.

No fire. No smoke. There was no trace of damage.

Illusion? Madness? His hair was singed, his skin scorched.

David stood panting, blinking. With heartsick abruptness he forgot his own pain, remembering—Melanie.

His blackened face jerked toward Sprague's. Flares. He broke into a labored run toward the Scout.

The shelterbelt of woods lay darkly against the shadowed lawns. No nightbirds sang. The restored manor stood bone-white against the few stars as if unnaturally forced upon the land, its eaves etched in stark angles, in black masses rising to the cupola, which now had the appearance of a gigantic misshapen head.

Fog was rising from the river below. It clothed depressions of the lawns in cold gray, creeping into the black trees.

From the edge of the tree shapes emerged another shape. Gliding and crouching, halting, moving again through the patches of fog, it was silhouetted against the dull pallor of the great house. Something lay across its arms. It was the nude unconscious body of a human female child.

The thing crept toward the rear of the manor where its master waited in a black doorway with lifted open arms, his blind eyes two fiercely watchful gleams.

David gunned the Scout down the brick drive. It broadsided into blacktop, tires screeching, engine racing. David's foot ammed the pedal to the floor, both fists white-knuckled on the wheel.

He snatched the C-B mike from its hook and keyed the emergency channel. Somebody was chattering about catfish. David shouted into the mike.

"Tell Dewey Pounds this is David Rawlings—I'm headed for Sprague's to kill the sonofabitch!"

Foot jamming the gas, he threw the mike aside, the radio filling with excited jabber. He grinned bleakly, knowing he had said the only thing guaranteed to bring Pounds quickly to Sprague's manor.

A quarter-mile from the restored manor, the last curve in sight ahead, David squinted in sudden blinding light. In spite of the intensity his eyes widened as the light came at him; he saw the dark bulk of a locomotive shaped around the light in the middle of the road, felt the thunder rising through the floorboard and seat.

Screaming, David snatched wildly at the wheel. He saw the light-glaring steel nose towering, then the Scout was headed into shadows. He saw the ditch and wrenched the wheel back toward the road with an effort that ground his teeth and clashed his eyes shut. He felt the Scout dip, tires shuddering, then an explosion of glass and steel. He was floating on a pillow of air. The ground came at him. He hit a wall of grass and earth and rolled.

David sat up and vomited. Through spurts of sullen twinkling light he saw the Scout upside down in the ditch like an animal twisted in rigor.

He tried to stand but fell the first time. No bones broken, he knew, crawling to the Scout through waves of nausea.

The bundle of flares lay by a twisted door. The smell of gasoline was strong. He gripped the flares, stood drunkenly, and staggered up onto the road. Behind him the Scout burst into flame.

He tried to run. The sickness rose. Limping, grinding his teeth, clutching the flares like a savage, his singed clothes flapping from him in bloody tatters, he saw the manor loom in frightening pallor through black trees, blind windows staring down contemptuously as his feet struck the lawn.

He halted, struck by the enormity of evil he sensed. Fear rose like a hand thick in his throat. He knew Melanie was somewhere inside and his anger burned the sickness away, his fists tightening on the flares.

Advancing again through the magnolia shadows, he came to the front veranda. He climbed the tall steps and came between towering columns to the doors. They were locked and strong. His shoulder made no budge. The windows on either side were black, throwing back a faint starlight. A shudder passed through him. He realized ironically that if he had not been a doctor he might have already been in shoc

r have destroyed himself from the trauma caused by things
e had seen. Even as that thought struck him, he stiffened
nd leaned closer to the doors.

His pulse quickened—from within came a deep muted
hanting that made his flesh crawl. He remembered the
voodcut of the sorcerer and demon, of a young girl on an
ltar; he remembered his father's journal and thought with
resh rage of Holly and her little girl, and of his own.

David removed his shirt. He wrapped it round his right
ist and smashed a veranda window with a muffled blow. He
rawled inside over broken glass.

Standing in the dark room he heard the chanting louder,
ts tones sinister and beseeching but no clearer as if coming
rom below ground. He remembered the cellar room his
ather had described.

Now, a cold clarity siezed him. Melanie must be saved or
fe itself would be a madness.

In a crouch he moved forward through shadows, two
ares thrust under his belt, a third unlit in his fist as he
dvanced.

He passed the piano room. Stiffening, halting, he heard
he black instrument thrum of its own accord.

Thirty

Melanie was a whitish long shape on the dim stone loor. She lay on her back, nude, sleeping, arms by her sides, egs together, hair streaming over the stones under her head. he did not hear the chanting of the man nearby.

Murmuring, head lowered, Sprague wore a robe that was ardly more than a rag. It had been black once but was aded. Heavy gold threadwork frayed loose in its wide sleeves. Vorn draping folds fell about his bony naked feet. He stood vithin a chalked pentagram, its lines faintly phosphorescent, ach angle marked in symbols. A black peaked cap rose from he back of his head into the gloom. In the darkest corner, nother shape squatted, listening.

Sprague's arms lifted. The tattered sleeves hung nearly in hreds. By his feet within the pentagram lay his cane and an ronbound book that lay open; his eyes studied the curled archment pages scribed in fading brown ideograms and cript.

He gazed at the human female child. The lines of his face wisted in dark exultation and mockery. His lips parted and is chant resumed like a whisper of glass grating under claw-ipped feet.

"Cernunnos, Lord of my Fathers, Lord of Ages, I summon hee. Lord of Agonies, of Carthage and Hiroshima and Doomed Great Ones, I summon thee to wed and to sup. Rise rom thy eternal legions and I shall perform thy shapely ntroduction as ages ago I vowed in time upon time upon me to fulfill. . . ."

He listened, face lifted to the dark ceiling. Bending, he grasped the tip of his cane, bending forward, letting its golden bestial head move over Melanie's body. Masses of darkness in the room shimmered as if with energy. Melanie moaned. Her lashes fluttered. A seeming wind stirred the shadows.

"Thy time is again at hand, Unholy One, the slant of the moon and the Serpent in the house of the Elephant, thi offered fruit in flavor most sweet and ripe and pure. . . ."

The distant thrum of a piano sent Sprague whirling, eyes blazing over his shoulder, his chant replaced by a savage hiss of rage and surprise.

His robed arm shafted toward a low door in the darkest part of the stone room.

The thing watching its master rose and was gone.

Thirty-one

In the dark hall, David heard the chanting resume, still muted but definitely closer.

Abruptly, his eyes caught vague motion in the deep shadows ahead. He halted. Fist tightening on the flare, he strained his trembling vision. Something was growing larger, loping, coming straight at him.

David struck the flare.

In the burst of dazzling red light he saw Sprague's familiar towering over him, halting from the flare as if dazzled, height doubling even as David stared in disbelief and hatred. The black eyes mirrored the red crackling blaze. The mouth opened in a lion's roar that staggered David back on quaking heels.

A rumble from behind turned David's head. He saw a bookcase grind into the hall from another room. It careened at him. He dodged through a doorway as it collided with a wall where moments before he had stood.

The room was huge, David's flare casting reddish shadows, the familiar towering over him again.

A writing desk moved from a wall, almost pinning him, almost making him drop the half-burned flare. With a desperate cry he lunged at the gigantic shape that kept pressing his back.

In the dark stone room Sprague's chant rose in alien tongues. The darkness stirred, shadows clotting, massing against the wall nearest the semi-conscious child.

Sprague hissed in delight as the monster slid noiselessly

through the wall. Its crouching mass and familiar scent made him smile; its gnarled bulk swayed near the child as if sniffing spoor, the shoulders stooped against the stone ceiling, two red gleams blinking from the neckless head so that even Sprague's flesh beaded in clammy sweat.

"Here is no pit of charred bone such as others offer," Sprague dared to whisper, waving the cane over the child, careful not to extend his hand beyond the pentagram. "Here is the succulent young life you have learned to expect, which I give and will continue to give!"

Lesser shapes writhed now like parasites at the clawed feet of the shadowed beast. The darkness vibrated with singing more discordant than insects'. The stones and Sprague's cane warned them away from the yet untouched pale form awakening now on the dim floor.

Melanie opened her eyes and saw the thing gazing red-eyed down upon her in lust and hideous curiosity. Her mouth opened in ululating screams, yet she could not move.

David heard his daughter's screams pierce the halls and rooms of the house. His flare dug wildly into the shape confronting him. He heard a catlike howl and the way was clear ahead.

Racing into the ballroom his flare fizzled and waned. Even as it burnt out the thing appeared in a doorway. His hands clawed a flare from his belt, his feet staggering back. A grind of broken plaster tore his eyes upward. He leaped and rolled under a heavy table as the massive chandelier dropped with an explosion of shattered crystal that showered the floor.

He was up with another flare sputtering. It was old. In its feeble uncertain light he cursed the thing gliding toward him in attack, its arms stretched wide, black eyes lancing into his own. The flare suddenly blazed up. He thrust forward, the red flame cutting the dark like a sword. He felt razor-sharp nails rake his face. Staggering back, he fell. The flare rolled from his hand, the thing rose over him like a hood of night.

One side of the ballroom abruptly flooded with white light through every window. Car doors slammed outside. The thing turned its maddening black gaze from David. It whirled toward the light and David scrambled to his feet, clutching the dropped flare.

The shouts of men came from outside. The thing glided through the dark rooms toward the front of the house. David paused in a doorway for only an instant to watch it go. He heard Melanie cry out again, a shriek that drew him furiously down the corridor. He found a door and snatched it open. Below him ran stone steps. His flare ate into subterranean darkness as he raced downward, the chill air bearing a bestial stench.

Dewey Pounds jumped from his cruiser. Headlights of semicircled pickups and cars focused on the front of the restored mansion, vehicles of the hangers-on who heard David's radio message to Pounds. Men ran with Dewey across the lawn through their own headlights, shouting, the car doors of fresh arrivals slamming behind them.

Halfway across the lawns Dewey and eight men halted, gaping. The huge front doors of the house erupted from their orifice. The two massive slabs of wood shrieked through the air. The men tried to scatter but the doors tumbled end over end through their rank, carrying three broken bodies with them. Dewey and the others stood stunned in a settling mist of blood.

But they had no time to gather their wits. A man screamed and Dewey saw the thing coming from the gaping doorway.

At the base of the steps, David's flarelight showed the cellar described in his father's journal. The accoutrements of sorcery were there. He could hear the chanting but the room was empty.

He went to a wall, quickly feeling for niches, for cracks or hidden seams. Melanie screamed. He ran to the opposite wall and felt the telltale seam and shouldered the cold stones with muscle-bursting desperation.

Stone grated, then the door swept open. David stood frozen in a moment of mind-bending horror at what he saw.

Within the room, Sprague turned hissing at the blasphemous interruption. Melanie screamed, trying to rise from the floor. The gnarled black immensity looming over her swarmed with lesser beings. Its red eyes flicked from Melanie to Sprague as the stone door scraped open.

The red flare blazed, David advancing into the dimness. Obscene howls filled his ears, his mind, and he saw Sprague leap from the pentagram.

Sprague snarled in rage, jabbing at David with the cane. A sheet of brick materialized but David thrust the flare through it and it wavered and dissolved.

Sprague's eyes twisted back in fear toward the massive thing behind him. It was moving. He jabbed wildly at David.

The tip of the cane brushed David's arm. The muscles went cold. The flare dropped from his numbed hand.

"Cernunnos!" shrieked Sprague, "seize the virgin fruit and begone!"

David reeled to a thunder which shook the stone room. Melanie was crawling toward him but the thing's red eyes were fixed upon Sprague, and his in terror upon it. David kicked at Sprague's hand. The cane flicked away, clattering on the stones. Sprague saw it with a cry but David had it first, and saw Sprague backing from it as if it were a snake. New thunder crashed through the room, followed by a steady earthshaking rumble.

The thing of darkness wavered, its host shrieking, its maw opening like a furnace door, flames escaping through bared fangs. Backing from David, Sprague's cloak brushed the fallen flare and burst into flame. Sprague shrieked. Flames covered him. Shadows raced about the watching shape.

Melanie reached her daddy's leg, gripping an ankle. David lifted her wildly as a tremor shook the room.

Outside, the familiar ceased its attack upon Dewey and his men. Half of them laying moaning and battered, some with grotesque wounds. Lightning slashed across the black sky through gathering clouds. Drops of rain began to fall as an earth tremor shook the ground. The familiar shrank to a raven racing through falling rain, smoking as droplets struck its body, flying into the gaping mouth of the house. A fresh tremor would have thrown Dewey to his feet had he been standing. On hands and knees, he looked at the house with eyes utterly insane.

Clutching Melanie, David saw the familiar at the door. Its eyes were no longer passionless, riveted with despair as they were upon the sight of its master ablaze.

David rolled with the impact of a tremor. Half-conscious, he was aware of terrific heat and noise. He saw the monstrous thing wrapping itself around Sprague, heard Sprague's screams drowned in the earthshaking roar; he saw the familiar leap at that same instant to attack him. But the black thing was dragging Sprague through a sudden rift in the stones—the familiar seemed caught in midair, its malignant face becoming, in rapid and dissolving succession, Streak, his father, his mother, Woody, then Sprague himself fading in midair. The earthquake redoubled and David saw the rift shriek wider. He glimpsed Sprague's face once before the thing pulled him down, Sprague's blind eyes wild with awful surprise and then sheer terror.

David clutched Melanie tighter and staggered from the small room. Blocks fell from the ceiling. The second room was collapsing. He made the stairs, groping upward through thundering blackness, Melanie screaming in his ears.

Through the shaking rooms he ran with her, ceiling dropping plaster, walls caving in.

Then they were in the rain outside. The earth and sky roared. Men gibbered like wounded insane animals in the downpour.

Holding Melanie tight, David saw lightning attack the house. Bolts struck it again and again, never missing it, none striking elsewhere.

In a daze he felt himself crawling with his child away, yard by yard. Behind him the great house was falling in upon itself. Dimly he heard Melanie mouthing the Lord's Prayer in his ear as he dragged her through the rain.

The ground heaved and split beneath the house. Lightning bolts ravaged the massive crumbling block of earth that fell away into the river carrying the last of the house with it into the rainswept belly of night.

Thirty-two

At Whitewood the morning was clear. The storm had ravaged a few trees. The manor stood undisturbed, glistening with moisture.

A crew of men labored in front, hauling the stone gargoyle back to its place on the lawn. Birds sang in the trees, squirrels played.

David held Melanie's hand. They watched attendants wheel Sandra to the open ambulance doors and lift her stretcher. Melanie wept. David had no more tears. His gaze had the inhuman quality of steel.

The ambulance drove away, lights rotating. David and Melanie climbed into the Scout to follow, its hatch space oaded with their suitcases. The Scout went down the long brick drive.

On the two-lane blacktop, hundreds of people stood rubbernecking at the place where the night earthquake had reduced a great mansion to rubble and dumped land and all into the river. An ambulance and a yellow Scout had difficulty getting by.

At Whitewood, in a kitchen corner, a pile of torn and wet clothes lay on the brown tiles in a corner. The jeans quivered. The long nails of two fingers poked from the pocket like animal eyes peering from a burrow.